# MINDJACKER

## Sean Patrick Reardon

"Think Koontz's "Night Chills" and "The Key to Midnight" and you'll have a good idea of what your in for when reading "Mindjacker". The author has come up with a great antagonist in Dr. Joel Fisher, who's both a psychologist, and a sociopath"

"A taut, fast-paced thriller that kept me reading until the end"

"Fast pacing, plot twists, and excellent dialogue made this an enjoyable read that I finished in two sessions"

"Cracking dialogue in a molotov cocktail of Repo Man and Pulp Fiction, with twist of The Twilight Zone"

"It's a wild ride, taut as a drum, a great read that'll keep you turning the pages right to the end. Highly recommended"

"Non-stop action, fast cars, a great sound track (that will have you digging through your old classic vinyl)"

"Like a combination Tilt-A-Whirl and Wild Mouse . . . in the dark . . .with really great music"

"Entertaining, fast paced story. A lot of action, fast cars, and a great soundtrack."

First edition

For Tommy Lagg

# JOEL & SCOTT

**June 2007**

Scott Haskins stared at the table with "the view" in the Sunset Tower Bar, thinking they must use a tape measure to place it exactly in front of the five floor-to-ceiling windows showcasing downtown Los Angeles. The table to the left got you a view of the fireplace. The one to the right squeezed you into an alcove with a small double window, overlooking nothing of significance. From his seat at the bar, although only fifty-feet away, he might as well be in the nosebleed section at Gillette Stadium. Back home, Scott had season tickets behind the Patriots bench.

He watched the three people currently occupying "the table". Being at the table meant you were somebody. Sitting in the seat facing the window, meant you were "the man". Scott pegged the current man du jour for either a music or studio exec as he held court with the two guys sitting on each side of him.

Mr. Bigshot looked like a caricature of someone Scott had seen before. His black beard was cropped tight to the face. His receding hair, which Scott figured got colored regularly, was slicked back tight to his skull and fed the piece de resistance.

The ponytail.

*No one has the balls to tell him that corporate ponytails went out of style twenty years ago. Probably wouldn't give a shit what anyone said anyway.*

"Would you like another sir?" the bartender asked, breaking Scott's thought process.

"Sure." He drained the last of the club soda and lime, put the glass down on the bar.

Scott didn't want another, but didn't feel like leaving just yet. It was only ten o'clock and sleep would be hard to come by.

Two years without a drink and the cravings and insomnia still reared their ugly head whenever he was away on business. At home, surrounded by the familiar, it was easy. Now, it was white-knuckle sobriety. Back in the day, he would have thought of a way to introduce himself to the Man. And the Man would accept his company, gratefully. Scott might not have the drink in his arsenal anymore, but he still had the looks, physique, and his secret weapon.

The smile.

Scott smirked. *The ponytail versus the smile.*

If Scott was going to move his family from Bedford, New Hampshire out to L.A. early next year, he damn well better bring his A-game. Sure, it was a challenge, but that's what he lived for. Brains and lacrosse had taken him to the Groton School and Harvard. After a few seasons playing box lacrosse for the Boston Blazers, he decided that Harvard Law was a more secure career choice.

"Here you go sir." The bartender placed the glass in front of him.

"Thanks pal," Scott said, catching a glimpse of the three guys at the table as they stood up.

Scott noticed the paleness of the other two's skin, compared to the Man's bronze complexion and hands.

*Foreigners.*

***

"Gentlemen." He put a bronze hand on each of their shoulders. "This is the dawn of a new age. We will thrive and we *will* conquer. John is waiting for you downstairs. We'll talk soon. Have a safe trip."

They shook Joel Fischer's hand and headed toward the exit. Fischer grabbed his drink off the table and finished the last of it.

He walked over to the window, talking on his cell and staring out over the city. To Scott, it looked like Fischer was telling L.A. he was on his way home and it better be ready for him to tuck it in for the night.

Scott was caught off guard when Fischer turned and walked toward the bar. Scott guessed six-foot two, about the same as him, but knew the blue suit was Versace. Fischer stood next to him, whistling, twiddling his thumbs and glaring at the bartender, who was busy making small talk with a couple of twenty-something girls, who were there chumming the waters with peroxide, cleavage, and imitation Chanel.

One of the girls noticed, or felt, Fischer's stare and tipped off the bartender.

"How are you this evening Michael?" Fischer asked him.

"I'm doing okay Mr. Fischer. How about you?"

"Absolutely splendid. Where's Jeffrey tonight? You would think the owner would be more visible."

Fischer considered the owner, Jeff Klein, a friend. Klein considered Fischer a pompous asshole, and made himself scarce whenever he got a heads up that Fischer was in the house.

"I'm sure he's around here somewhere. You just have to know where to look. You need something?"

"A drink would do nicely. You know where I can get one? I heard the service is less than desirable here."

Scott laughed as Fischer sat beside him.

"Joel Fischer," he said, extending a hand. "What are you drinking?"

"Scott Haskins." Scott shook his hand, dreading the rest of the reply, knowing this was just a taste of how it would be when he moved to L.A. "Club soda…and lime."

"Crown rocks." Fischer looked over at Scott. "Make it two?"

*Fuck it,* Scott thought, then said, "Sure, why not. Thanks."

"I detect an accent. Boston?"

Scott noticed Fischer's eyes were extremely blue, like crystal marbles. The oversized, porcelain veneers dominating his mouth looked like they were made of ivory. "Is it that easy to tell?"

"Of course it is. I used to spend a lot of time there myself. It is a wonderful city."

The bartender brought the drinks. Fischer held his glass out to Scott. "To Bawston."

"Cheers." Scott sniffed in the vapors as the Crown made its way down his throat.

"So, what brings you here Scott?"

"I'm thinking of moving out here next year. Been checking out real estate, locations, things like that."

"What are you into? Where are you staying?"

"Lawyer…sports. Been thinking about maybe branching out into entertainment. I'm staying in this place for a couple more days."

Fischer raised his eyebrows, taking mental notes. "Any luck so far?"

"A few prospects, but I'm still looking around. Hopefully it's all set in a few more months."

Fischer figured Scott was early forties and…had a problem with the bottle, maybe drugs too, but didn't think so. He noticed the golden shackle on Scott's left index finger, while organizing the facts in his head.

"Married?"

"Yeah." Scott finished the last of the drink, already feeling it work its magic. "Have a couple kids too, a boy and a girl."

"Marvelous, join me in another?"

"If you insist." Scott smiled, pushed his empty glass aside.

"Michael." Fischer made a peace sign and then turned it upside down.

"Tell you what." He stared into Scott's eyes. His thick brows raised high on a Botox paralyzed forehead. "I'm throwing a little soirée at my place in Sherman Oaks tomorrow night. And since you will be in town for a few days, maybe you would be interested in stopping by. I think you would enjoy yourself. There might even be a few people there that could be of help to you. What do you say?"

"I just might take you up on that."

Fischer reached into the breast pocket of his jacket, handed Scott a shiny, gold business card with black lettering.

**Joel W. Fischer Psy.D.**

**TALK TO ME**

**888-HEDGAME**

*A fucking shrink?* Scott thought, let down by his initial guess at how Fischer paid the bills.

Scott put the card in his wallet, wondering how many famous clients Joel had on the roster and how that might work in his favor. At the same time, Fischer thought he just found the perfect guinea pig.

The bartender put the new drinks in front of them.

"If you decide to come, and I hope you do, give me a call. I'll send my driver over to get you. Which reminds me." A Rolex popped out of his jacket sleeve when he extended his arm, like a turtle's head from its shell. "I need to call him to come get me." He took a sip, winked at Scott. "After one more round of course."

# DERRIK

## December 23, 2007

Derrik Jackson relaxed on the bed at the Marriott in Burlington, Massachusetts, thinking he needed to start getting in better shape when he got back to L.A. Ten years ago, playing cornerback for Tulane, two hundred and ten pounds looked impressive on his five-eleven body. Now, twenty pounds heavier and a lot less muscular, he looked sloppy. Like any athlete does when they stop lifting and running, but still hit the training table with the same ferocity. Derrick watched the time on his cell change to one-thirty. Just as planned, the ringtone went off. He answered.

"What up?"

"Is everything under control?" Joel asked.

"Good to go and ready for the show."

"Excellent. Scott is scheduled to leave early tomorrow morning from Logan. How's the weather treating you?"

"Cold as a motherfuckah. I ain't used to this. Got no desire to come back either. Supposed to be a storm comin' too."

"I know, but you'll be fine. Everything you need is waiting for you. I suggest heading out soon, while it's still light out. I know from experience how tough it is driving in Boston. You have GPS in the car right?"

"Shit yeah."

"Okay. Do you have any questions? More importantly, do I have any concerns?"

"Nah, we good. Your only concern is gettin' me back to LA."

"I just called Santa, he'll give you a lift tomorrow night." Joel laughed.

"I better have a little somethin' under *my* tree when I get back."

"That you shall. I have go. Just be very careful…and good luck."

"Everything's under control. Adios." Derrik snapped his cell closed, then thought about what to do for the rest of the night. Room service? Maybe a little porno? That fucking skinflint Fischer. More money than he knew what to do with, but always keeping an eye on the bottom line. Probably be asking Derrik for itemized receipts when he got back to L.A. Fuck him, and the Mercedes he rode in on. Derrik needed a little "me time".

## MERRI

### Christmas Eve 2007

"Simplicity is elegance." Merri Haskins admired the picturesque scene from the driver's seat of her Lincoln Navigator, as it idled in the entrance of the long driveway that lead up to her house.

An electric candle glowed in each of the sixteen front windows. A lawn spotlight aimed at the center of the house highlighted the large, handmade wreath on the front door.

She turned around, looked at Molly and Max in the second row seating.

"Always remember that."

"Remember what?" Max asked.

"You idiot," Molly sniped. "Less is more. Right mum?"

"Don't talk to your brother like that."

"He's a stupid little baby."

"Enough," Merri yelled. "Just be quiet...okay?"

She composed herself, looked in the rearview mirror.

"You're right though, especially with Christmas lights. Less *is* more. There's no need for colored lights and ridiculous lawn ornaments. It's *way* too much."

Merri pulled into the first bay of the three-car garage, thinking about the dead cell phone in her pocketbook, trying to remember where in the house she put the spare battery.

She'd already browbeat herself all day for not charging it before they left that morning. To make matters worse, the goddamn car charger wasn't working either.

Somehow, she had made it through the entire day without the cell, dealing with it, but not liking it. Christ, she might as well have been on Gilligan's Island without it. The piece of shit battery, or the phone, was junk. That was the only logical explanation she could come up with.

The kids bailed out, fighting to be the first into the house. Molly won, using her four-year advantage to out muscle six-year old Max.

Merri hoped the car service had already picked up her husband Scott at Manchester Airport and he'd be home soon. Halfway to the kitchen, she heard Scott's muffled voice mixed with the kid's bickering.

"Dad isn't coming home tonight," Molly screamed. "The airport in New York is shut down because of a snowstorm."

Merri dropped her pocketbook on the hardwood floor, pointed a finger at them. "I told you guys not to touch the answering machine. Get the hell away from there."

She replayed the message, fighting back the urge to either cry, or put her fist through the cabinet. If the kids weren't there, both seemed like worthy options.

As pissed as she was, the huge money Scott was making the last six months, would make furnishing her dream house in L.A. that much easier.

After hearing he'd try to get the first shuttle out in the morning and he'd tried to rent a car, but there were none available, Merri pushed the stop button, cutting him off mid-sentence.

She opened the junk drawer, raked her hand through the mess and pulled out the spare cell battery.

"Is he coming home? Is he coming home?" both children badgered her.

If they didn't give it a rest, they'd be getting an expletive-ridden tirade for an early Christmas present, instead of a Neiman-Marcus stocking filled with goodies. A couple Xanax with a hot cocoa chaser would be good right about now.

"No, he won't be home tonight, but he promised that he'll be here in the morning. Now get upstairs and get your pajamas on. Daddy told me yesterday that *A Christmas Carol* is on tonight." She looked at the microwave, noticed it was six-thirty, and felt sad that Scott was missing this tradition. "It's on in a half-hour. I'll get some cookies and make some hot cocoa."

The kids raced out of the kitchen, stomped up the stairs. Merri grabbed her pocketbook off the floor, pulled out the cell, swapped out the battery. It remained lifeless.

"Goddamn piece of shit," she said aloud, then thought, *maybe it just needs a charge.*

She plugged it into the wall charger cord, tried again. The activation jingle played and it synchronized with the network. The display informed her of seven missed calls and five new voicemails.

The messages from Scott told her what she already knew. She called his cell. They argued. Merri hung up on him.

A half-hour later, the three of them were under blankets on the couch, watching Merri's favorite version of the movie starring George C. Scott.

It had been a long day of last minute shopping. She wasn't surprised the kids hadn't made it through the whole movie. She looked at them sleeping, noticed how much they resembled Scott, and wondered why neither one inherited her curly blond hair, or pale blue eye color.

Brown eyes and brown hair were boring.

Merri hated to wake the kids, but without having Scott to carry them up to bed, she jostled them until they woke up. Then lead them up to their rooms. She tip-toed up the unfinished stairs leading to the walk up attic and started bringing the kid's presents downstairs. It took four trips to lug them down to the family room where the fourteen-foot tall tree was.

She selected the Christmas music channel on the TV, lowering the volume on The Supremes as they sang *"My Favorite Things"*. Ten minutes later, she admired the final display of presents, crying, while *"O' Holy Night"* played.

Satisfied with the arrangement, Merri went upstairs and checked on Max first, then Molly. Both got a goodnight kiss on the forehead. She went into her bedroom, changed into pajamas, and stood in front of the mirror above the double vanity, getting ready to take out her contact lenses.

The left lens came out easily. The right one shifted toward the outside corner of her eye. She moved in closer to the mirror, spreading her eyelid apart. Holy fuck! The shower curtain ripped open behind her. In the reflection of the mirror, she saw the black ski mask and the latex gloved hands. One covering her face, the other attached to the arm that wrapped around her chest and lifted her body off the floor.

***

When Merri came to, her first thought, *I'm dead.* Paralyzed limbs and complete darkness convinced her she nothing more than a soul, existing in a black hole somewhere in the universe. Hearing the bursts of air coming from her nose and the muffled sounds trapped in her mouth, let her know she might still be alive.

Merri recognized the sound of a zipper being pulled and knew something very bad was happening. A body bag flashed through her mind. Before she could process any more information, the duct tape covering her eyes was ripped off in one quick, stinging pull. A hand reached under her neck and tilted her head forward off the pillow.

He stood, leaning over her. The headlamp light secured to the outside of the ski mask blinded her. He pulled a strap over Merri's head and forced something onto her face, covering her eyes and cutting off all light. He let her head fall back into the pillow and pushed the headphone cups onto her ears. Merri, blind and deaf, braced herself for what she knew would come next.

She couldn't feel the needle tip as it pierced the skin on her arm.

***

When Merri stretched her arm out, her fingers touched something that felt like human skin. Her arm instinctively recoiled tight to her body as she rolled in the opposite direction toward the lamp on the nightstand. She reached across the darkness and turned the light on. She stared at the lump under the comforter, her heart pounding under her breast.

*What the hell is that?*

She pulled back the comforter, slowly. Her body stiffened when the muscles contracted around her spinal cord.

It lay motionless, with unblinking eyes, staring directly into hers.

Merri looked at the expressionless, naked infant lying there. It was a boy with rose tinted skin, albino blond hair, and beautiful, pale blue eyes. He kept staring, not moving or showing any signs of breathing.

Merri felt a sense of calmness wash over her and reached out, gently touching his hair. He extended his arm upward with a pointed finger. She wrapped her fingers around his tiny hand. It was ice cold. She tried to pull away, but he clenched her thumb with such a powerful grip, she wasn't able to.

***

Merri looked at the horrific accident scene in front of her. Traffic was backed on both sides of the road. New Hampshire State Police cruisers, ambulances, and a fire truck, obstructed her view of the wreckage. Pieces of Christmas wrapping paper blew around on the ground like tumbleweeds and remnants of the presents littered the highway. Merri heard the two state troopers talking.

"It's a triple fatal. What a fucking shame. Just as the guy was dying he says to me, 'Are my kids alright? Tell my wife I love her, it wasn't my fault'. Poor bastard, of all times Christmas Eve. It doesn't get any worse than this. I got a couple kids myself. We're trying to contact his wife, but so far no luck."

Merri moved closer, staring at the remains of what looked like an upside down, black SUV. The roof was caved in and the glass had blown out of the rear window. Her eyes focused on the license plate as she tilted her head to the side, trying to get a good look at it.

*MERRI-4?*

Her legs gave out and she fell to her knees. She looked away and saw the three yellow body bags laid out on the snow covered embankment.

Merri curled up on the ground, crying uncontrollably, oblivious to everything around her. When her head rose from her cupped hands, she was back in her own house, looking at an image of herself sitting alone in a chair. The newspaper on the coffee table was dated December 25th 2008, a year into the future.

Merri's heart ached seeing herself with swollen, red eyes and staring across the room like a zombie. A voice came from the kitchen.

"Ma, are you alright?"

Merri heard footsteps and looked across the family room.

"Ma? I'm right here, you okay?"

A man came into the room, tall, handsome, wavy blond hair, and pale blue eyes. Merri guessed he was mid-twenties.

He bent over and comforted the grieving woman. Merri could barely see the image of herself, because his large body completely blocked it. His comforting words and hugs were not recognized though. He was in the same clandestine form as Merri.

"You still have me Ma. I'll take care of you."

His head turned, eyes staring directly into Merri's. "Even though you killed me, I'll still love you and take care of you."

Merri screamed, but his eyes stayed locked on hers, like he was looking through her eyes and into her soul.

She forced herself to look away. A burning sensation enveloped her sinuses and overpowered her face. Her eyes filled with tears and overflowed so quickly, it temporarily blinded her.

She wiped her eyes and was back in her own bed.

The infant boy lay across her chest, sleeping, his arms wrapped around her. She felt the warmth of his body, the slight movements of his chest as he breathed. Merri cried, holding him tight to her chest.

"What was I supposed to do? I was only sixteen years old. My parents would have disowned me. What kind of future would you have had? I am so sorry. Please, please forgive me. Oh God, what did I do?"

He turned his head, opened his eyes and smiled at her, exposing a full set of miniature adult teeth.

"Da-da."

***

The bedroom door burst open. Molly and Max ran in, got right in Merri's face, and started shaking her.

"Mum, wake up, Dad's on the phone," Molly yelled. "He just landed and he's getting a cab. He'll be home in forty-five minutes. Can we start opening presents now?"

Merri's eyes opened. She tried to focus through the blurred vision, while her hands swept over the comforter, feeling for the shape of the infant. The alarm clock showed it was five fifty-seven in the morning. Her vision slowly clearing up, she tried to compose herself.

"Give me a minute, will you. I'll be right down."

"Come on, hurry up. We can't wait," Max begged.

Molly pulled him out the door by his shirt.

Merri stared at the ceiling, shaking, trying to comprehend what had happened. She shuffled into the bathroom, feeling dizzy, and put her glasses on and took off the damp pajamas. The phone startled her when it rang. She answered. The mechanical voice announced an "unavailable" number.

"Hello."

"Hi Ma," the man's baritone voice said. "I miss you."

The line dropped and the phone fell from Merri's hand, landing on the rug.

***

Merri tried to concentrate on making Molly's bed, but the images from the dream, the nausea, and her mounting guilt wouldn't let her. When Scott got out of the shower, Christmas Day or not, she had to talk to him about it. The abortion was a heart wrenching experience, but that was so long ago. They were just kids themselves with their whole life ahead of them.

"Mum, your phone is beeping," Max yelled from the kitchen for the second time.

"Bring it up to me."

Max bounded up the stairs and handed her the phone.

"I want you in the shower as soon as your father gets out," Merri told him.

"But I'm still playing with my Christmas presents," he wined, and took off down the stairs.

Merri looked at the display on the cell. One missed call from a private caller and one new voicemail. She logged into the voicemail account, played the message.

"Hey there lover, it's Chrissie. Hope you made it home okay. I'm heading home tonight. It's a Christmas to remember, that's for sure. Give me a call Scott. Talk to you soon, I hope. Bye."

# FELIZ NAVIDAD

Derrik called Joel as he drove the rental car down the access road leading to Manchester Airport.

"Are you on your way to the airport?" Joel asked.

"If that's what you want to call this place. I'm already here. What am I fuckin' flying on, a crop duster?"

"Please, you're in first class. I don't want to hear it. You will be back soon enough. It will still be Christmas Day in LA. Did you dispose of everything?"

"Yeah, everything but Miss Merri Christmas. I'm tired as shit though."

"You can sleep on the plane. Call me when you land. John will be there to pick you up."

"He better be. Don't keep me waitin'. It's bad enough I have to stop over in Vegas."

"Play some slots, maybe you will get lucky. Have a safe trip, see you soon."

The line dropped and Derrik pulled into the Avis rental to return the Impala.

# DR. MARI

## August 2008

Joel sat behind the desk in his office, put the headphones over his ears and plugged into the audio jack of his laptop. Dr. Mari had called him earlier, looking for the latest report and treatment recommendations on Scott Haskins. Joel figured another hour wouldn't matter, especially for a little pissant like Mari. He turned out to be a real pain in the ass, didn't know the meaning of the word patience. Looking for updates and treatment plans, when he knew damn well what the fuck the plan was. If he kept it up with all the cover your ass bullshit, he'd be the one getting a treatment plan, courtesy of Derrik and James.

Joel pulled a CD case labeled *S. Haskins* out of the desk drawer, took out the disc and put it in the DVD drive. His fingers rapped a nervous drum roll on the desk as he stared at the screen. He clicked on the play icon. The acoustic guitars of *"Ventura Highway"* came over the headphones and he leaned back into the leather captain's chair, oblivious to everything, but what played on the screen and in his ears.


## INSANE IN THE BRAIN


*This can't be a coincidence,* Scott Haskins thought when *"Ventura Highway"* started playing as his convertible cut through the darkness at eighty miles per hour. Both mind and body in perfect harmony from the three glasses of Bushmills he treated himself to in the sanctity of his office thirty minutes ago.

The wind rolled off the windshield, aerating his hundred-dollar haircut and filling his nose with the fragrance of Eau de Southern California.

Scott just signed a second round pick of the L.A. Clippers and now he was flying down Ventura Highway in a hundred thousand dollar car, listening to America sing about the very road he was on.

In this moment of time, he was the man with a fucking plan.

The first waft of a chemical stench assaulted his nostrils, interrupting the serenity of the moment.

He focused on the faint, amber colored light a half-mile ahead of him. Seconds later, seeing the flames shooting out of the ground, he down shifted the Dodge Viper SRT-10.

A huge fireball lit up the right shoulder of the highway. Scott cut the wheel hard right, stomped on the break pedal and shut down the engine. He ran toward the burning wreck, but the intense heat forced him to stop thirty feet away.

*No skid marks. Full-speed collision. No one could have survived.*

Other cars started pulling over. He flipped his cell open and dialed 911.

Scott moved closer, scanned the surroundings and saw something he knew was human sprawled out on the grassy hill lining the overpass. He sprinted toward it, dropping to his knees when he reached the boy, who was unconscious, but breathing.

"Oh man, fuck. You'll be okay. Come on kid wake up."

Scott stroked his hand through the boy's wavy, blond hair, trying to provide some form of comfort. Bedside manners were not something he had experience with. If the kid was a lottery pick, he'd carry him to the hospital on his back. The boy's pale blue eyes opened, rolled around a few times, and closed. A muffled moan came from his unmoving lips.

The cadre of emergency responders that arrived had reduced the wreck to a smoldering carcass, covered in white foam. The mix of chemical odors still dominated the air. Scott watched as the legs of the gurney collapsed and the boy was loaded into the ambulance. A C.H.P officer approached him, ready to take Scott's statement. It didn't occur to Scott that the Bushmills might be lingering, but the officer noticed and decided it wouldn't be a factor, given the circumstances.

"How many people were there?" Scott asked.

"Two, well three, if you count the kid. That's about all we know at this point. The two in the car were burned beyond recognition. Once we can talk to the kid, we'll know more. Are you okay Mr. Haskins?"

"Yeah, I'm alright. Where did they take him?"

"Cedars-Sinai."

"Hope he's okay."

"You did all you could do Mr. Haskins. Did he say anything to you?"

"No, he was just groaning."

"Okay, that's all I need. If we have any more questions, we'll contact you." The trooper looked at Scott with a serious, but not quite accusatory look in his eyes. "Are you okay to drive Mr. Haskins?"

"Yeah, just a little shook up that's all," Scott said, recognizing that alcohol, not his mental well being, was the driving factor for the question.

It was a surreal ride back to his condo. The smells of the wreck were still imbedded in his nose. He needed a stiff drink and shower, in that order, maybe at the same time. Scott thought of the kid in the accident and it a made him think about his two kids back in New Hampshire. He missed them and thought about how so much had changed since last year, when a single voicemail destroyed his family. He didn't need to be in New York on Christmas Eve last year and could have got out of it, if he wasn't so goddamn career driven. Crystal swore she had called the cell number *he* had given to her. Scott still wasn't sure if she was lying or not. The drink created reasonable doubt on the night in question. It was times like this when the guilt and loneliness were almost unbearable for him. Life had become a never ending series of extreme highs and depressing lows. This night served as a perfect example.

***

The latest Brooks Brothers catalog was the only thing of interest in the mail.

*Boston blueblood Brahmin*, Scott thought, looking at it. That was his style and he remained loyal to it, even in California, despite the constant pressure to succumb to a more laid back "SoCal" style.

He heard the phone ringing inside as he unlocked the door to his Hollywood condo. The robotic voice of the cordless phone indicated a private caller. The call went unanswered, then to the answering machine. It sounded like a male in adolescent purgatory, the Adam's apple desperately trying to lower octaves, but not quite succeeding.

*Peter Brady?* Scott smiled at the childhood memory.

"Hello…hello…Mr. Haskins? This is Tom."

*Tom?*

"I'm the boy, um, who was in the car accident."

Scott snatched the phone and pushed the talk button.

"Tom, oh man, how you doing kid? I just got in."

"I'm okay. I'm pretty much all better now and I, um, just wanted to thank you for helping me back then."

"That's awesome. It's great to hear from you. What can I do for you?"

"Well, I won this contest, and I get to take someone, and I was wondering if you would go with me."

"Wow, that's great. What kind of contest was it? Where are you living now?"

"I live in Westlake with a new foster family. It's okay I guess."

*Can life get any worse for this poor fucking kid?*

"Will you go with me? It's this Saturday night in Ventura. There was this contest on the radio, and ten people got picked to be the first ones on this new virtual reality ride they're opening. All the winners can bring one person with them. It would mean a lot to me if you would go."

"Saturday night? I don't think I can. I have to fly to ah…"

Tom interrupted, "Please, please will you? We get to take a limo."

The images of the accident flashed in Scott's mind.

"I guess I can reschedule. What the hell, sure. It would be an honor to go with you."

"Thanks Mr. Haskins. We have to be there at seven, so the limo will pick me up at five o'clock. And we'll pick you up at five-thirty. Is that okay?"

"Sure kid and please, call me Scott. I'm looking forward to it. It's supposed to be a good ride huh?"

"Yeah, I can't wait."

"Let me give you my address."

"Nine thirty, North Doheny drive. Is that it?"

"How'd you know that?" Scott asked, a little freaked out.

"A police officer who was at the accident, Detective Carleton, came to visit me and I told him I wanted to thank you. And he gave it to me."

"Ah, okay then. I'll see you Saturday."

"Thanks again so much. It will be awesome, bye."

\*\*\*

Scott spent the first half of Saturday sleeping off the effects of a late night partying with Joel Fischer. Damn, that guy could put the drinks away. Fischer was still needling him about passing out last month and having to put him up at his place for the night. Not good, when you have to finalize a deal with a Clippers draft pick the next morning. Last night had started with a Black Crowes show at the Music Box @ Fonda and ended with too many Grey Goose and Red Bulls at the private party in the same venue. A workout and steam bath helped the recovery process. He passed the last couple of hours getting ready and fighting off the apprehension that a couple drinks could have easily cured, but held off.

The phone rang. It was Tom. He told Scott they were out front ready to go. Scott peeked between the Venetian blinds and saw the driver sitting in a black, eight-passenger Lincoln.

As Scott approached the limo, he saw the driver and Tom standing outside it. Tom had on cargo shorts, retro Thin Lizzy t-shirt, and black Adio sneakers.

*Handsome kid. Looks older than I remember. Probably around fifteen.*

Scott reached out and shook Tom's hand.

"Thanks so much for coming with me Scott."

"My pleasure."

Tom pointed to the driver. "Scott, this is John. John, this is Scott Haskins."

*Looks like Paulie Walnuts from the Sopranos.*

"Nice to meet you Mister. Haskins. Well, we better get goin'. It takes about an hour to get there." He opened the door, motioning with his hand and a slight bow. "Gentlemen."

A Stone Temple Pilots song played at low volume inside as they sat down.

"John, you mind if I put the divider up?" Tom asked.

"Go for it."

Tom sat slouched with his legs stretched across the back seat and reached for the glass of iced soda resting in the holder to his left.

"So what are we in for tonight?" Scott asked.

"It's supposed to be awesome, better than the NASA flight simulator."

"I'll take your word for it. My son would be all over something like this. I'll have to take him when he comes out here."

"How old is he?"

"Seven. I have an eleven year old daughter too."

"Are you…divorced?"

"Yeah, I am. How about you Tom? You said you live with a foster family," Scott inquired, hoping to find out more details of what happened.

"Well, actually they're my second one. The two people that died in the accident were my first one."

"I'm sorry Tom, I didn't mean to…"

"It's okay. They're cool, but Westlake pretty much sucks. I was living in Ventura before. I liked that a whole lot better."

"I hear that."

"You mind if I change this?" Tom asked.

"No, put on whatever you want. Anything but country that is."

"Country sucks." Tom started smiling. "Big time."

Tom scanned through the channels, chose a crunching, guitar rock song.

"Who's this?" he asked Tom.

"It's the Kings of Leon. They rock."

"Good stuff," Scott said, while thinking, *there just might be hope for music after all. Need to find out more about them.*

The limo made its way down Route 101 as they talked about school, sports, and New Hampshire. Scott still hoped to find out more details of what happened the night of the accident, but unless Tom brought it up, it wasn't going to happen.

As they entered into Ventura, Tom moved to the driver side seating and looked out the window.

"Look over there, it's two trees," he said, pointing out the window, implying that Scott join him for the view.

They looked at the two bushy-topped trees, set apart from each other at the top of a large hill.

"They're Big Blue Gum Eucalyptus trees," Tom informed.

"Interesting, I heard they were planted so ships could get their bearings," Scott offered.

"Actually, that's just a story. They weren't planted for any reason. In eighteen ninety-eight a guy had them planted just because he thought they would look good on top of the hill. There were thirteen trees at first. The guy had to use a horse to get the buckets of water up there."

"What happened to the others?" Scott asked.

"Five years later, a fire burned down eight of them. Fifty years later, some kids cut down three of them on Halloween night. The townspeople planted three new trees, but in nineteen sixty-six someone cut down three of the five."

"That's a fascinating story."

"One of them is an original and one's not. You can't see my favorite one though."

"What do you mean?"

"It's the stump of one of the original trees that's still sticking out of the ground. I feel bad for it. They killed it for no reason and it never had a chance to grow. It just sits there. I hope the people who did it were cursed."

"Yeah, me too, that's a bummer."

The limo exited the off-ramp and headed down Ventura Ave. An old Rolling Stones song came from the drivers section of the car as John lowered the divider.

"We're almost there. About fifteen more minutes," he told them.

"Awesome. Great job John." Tom lowered his window and Scott did the same on his side.

The car turned right and continued for another four miles. They were out of the urban surroundings and facing the vast, mountainous terrain. The limo slowed down, turned right, and Tom yelled, "Muluceps Drive, this is it."

When they pulled up to the gatehouse, an ancient, meek looking security guard waved them through. Multiple buildings comprised the enormous complex in front of them. Five, one hundred and fifty-foot smokestacks towered over the building roofs.

"This used to be the old Deyancey Flour mill," John said. "If you ever ate a Nabisco product, chances are this place had a hand in it. It's been abandoned for a long time now. At least they're finally doing somethin' with it."

"This is where they built the prototype of the ride and tested it," Tom said. "We get to be the first ones outside of the company who get to go on it. They'll manufacture it here if all goes well."

"I guess we're in the right place," John said, pointing to the various white and black limousines parked in front of the largest building.

John pulled alongside the seven parked limos as two more made their way down the access road heading toward them. Incubus blared from speakers mounted on top of a black van with WGYN 107.3 stenciled all over it. A couple of the drivers remained in their cars, while the others talked among themselves, or on their cell phones. Their outfits were standard limo driver: black pants and jackets, white shirts, sunglasses. A couple of them wore old-school driving caps, like John's.

*Burnt Offerings* flashed through Scott's mind. The evil chauffeur had scared the shit out of him as a kid. Still gave him nightmares once in a while. Joel had laughed when Scott mentioned this during one of his therapy sessions. Two weeks later, the movie poster was delivered to his house, Fischer's idea of a prank. Scott threw it out.

"When in Rome." John opened his door, preparing to step out of the car.

"Hey, thanks John, see you in a couple hours," Tom said.

"Yeah, I really appreciate it John."

John tipped his cap as he got out. "My pleasure gentlemen, I hope you enjoy yourselves."

He lit a cigarette and made his way over to join the other drivers.

Tom turned off the radio. "Ten cars, looks like we're all here. It's six forty-five. Only fifteen more minutes. Should we get out? Everyone else is."

"Yeah I think so. I wouldn't mind stretching my legs."

Everyone lingered around their respective limo, making small talk and discretely glancing at each other, while Nirvana blasted from the van. Scott looked around, took a mental inventory of the others.

*Ten adults including me. All males. Each one with a teenager. Six boys and four girls. Eight white guys and two black. One of the black guys with a white boy. One of the white guys with a black girl. Everyone looks fairly the same. Decently dressed, most likely professionals. The kids all look like typical California teens.*

"This is so cool," Tom said. "It's seven. They should let us in soon."

The music abruptly stopped. A professional radio voice boomed from the van, drawing everyone's attention to it.

"Ladies and gentlemen are you ready to experience the thrill of a lifetime?" the Voice proclaimed.

Scott wondered if Michael Buffer was holed up in the van.

A large loading dock door opened, revealing two men dressed in tuxedos. One was black, less than six feet tall, heavy set, with a short, cornrow hairstyle. The other was white, over six-foot, muscular build, and shaved head.

The Voice inside the van continued, "WGYN 107.3 proudly welcomes you to beautiful Ventura California. You are the lucky, the chosen…the pioneers. Congratulations, you'll be going where no one has gone before. Now, if you will, please head up the stairs to meet your tour guides. Who will take you on the adventure of a lifetime. WGYN bids you Godspeed and good luck."

\*\*\*

The massive rectangular space had neglected wooden floors and unfinished, twenty-foot tall pillars supporting the floor above. The longer walls on each side were lined end to end with five-foot long split windows that allowed the outside light to filter in. There was no artificial lighting inside.

"Welcome everyone. Please follow me," the black guide instructed.

He led them through the space, then up a fire-escape style set of stairs that hugged the interior wall, until they reached a yellow door at the top. They followed the guides through the door and entered the second floor of a separate building. The equally massive room had an aged, concrete floor covered with dark stains, and fewer windows. Antiquated skylights provided additional lighting. Remnants of machinery were scattered along the floor and vintage industrial signage remained mounted to the walls.

"This must have been the baking room. Do you smell cookies?" Scott whispered to Tom.

Tom laughed. "Yeah, I thought the same thing."

They stopped at an obviously new brick wall that sealed off the remainder of the space. A large steel door was centered in the middle of the wall. The white guide pulled some papers out of his leather satchel bag as he addressed the crowd.

"Well, we've made it. In a few minutes we can enter. Before we do, I need each of you to sign a waiver form."

He handed a form and a pen to each adult. Everyone signed, handed them back in, and gathered in a semi-circle around him.

The black guide entered a code into the keypad mounted on the door, turned the large handle, and pulled the door open. "*Magical Mystery Tour*" thundered from the state-of-the-art sound system inside. They followed the guides into the room. Multi colored, wall mounted lights reflected off a huge, spinning, mirror ball suspended from the ceiling. The fast moving colors bounced off the white walls and shiny varnish of the wooden floors.

# MR. KITE

"This is totally insane," Tom shouted into Scott's ear.

Scott nodded in agreement, mesmerized by the ride in the center of the room. It reminded him of the Sizzler, or the Turkish Twist he used to ride at carnivals when he was a kid. The ride was circular with twenty, seven-foot tall stations around its perimeter. Full length dividers separated each unit. Each one had a round platform to stand on.

The rear wall of each unit was padded and provided the connection point for the adjustable torso restraints. A flexible cable attached to the top of each station, supported the dangling devices that looked like large, upside down, black bowls.

The volume of the music increased and thousands of imbedded, blinking, neon lights swarmed the ride as it came to life. Strobe lights started flashing and a structure began rising from the middle of the ride. The first thing Scott saw was THE ASPIRATOR, in large, yellow, neon letters. Everyone yelled wildly with excitement, punching the air with their fists.

The structure kept rising, revealing a longhaired man in a top hat and black, crushed velvet jacket, sitting in an oversized leather captain's chair. He was hunched over a large control panel and his gloved hands moved around it, pressing buttons and turning knobs. He seemed unaware of his captivated audience.

*Willy Wonka!* Scott thought. *The radio contest. Tom inviting me here. The secret nature of the whole thing. And that character sitting up there, damn, it's all part of a new age version of Charlie and the Chocolate Factory. What a brilliant fucking marketing gimmick.*

The upward movement of the platform stopped. The man's hand motions on the control panel indicated he was slowly fading the music.

He abruptly stopped and looked up, keeping his head still, scanning the crowd with animated back and forth eye movements.

"Welcome everyone. I am Mr. Kite, and I will be your host tonight. I would now ask all of you to select a pod on the ride and stand inside it."

"Which one do you want?" Scott asked.

"Those two." Tom pointed at the pods directly in front of them.

After everyone had selected their spot, the host ran a hand over his close-cropped beard and continued.

"Thank you very much. In a moment, the shoulder restraints will be lowered. They will feel rather confining, but that is because they need to be. This is an extreme motion ride."

Kite pressed a button, initiating the downward movement of the restraints. They automatically stopped after making contact with each person's shoulders. The two guides went around to each pod, checking each restraint, until it fit tightly on every rider.

"Good luck." Scott extended his hand across to Tom.

Tom shook it. "Thanks, you too."

*His hand is ice cold,* Scott thought, as Mr. Kite continued.

"We are ready to begin. Your headsets will now be lowered. Please position your head in the center as it comes down. You will feel it gently touch the top of your head, and then it will raise two inches."

He pushed a button and the process happened just as he described. The headset completely covered Scott's head and rested just above his shoulders.

"Shall we begin?" Mr. Kite's voice came over the stereo speakers inside Scott's headset.

The entire inside of his headset became a three hundred and sixty degree video screen of blue sky with clouds rolling by.

*These guys are going to be millionaires.*

"Enjoy the show," Mr. Kite's voice whispered through their speakers.

"*Ballroom Blitz*" blasted inside Scott's headset and the ride started. He really did feel like he was sitting behind the wheel of a car driving at night. The ride moved his body with the visuals. Everything about it seemed realistic. The road was familiar and Scott recognized it was the 101, as the headlights beamed out over the road ahead of him. Suddenly, he saw something speeding toward him on the horizon. It flew at eye level, gaining speed, and then stopped in freeze frame just as it was about to smash into the windshield. Scott saw it had Tom's face. The screen unfroze and the naked, black-winged figure with Tom's head veered to the right, landing in the grass on the shoulder of the highway.

The car cut hard right and crashed into the overpass abutment, slamming Scott's upper body against the torso restraint. The screen went black. Scott struggled to push the headset off, but it wouldn't move and he couldn't squirm out of the shoulder restraints.

*Get me out of this fucking thing.*

The shrieks and profanity laden screams coming from the other adult riders caused Scott to struggle harder.

Mr. Kite's voice came through the headset, "I hope you have enjoyed the show so far. Now, we will move on to act two."

The headset began to move and Scott felt relieved, until it lifted above his eye level. Tom stood in front of him, staring into Scott's eyes.

"What the hell is going on Tom? What just happened? How did you get out of this thing?"

The restraint tightened. Scott's lungs emptied from the pressure against his chest.

Tom's closed lips formed the beginning of a smirk and quickly turned into an open mouthed laugh that sounded like a little child's. Two baby teeth protruded from the center of his bottom gums as he laughed and moved in closer, still locked on Scott's eyes.

"I would have been a good son. I would have loved you."

The sound of Tom's toddler voice caused Scott's body to shake. Tears streamed down his face.

"What *the hell* are you talking about?"

"Never mind daddy. It's okay. Molly and Max are their names. Isn't that right? I have to go now daddy."

Tom turned away and started following the other kids as they walked out the door. The sounds of childish laughter trailed off as the last one left the room and the door closed.

"Wait, come back here. Please, come back Tom," Scott begged.

Mr. Kite's voice came over the sound system.

"I trust that everyone enjoyed the ride. We will move on to the final act, the grand finale if you will. Now that everyone is ready, on with the show! Maestro, a little mood music please."

"*Dr. Feelgood*" overpowered the room.

"Lights!"

The colored wall lights and mirror ball activated.

"Action!"

The torso restraint tightened again, the pressure slowly crushing Scott's chest. A Plexiglas tube started rising from the base and slowly encased Scott in his own personal test tube. The headset lowered, until it formed a perfect cap on the top of the tube.

A cold, clear liquid gushed down from above Scott's head, soaking him as it ran down his body. The liquid rose quickly within the tube. Scott struggled to get out of the restraint, kicking at the sides of the tube, trying to put a hole in it. The bitter, salty taste sickened him and he heaved violently. His throat and nose burned when he involuntarily swallowed a mouthful. The liquid rose up to his chin. Scott held his breath as it covered his head, his insides boiling.

*I am going to die.*

He exhaled the last of his air, closed his eyes, and clenched his lips as the liquid reached the cap. He coughed and the air bubbles rose to the top of the tube. He sucked in more of the liquid and his insides burned. His eyes opened and the intense pain forced him to choke up a scream as his vision deteriorated, then went dark.

Scott hacked violently as the liquid started draining from the bottom of the tube. Crimson tainted syrup dripped from his mouth and nose. Blood oozed from the raw skin and open sores covering his face and arms. The excruciating pain let him know that he wasn't dead, yet.

"Please God," he whispered. "Let me die."

The bottom of the tube opened, but the restraints held Scott tight. His feet dangled above the hole. A loud noise, like the drying units in a car wash, pierced his ears and he felt an unbearable force pulling his body toward the hole. He shrieked when the vacuum pressure ripped his legs from his body. Ten seconds later, his arms tore away from his shoulders. The torso restraint released. What remained of his lifeless body, dropped through the opening at the bottom.

The cover automatically moved back over the hole and the Plexiglas tube started to disappear into the platform.

"And that's a wrap," Mr. Kite announced over the sound system to the empty room. He stopped the music and shut down the lights. The control structure he sat in started returning to the sunken area it came from.

Kite opened a hatch, revealing a staircase, and walked down it. At the bottom, he opened a door that lead to a large loading dock area. He walked toward the two guides, who were putting large, blue barrels into a cargo van.

"Nice work tonight guys." Kite told them.

"Thanks Boss," they said in unison, shoving the last barrel in.

"Same place as always right boss?" the white guide asked.

"Yes, *of course* in the same place. Come on guys, you know the drill."

## THOMAS

Fischer looked out over Los Angeles from the twentieth floor window of his office. His right hand stroked through his ponytail as he dictated to the digital recorder in his left hand.

"Doctor Mari, please find enclosed, along with this report, the complete audio of my sessions with patient Scott Haskins. I remain committed to my diagnosis of acute psychosis. I recommend that the patient continue to remain in the care of the Napa State Hospital, as well as maintaining a rigorous progr-"

"Joel, are you there?" A woman's voice interrupted over the intercom of his desk phone.

"Yes, Elaine, what is it?"

"A Mister Thomas Haskins is here to see you."

"Please, send him in."

The office door opened. A tall, blond haired man entered.

"Thomas, how are you? You're looking *very* sharp. What's the occasion?"

"No occasion, just came from an audition." He grinned. "I stopped by to tell you I'll be leaving for a while. I'm heading back East for a week."

"What for?"

"Nothing special, just a change of scenery."

"When are you leaving?"

"Tomorrow morning."

"Please, have John take you. I don't need him until the afternoon. What time do you want him there?"

"Ten-thirty works."

"Consider it done."

"Thanks, I appreciate it."

"I know you do. Enjoy yourself."

"I will. Okay, I have to split. Call me if you need anything."

"You know I will."

## JOHNNY

I decided to fly out of Orange County rather than LAX for the same reason I was flying into Manchester, New Hampshire, instead of Logan in Boston. I didn't need the hassle, simple as that. I needed a break and taking the stress out of the travel was a good start. John was taking me to the airport in the limo. I hadn't seen him in a couple weeks and knew he would be good for some laughs. I had no agenda or firm plans and it felt good. Things were going to happen at my pace and by my rules.

I waited for John in the entertainment room of the house in Woodland Hills that Joel owned, while "*Rollin'*" assaulted my eardrums by way of the MP3 player that I had just downloaded a new mix to.

My cell started vibrating on the coffee table. SALVATION blinked on the display. That was Joel's nickname for John, Johnny Salvation.

"What's up John, where are you?"

"Look out the window."

I went to the front room and saw the limo pulling up the long driveway.

"Get your ass out here will you?"

"I'll be right out, calm down."

I put my suitcase in the back, sat up front with John.

"To what do I owe the honor?" He reached over, patted me on the shoulder.

I pulled out a dollar bill, waved it in front of his face.

"I'll sit in back if you want, and then you can pop the trunk and put my suitcase in. *After,* you open the door for me of course."

"I was only shittin' you. Good to see you kid."

John, dressed in jeans, light blue cabana shirt, all tanned up, his silver hair combed back. He was a pretty handsome guy and looked about ten years younger than sixty-one.

"What's with the casual look?" I asked him.

"Hey, you think I *like* wearing that chauffeur getup?"

"I wouldn't think so, but I'm sure Joel loves you in it."

"Just another one of his fuckin' quirks."

"I hear that. Let's roll. I just want to get out of LA."

"Your wish is my command."

He put the limo in gear and we headed to John Wayne Airport.

The ride went smooth, until we hit a patch of traffic on the 405 in Long Beach. The radio had been on the whole time, but as we crawled along, I became more aware of it. Thinking it was the Beatles, I turned it up.

I looked over at John. "This isn't the Beatles is it?"

"No, sounds like em' though. It's the Dave Clark Five. Might as well be them though, it's called-"

"Let me guess, "*Catch Us If You Can*".

"Bingo."

The song ended and as I listened to the next one, my chest tightened, cheeks and nose burned.

"Turn this shit off, will you."

John turned it down. "What's the matter, you don't like the oldies?"

"That has nothing to do with it. I'm just not in the mood for this song, if you know what I mean."

He paused for a second, made the association, and turned down *"Cats in the Cradle"*.

"Sorry about that Tommy."

"No worries. You got any plans for the weekend?"

"Yeah, goin' to Vegas for a few days with Joel."

"I didn't know he was a gambler."

"He's not, but he's been workin' on a project with some guys out there."

"What kind of project?"

"Don't know many details, but the work he did with the Blue Man Group out there has something' to do with it. I guess some people liked what he did with that, and he told them about the work he's been doin' with the video stuff. Well, not everything of course, but the general concept. They liked it and want to meet with him."

"Sounds interesting. You flying or driving?"

"What do you think? They offered their jet, but he don't fly anywhere."

"Sucks for you."

"Eh, the drives pretty boring, but once we're there it should be alright. We're staying at The Venetian, carte blanche for everything."

Twenty minutes later, we pulled up to the passenger drop off at John Wayne.

"Check it out." John pointed to a huge bronze statue of John Wayne in full cowboy regalia.

"Wow, that explains it," I said.

"Kind of ironic ain't it? He fought to stop building this because he lived around here and didn't want all the noise. So what do they do? They put a huge statue of him right at the entrance. It's like fuck you Duke. They should have made it so he was giving the finger to everyone as they pulled up. *That's* the way he would have wanted it."

"You're a wealth of information John."

"So they tell me. Alright my friend you take care and stay warm. How long you going to be gone?"

"About a week. I'm sure you'll be picking me up when the time comes." I shook his hand. "Thanks for the ride man, been good talking with you."

I checked in, went through security, and headed to my gate. I found a place to sit and it felt good to relax. I put the MP3 earphones in and started reading a book Joel gave me, *Bless the Beasts and Children.*

An hour later, they started boarding my flight. It was two o'clock, which meant it was already five on the east coast and I wouldn't get there until ten at night. I grabbed my carry on, made my way onto the plane. My seat was in first class and I hoped to sleep through most of the flight.

I landed in Manchester, New Hampshire a little after ten o'clock. I didn't get the sleep I had hoped for because the book was too good to stop reading and I finished it. I again realized that Joel doesn't do anything without a purpose. As I waited at the baggage claim, I remembered that I needed to turn my cell back on. It came to life and I looked at the display.

Two calls, one from Joel, one from John. I had two messages and checked the first one.

"Hey Tommy, it's John. I know you're back East but this is important. Call me as soon as you get this. Talk to you soon."

I deleted it and the next message played. It was Joel.

"It's me. You need to get back here. I know it's late where you're at, but you need to get on the first flight back in the morning. Call me."

I called John first. It rang, went to voicemail.

"John, it's me. What the hell's going on? I just landed, call me back. I'm going to be staying at the Radisson in Nashua, New

Hampshire. I have to get the rental car and I should be there in about an hour. Joel left me the same message. I'm going to call him now. I was hoping to get a heads up from you. Call me when you get this, later."

*What could Joel possibly want me back there for? Should just let it go until tomorrow. Don't need this shit, need a break. Doesn't matter, he'll find me. He's probably with John right now, listening to my message.*

Joel picked up after the second ring.

"Why didn't you call me first? I'm here at the house, with John."

"What's up?"

"Obviously it's an emergency, or I wouldn't have bothered you. I know this trip was important to you, but it absolutely can't wait."

"So, are you going to get to the point?"

"Love to, but not on the phone. You need to trust me on this one. Okay?"

"Whatever you say Joel."

"Please, lose the attitude. You need to be back at the airport in the morning for a nine o'clock flight. It's all taken care of. Just make sure you are there."

"Alright, I'm staying at the-"

"I know, the Radisson in Nashua. Listen, when you get there, log into a Gmail account with user name dream weaver md, all one word. All e's no a's. The password is salvation eighty-one. All the details of your flight are in an email from glamgirl thirty-three. Once you have read it, reply back with the word bryce, B R Y C E, so I know you got it. Okay?"

"Yeah, I got it. Is that all? It's late here, and I still need to get the car. I'll see you tomorrow, alright?"

"Cheer up, will you. It's all good. See you tomorrow."

I got my bags and ended up renting a Chrysler 300. I entered the hotel address into the GPS, scanned the radio for some decent music, and headed out of the airport listening to *"Rooster"* on Rock 101.

"Turn right onto Route 101 east," the female voice on the GPS told me.

*Rock 101 on Route 101. Wonder how many people have noticed that?*

The hotel was nice, right off the highway. It looked like a big castle way up on a hill. I would have liked to stay longer, but knew I would be back. It was only a matter of time.

I was on the road at six-thirty the next morning, to catch a nine o'clock Southwest flight back to L.A.

Live Free or Die is on the bottom of every New Hampshire license plate, along with a picture of the Old Man of the Mountain. The lady at the front desk of the Radisson told me the "Old Man" was a rock formation on a mountain and when you drove by it a certain way, it looked like a man's face sticking out.

When I told her that I wouldn't mind seeing it, she said, 'it's too late, it crumbled and fell to the ground in two thousand three'.

I thought of these two things as I drove.

*Live Free or Die. The Old Man of the Mountain. The Old Man Lived or Died Free of the Mountain. The Free Man Lived or Died in the Mountain. The Old Man Lived Free or the Mountain Died.*

My mind game ended when *"Californication"* came on, reminding me that I was heading back to L.A., and bumming me out.

*Live Falsely or Die Trying. The Old Fake Titted Bitch in the Valley.*

## SABORO, GHEDE & BRYCE

I landed at LAX around eleven o'clock. I had been gone less than a day, but had a feeling of culture shock as I made my way through the masses toward the baggage claim.

I called John.

"You made it," he said.

"Yeah, I'm getting my bags."

"I'm out front. Enjoy your trip?"

I hung up on him.

I got in the limo and we left LAX.

"What's going on? What's so goddamn important?" I asked John.

"We're meetin' Joel at his place. He's got some big news about the project, and he wants you in on it."

"What kind of project?"

"Somethin' to do with what was supposed to go down in Vegas, but he changed his mind, so it's goin' down here now."

"You got screwed out of Vegas huh?"

"More like gettin' screwed out of *gettin' screwed* in Vegas, if you know what I mean. The place is crawling with hot broads."

"You would have loved New Hampshire. It's loaded with women. Some even had all their teeth."

We stopped at the front gates of Joel's house in Sherman Oakes. John entered the code, the gates opened, and we pulled up the driveway. A Cadillac Escalade, which I hadn't seen before, was parked behind Joel's Mercedes SL65 and Chevy Tahoe.

"Who else is here?" I asked.

"It must be the people from Vegas. The Escalade wasn't here when I left."

John pressed a speed dial on his cell phone.

"We're here...Is that right? I better say cheese then." John put his arm out the window, raised his middle finger, and waved it around. "Smile, we're on Candid Camera."

We pulled behind the Escalade. I noticed it had Vegas plates and wasn't a rental.

"Welcome to *Shangri-La,*" John said. "You believe he named this place, like it was a fuckin' boat."

"If I owned a place like this, I'd name it too, but not the Shangri-La."

"Not *the* Shangri-La, just Shangri-La. You know he's fussy about that."

We walked up to the double, ten-foot tall, glass doors. The glass was clear, but could be changed to white by remote control. I went to press the button on the intercom, but Derrik, one of Joel's two security guards, opened the door for us.

"We don't need no girl scout cookies." Derrik folded his arms across his chest and lowered his head, looking at John out of the top of his eyes.

"Too bad," John said, "I hear your cookies got a thing for the Girl Scouts."

"Fuck y'all, at least I'm always getting somethin'."

"Only when James is in the mood." John winked at me.

"I'm gonna tell him you said that, when he gets back."

"Call him now." John pulled out his cell. "He's over at your girl's place isn't he?"

"Where are they?" I Interrupted.

"They down in the media room, where else you think they gonna be?"

"They could have been out at the pool," I said. "Or getting the soap and wax you'll need for the limo, while we're here."

John and Derrik looked at each other and laughed, impressed by my wisecrack.

We walked through the great room, which had shiny, hardwood floors and a high, truss beamed ceiling, and headed to the media room.

Joel, two guys dressed in suits, and another guy, who looked like he was around my age were all seated around the huge, black leather sectional. A bottle of Dewars and some glasses sat on the large, black marble table in the middle of the sectional area. The media room was Joel's pride and joy. The walls were covered top to bottom with black velvet drapery, with the exception of the eighty-inch plasma screen mounted on the wall in front of the sectional. The carpet was short, black shag and the twenty recessed lights in the ceiling were dimmed to create an atmosphere of screening room chic.

A mellow Rod Stewart song was coming from the surround sound, just loud enough to hear. A show I didn't recognize was on the plasma and the volume was muted.

Joel stood up, drink in hand. "Thomas, glad you could make it. John, I like the casual look. Come, have a seat, join us for a drink. But first, introductions are in order."

Joel looked at the three guys sitting down, then pointed toward John and I. "Gentlemen, this is Thomas, and his cohort is John. They are both very good friends, and confidants of mine." He looked toward the first guy in the suit. "Thomas and John, this is Robert Saboro. Seated next to him is Jason Ghede, and this handsome devil is Bryce. Robert and Jason come to us from Las Vegas, and they are here to discuss my latest venture. Bryce is from Ventura, and will be joining the team. He'll be working closely with you Thomas. In fact, I told him that he'll be taking up residence with you in the Woodland Hills house. I'm sure you'll extend every courtesy to him. I think you'll find the two of you have much in common."

"Yeah, no problem," I said, looking at Bryce.

"Thanks bro," Bryce said.

"Nice to meet all of you," I said.

"Likewise," John said.

We went around and shook hands. Joel handed John and I a glass of Dewars on the rocks.

"Excellent," Joel said. "I've also leased a Mustang Bullitt and a Dodge Challenger that will be delivered to your place tomorrow. You two can flip a coin, or do whatever to decide who drives which one. I'll leave that up to you. It goes without saying that you *will* take care of them."

He looked at me, then Bryce, expecting a response.

"Will do," I said.

"No worries," Bryce said.

"Now that we're all settled in, we can get down to business." He looked at Jason and Robert. "Is everyone good on drinks before I start the video?"

No one needed a refill.

"Excellent. Shall we then?"

Joel used the remote to stop the music, pressed it again, and the plasma changed over to a blue screen. He dimmed the lighting to almost darkness. One last push on the remote and the screen went black.

"*Toys in the Attic*" started blaring from the surround sound. The footage on the screen showed a birds-eye camera view, moving rapidly over the ocean, headed toward mountains on the horizon. Within seconds, it was above a volcano and immediately nose dived into the opening.

The screen went black and repopulated with Kite Industries in red letters that looked like they were dripping down the screen. The screen slowly dissolved and refreshed with DreemWeever VR in the same font style.

The screen changed and showed a close up of a man's face. A black headset that reminded me of large ski goggles covered his forehead and eyes. Attached headphones covered his ears. He was smiling and beads of perspiration ran down his face. The music abruptly stopped and the face on the screen screamed over the surround sound. It startled all of us, except Joel. The screen continued zooming in on the man's face, focusing on his wide open mouth, until it showed only the dangle at the back of his throat. The screen went black and Joel turned on the lighting.

Joel scanned the room, knowing he had impressed everyone and had our attention. The suits sat upright and stiff on the edge of the sectional. Bryce nodded his head in approval. John gave a low round of applause and I followed his lead.

Joel looked at the Vegas guys. "This, gentlemen, although a rather primitive example, is the vision of DreemWeever VR. An experience so real, so vivid, to both the visual and audio senses, that it crosses the line between reality and fantasy. It has the ability to produce physical and mental reactions to the stimulus it has provided."

Joel paused for effect and reaction, and continued.

"I'm sure you have many questions, and I'm quite confident that I can provide the answers to them. I suggest that we continue this discussion here, while Thomas and Bryce take the time to get to know more about each other. The pool area is quite adequate for that purpose. John, you're free to leave, but we will require your services at five o'clock, as Robert, Jason and I will be taking a trip out to Ventura."

Joel raised his drink to the group

"I look forward to the many great things we will accomplish together during our partnership. Cheers."

We all took a drink.

"Catch you later John." I looked over at Bryce. "Let's go man surfs up."

"Sounds good," Bryce said.

"You'll find towels and bathing suits in the cabana if you need them," Joel told us. "Help yourself to the bar as well. We'll be busy for some time. When, or rather, *if*, you want to leave, ask Derrik, or James if he's back by then, to drive you back to the house."

"Will do," I said.

***

Bryce looked around the property of Shangri-La. "This place is sweet."

"Yeah it feels like you're in your own private resort back here. Doesn't it?"

"Like a hotel."

It *was* phenomenal. We had to walk down a long, sloping set of stairs off the back of the house to get down to the pool area. The huge back yard was secluded by large trees around the entire perimeter, providing total privacy. The pool was shaped like a Gibson guitar without a neck. Both the pool and oversized Jacuzzi were encased by custom cement that extended out ten feet at the smaller end toward the house, and thirty feet at the opposite end. Flowers, plants and shrubs were everywhere around the tree line and cascaded down the slope from the back of the house.

We walked around the pool toward the huge granite bar that was built into the cement at the far end.

"That's the *cabana*?" Bryce said, pointing to the left.

"Oh yeah, it's really a guest house. He calls it a cabana. It's an ego thing. Come on check it out."

The cabana was off the back side of the pool in a secluded grassy area. We walked along the thirty foot brick walkway that cut through the grass.

It was forty feet long and twenty feet wide with double glass doors on each side. Two sets of the same style doors were separated by a solid white entrance door in the front. The flat roof hung over the house by three feet on the sides and front. A concrete patio, five feet wide surrounded the whole thing.

"This is insane," Bryce said.

"Wait until you see the inside."

We went in and I gave him the tour. It had a full kitchen area, granite on the counters and island, and white marble tiles on the floor. Behind a door to our right was a huge bathroom with a

Jacuzzi tub. Through a door to the left, was a fully furnished bedroom that had a large plasma screen mounted on the wall.

"Here's the best part," I said.

We walked straight ahead, into the entertainment room. The same leather sectional as the one in the house, except in white, took up most of the center of the room. A large oak table was in the middle of the sectional. The fireplace on the side wall had shelves of CD's and DVD's on each side of it. A sixty-inch plasma was mounted on the wall in front of the sectional and the carpet was a light gray berber.

The DVD and CD players rested on a marble table underneath the plasma. The surround sound speakers were recessed into the ceiling and walls.

"Man, he loves his music," Bryce said, inspecting the CD's.

"Oh yeah, he's a big fan of the seventies, as you can see. He's got a pretty diverse collection though. As long as its rock, it's probably in there somewhere. The music out at the pool is controlled from in here too. Find something and put it in. What you choose, will tell me a lot about you."

Bryce scanned the collection, made his choice, handed me a Cult CD.

It caught me of guard, but a decent choice.

"Start it at track seven," he said.

I grabbed the remote from the coffee table, put the CD in, skipped it to the track and turned up the volume.

"*Love Removal Machine*" filled the room.

"We'll get along just fine," I said, giving him a hippy handshake.

"I thought you might like that."

"Let's go outside, you up for a drink?"

"Sure." Bryce said.

We went out to the kitchen. I pressed the button to activate the music out at the pool area and inspected the liquor selection.

"Let's see, we have Grey Goose, Jack Daniels, or Bacardi. Which one you want?"

"I'll go with the Jack, on the rocks." Bryce said.

"Nice, I think I'll have the Goose with a splash of cranberry. Why don't you load up the disk changer, while I make the drinks."

## BIRDS OF A FEATHER

We took up residence at the large granite table behind the Jacuzzi. Bryce had brought along the bottle of Jack Daniels and a couple glasses.

Something about Bryce felt familiar. The way he looked at me when he handed me the CD and watched for my reaction when the song started, like he was telling me 'I'm in on the joke. I know exactly what you are about, Joel told me everything'. I had never met him before, but felt like I had known him a long time.

"So you're from Ventura huh, always lived in California?" I asked.

"Yeah, what about you?" Bryce poured some Jack, slid the glass my way.

"Same here, a native LA'er. How old are you man?"

"Twenty-eight." Bryce poured himself one, capped the bottle. "And you?"

"Twenty-six. How'd you meet Joel?"

"Long story, but basically, he's my therapist."

"Hey no worries, that's actually how I met him too."

The drinks were loosening us up and I sensed that, like me, Bryce wanted to loose the pleasantries and cut to the chase. Besides the common thread of Joel, I noticed the physical similarities: both of us about six-two, lean muscular builds, and shoulder length hair. We both had clefts in our chins. The major differences, my hair was dirty blond and wavy, Bryce's was light brown and straight. He had brown eyes, mine were pale blue.

\*\*\*

Joel walked John to the door of the media room, after Bryce and Tom left for the pool area. John rapped a new pack of Marlboros against the palm of his hand.

"You are *not* smoking in the car are you?" Joel chided john.

John gave him a sly grin. "Would I do that?"

"I check the driveway for cigarette butts."

"You're wasting your time. You should look harder."

"I will now. Remember, five o'clock." Joel put his hand on John's shoulder. "What would I do without you John?"

"Learn to drive?"

"Go feed your tumor."

Fucking prick, always having to get last word in.

Joel closed the door as John left and pushed the dead bolt into the locked position. He pressed a button on the remote as he walked back toward the couch. The plasma changed to an eight panel display of color surveillance feeds. He pressed it again, changing it to a split screen of the pool area and the entertainment room inside the cabana.

Robert and Jason, impressed, nodded in approval at each other. They continued the conversation in Russian.

"The power of modern technology," Joel said, putting his hands behind his head. "I could turn on the audio as well, but I will let them have their privacy. Besides, we have much more important technological matters to discuss."

Robert took off his glasses and cleaned them with a silk handkerchief he pulled from his pant's pocket.

"Yes, we are both very curious about your enterprise, and the advances that you've been able to make."

Jason leaned forward, placing his empty glass on the table and looking agitated.

"We are here for you to make believers out of us. You have done nothing but tell us of your breakthroughs, yet you have *shown* us nothing. We came here to see evidence of your claims, yet you do not-."

Joel put his hands up. "Patience gentlemen, I shall provide you with what you are looking for, and could, if I wanted to, show you much more than you would want to see. I am the one who should have the concerns, not you."

"I didn't mean to offend you," Jason said, "but as you know, it is more than just the two of us who are waiting on this, and have also invested a lot of money in the development."

Robert interrupted. "What he means is, we have provided financing and in return, have received nothing but speculation. You invited us here with the promise of results and it results we must see. That is all."

Joel pointed a finger at him. "And results you shall get, and more wealthy we *all* will get."

These two were really starting to get under Joel's skin. Not to mention, both of them could use a couple weeks in a tanning salon. And the suits they had on, oh brother, must be showing re-runs of Miami Vice on every channel back in Russia. Sure, they had given him a shit-load of money. But it was fucking peanuts in the grand scheme of things. You think people told Thomas Edison, or Michelangelo to fucking step it up? Perfection took time, couldn't be rushed.

Joel pressed the remote and a square portion of the carpet started rising from the floor under the plasma screen. A large, black safe with a digital keypad appeared. Joel walked over to it, entered a sequence of numbers and it automatically opened. He took out a folder, removed a disk and shut the door. The safe began sinking back into the floor.

"Before we start, I think a drink is in order. Do you agree?"

"Certainly," Robert said.

"Please," Jason agreed.

Joel placed the disk into the DVD player, walked back to the table and refreshed the drinks. He sat between them and raised his glass. They did the same.

"Gentlemen, I promise you will not be disappointed. We shall have success beyond our wildest dreams."

Joel pressed the remote, the screen turned black, and Metallica started into "One".

Kite Industries, in white letters shown on the center of the screen, then transitioned to a street view of a large, seven-story, brick building. It seemed like a ghost was walking with a digital movie camera, continuing up a long set of stone stairs, through a set of double doors, and down a long, white hallway.

It moved slowly past men laying on gurneys and sitting in wheel chairs. Every one of them either missing limbs, disfigured, or bandaged.

It moved to the end of the hall, turned to the right, and stopped at a metal door as it slowly opened and focused on a hospital bed. An oxygen tent covered the bed, distorting the image of the person lying inside it. The hoses coming from two suspended IV bottles snaked into the plastic near the headboard. A large, air compression machine beside the bed moved up and down. The phantom filmer moved closer, until it was at the side of the bed. A hand, covered by a blue surgical glove, reached out and opened a flap in the plastic.

The person in the bed was a male, his face badly burned and horrifically disfigured. The image on the screen slowly zoomed in, until the burn victim's face dominated the screen, showing the raw, pink skin, glistening from burn salve. Fresh blood leaked from his closed eyes, nose, and forehead. Clotted brown scabs dominated his cheeks. A large feeding tube snaked its way out of his swollen, burned lips. The chin and ears were wrapped in blood stained, white gauze. The top of his head, starting at the hairline, was wrapped in blue cloth.

The hand reached out and touched the cloth, remaining there for a few seconds, until the screen went black.

Joel pressed the remote and a game show populated the screen.

"So, what do you think?" Joel asked.

"What is the meaning of this?" Robert stood up, looked at Jason, then at Joel. "What does a video of a burned man tell us about what you are working on?"

"Yes Joel, I must agree with Robert. While this was disturbing, it doesn't shed any light on what we have come here for."

Joel massaged his eyes, took a deep breath. Another round of good copski, bad copski. What the fuck?

"Gentleman, you judge too hastily. I can understand that all you see is a movie of a suffering man, and you did not come here for lessons in compassion…or empathy. But, when I tell you that everything you saw, every single frame, was created using computer graphics. Then, I think you will have a much different interpretation of it. Am I correct?

"Is this true?" Jason asked.

"This cannot be. It was much too real to be created in this way, even with the most sophisticated technology," Robert said.

Ah, no shit, isn't that why you are paying me all that money? Joel almost said, but thought the better of it and continued.

"You came here for progress. That is what I have provided, and now you *question* me?"

Robert and Jason looked at each other, smiling and nodding.

"You have our apologies. You must understand our skepticism at seeing something like this. It was so realistic, more than we could have expected," Robert said.

"Yes Joel, please do not take any offense. As businessmen *and* investors, we were naturally apprehensive about this. Now that you have shown us this, we shall not doubt you in the future."

"I'm happy to hear that. You now know what has taken the extra time, but it has been worth it. With this technology, there is absolutely no difference between what is real, and what has been digitally created. I'm sure you will agree that it was worth the time, and that the possibilities of its uses are unlimited."

"Surely, you could have shown us other examples of this. Why did you choose this one?" Robert asked.

"Ah, that is a valid question, and our friends Thomas and Bryce that you met today, are part of the answer. You see, they are essentially my human version of guinea pigs. That is an extremely crude way of saying it, but it is the most basic and most appropriate analogy. There were a couple others before them of course, but that was rudimentary testing, and dramatic improvements have been made since that time."

"What do you mean by this?" Jason asked.

"The two of them are the first examples of what can be done with this technology. With them I have, and will continue to prove, that this can be used to manipulate the mind to believe things that are not reality. This particular video was my original method of manipulating their past from what it was, to what I chose it to be."

"What significance does the video we watched have on that process?" Jason asked.

"Good question. First you need to understand that these two gentlemen were nothing more than destitute narcotic addicts, before I abducted them. Thomas was the first, and Bryce came later, after I had completed my first successful trials with Thomas. My original plan was to have them believe that they were severely burned during their military service in Iraq. What you saw was a portion of the DreemWeever feed that I used to accomplish this. Using a process of many other feeds over a period of time, they came to believe that it was I who took them from that place, with the guarantee, and eventual delivery, of full reconstructive surgery."

"But this is not what you decided to do?" Jason asked.

"Correct. As I thought more of my ultimate goal of using the DreemWeever to not only manipulate minds, but to do it in such a way that certain audio or visual stimuli can trigger specific actions, I came up with a more intricate plan."


## JAMES


"What's up ladies?"

Bryce and I looked up across the pool and saw James standing on the terrace at the top of the stairs that lead down to the yard. His skin tight, black T-shirt could have passed for Under-Armor from where we sat.

We were deep in Jack Daniels and conversation and hadn't noticed him come through the sliders and outside.

He stood still, arms crossed over his chest and hands under the biceps, pushing them forward to add size. With the shaved head, he looked like Vin Diesel as he stared us down.

"What's with the pussy shit music?" he yelled, referring to the Hole tune that was playing.

"If we knew you were coming we would have had some of Joel's finest Bee-Gees waiting for you," I yelled back.

James smiled and made his way down the stairs to join us. His jeans were as tight as his shirt and his cowboy boots clicked off the concrete as he walked.

"Got to love the belt buckle," Bryce whispered to me.

It was metallic with the Aerosmith wings logo written on it and changed colors, like an opal ring, as he walked.

"What's old is new," I said.

James stood over us and extended his right fist across the table toward me, implying he wasn't making the effort to go around the table to initiate the greeting.

"What up slick?" he said.

"Same old man," I said, leaning forward, bumping his fist with mine.

"How's it going James?" Bryce said, bumping him.

"Had better days, but ask me again in thirty seconds and I'll rethink my answer."

He picked up the bottle of Jack Daniels, raised it to us, took a long power drink, and put it down on the table.

"How's it going James?" Bryce said, half laughing.

"Fan-fucking-tastic."

He pulled out a chair, sat down and stretched his legs out.

"Big doings at the Shan-gree-La today, huh boys? Joel's got himself holed up behind close doors with them weirdo's from Vegas. He told me over the intercom at the gate 'not to disturb him and go right out with you guys'. The Tahoe's here, where the fuck is Derrik?"

"He's in with them. Oh yeah, he was talking some shit about you too," I said.

"That fat, nappy headed fuck should be talking about treadmills and jogging. One of these days he's going to be trying to talk out of a jaw that's been wired fucking shut."

James took another drink from the bottle.

"You better take it easy," Bryce said. "Joel says you or Derrik need to take us to Woodland Hills when we're ready to go."

"I got news for you. I'm not doing anything but getting hammered, and you two are joining me. You're not going anywhere." He pointed at the cabana. "When the time comes, we're going to crash in there. How's that sound?"

"Cool," Bryce said.

"Right on," I said.

"You guys are too fucking good to me."

# PAUL & LUKE

"Yeah, this is perfect, near those cars over there, next to that truck," Luke Wadely said. "Turn that shit down."

"Chill man, I got it under control," Paul Roenik said, still strumming the chords to "*Dirty White Boy*" on his knee and fretting them on the steering wheel of his Ford Ranger pickup. "What the hell do they need such a huge parking lot for, if only a hundred cars are here?"

Luke pointed to the large, brick office building two hundred yards away from them.

"Look at the size of the building. Back in the day this place was filled to the max. I saw about three-hundred more cars here yesterday afternoon. Still, they're half of what they used to be. This is the second shift. They get off at midnight, and another crew comes in for the third shift."

Paul shut down the engine and looked over at Luke. "How far do we have to go?"

"We have to head that way." Luke pointed toward the boundary of the lot one hundred yards away, where Engelmann Oak trees grew along the entire inside perimeter of the ten-foot-tall chain link fence. "Once we get on the other side of the trees, you'll be able to see it. It's about a half mile walk from there."

"How hard is it to get in?" Paul asked.

"Should be a piece of cake. It's surrounded by fence, and there's a couple of security guards there twenty-four seven, but they don't give a shit. If we don't find a break in the fence, we can go over it. We just need to be careful of the razor wire on the top."

"Alright, let's do it," Paul said, high-fiving Luke.

Paul reached back into the extra cab space, grabbed a backpack and dumped it in Luke's lap. He pulled out another one and rested it between his thighs and the wheel.

"Make sure we got everything," Luke said.

"I know I got it all. I packed it right before I picked you up."

"Dude, just do a double check."

"We don't need everything anyway." Paul made binoculars with his hands, fitted them over his eyes. "This is just recon tonight, right?"

"You never know man. Just make sure you got everything."

"Whatever."

They walked across the expanse of the empty lot, headed toward the fence. The lighting had been turned off the last fifty yards. Paul followed Luke's lead into the semi-darkness.

"Those are some big ass trees," Paul said.

"This used to be all trees, before all these buildings and companies came around. I imagine they left these trees because you can't see shit behind them. Like Mother Nature's fence."

"Speaking of Mother Nature, how's about we-"

"No fucking way, not now." Luke walked a few more steps, stopped in front of the fence, and pointed at the massive building complex in the distance on the other side. "There's no lights in there, but you can see the outline pretty good.

They leaned against the fence, fingers locked in the mesh holes.

"Holy shit," Paul said. "Look at the size of those smoke stacks. Man, the place is huge."

"I told you it was." Luke pointed down the hill to the left. "See that little house type thing down there?"

"Yeah."

"That's the old guard shack, where the flunky security guys are. The only thing they do is make sure no one comes in through that main gate. This place is abandoned, so they don't do shit. They just sit in there all day and all night. Three shifts a day."

"Wonder if their hiring?"

"What's the matter dude, the body shop doesn't pay you enough?" Luke asked.

Paul gave Luke's shoulder a smack with the back of his hand. "I was talking about you."

"Come on man, the pizza gig is just until the-"

"Yeah I know, just until the band gets a big break. I'm only fucking with you. Which way are we going?"

Luke pointed toward the right side of the complex, one hundred yards away.

"We need to go around toward that way. That's the back of the whole place. Once we get through the fence we're golden. We'll go all the way around to the right, that will get us to the entrance of most of the buildings."

"You want to try out the Night Vision?" Paul asked.

"Not yet. Wait until we get inside the fence and we can try them out. Come on let's go."

They walked along the top of the grassy hill, until they reached the back of the compound and looked down on the flat roofs of all the buildings. The silhouettes of the five smokestacks rose into the sky, well above their eye level.

"We can cut down here," Luke said. "Watch your footing going down."

They made it down to the fence and stared at the three separate coils of razor wire running along the top of it.

"A little overkill don't you think? What did they make in this place, nuclear weapons?" Paul asked.

"No shit. Believe it or not they made flour and bakery products. Must have had some top secret recipes they didn't want spies to steal. You know, maybe like a flour bomb or some shit like that."

"Come on let's see if we can find an easier way through. I'm not even going to think of trying to get over this mess. We'll get cut to shreds."

The opening guitar riff of "*Secret Agent Man*" invaded the silence.

"Shit," Paul said, whipping off his backpack.

"You idiot, put it on vibrate. Don't answer it."

Paul unzipped a side pocket on the pack and pulled out his cell phone. He flipped it open, pressed a few more keys, and it vibrated. He looked at the display, snapped it shut, and put it back in the pack.

"I didn't want to talk to her anyway. She's a pain in my ass. I told her I'd be out tonight."

"Not good man if she's already checking up on you. You good now?"

"Yeah, while I got the pack out, I'm putting my headlamp on," Paul said.

"Might as well, but don't turn it on yet. Wait until we get up near the building."

They strapped the headlamp bands around their heads and tightened the forehead straps.

"Put your pack on, let's go man," Luke said.

They moved on, looking for a breach in the fence.

"How much further we gonna go?" Paul asked. "There's no opening in this thing."

"Your bitching isn't going to get us through it any easier. We're going to have to cut through it."

Luke opened his pack, pulled out a rubber gripped chain cutter, and cut two vertical lines, three feet apart.

"That should do it." Luke grabbed the bottom of the fence at the cut points, lifted up the flap, and looked at Paul. "Go ahead."

Paul took his pack off, pushed it through the hole, and then got on his knees and crawled through. Luke let go of the fence and it snapped back into place.

"Now pull that toward you," he told Paul.

Paul pulled it open. Luke pushed his pack through and crawled under.

"Let's go this way," Luke said, pointing to his right. "We'll see what's back there. Stay close to the buildings and put on the red lamp."

They pressed a switch on the headlamps and a red beam of light came on. They made their way across the pavement, until they were a couple feet from the four story wall of the building, then walked along the perimeter.

"Man," Paul said, "it's kind of eerie back here. This place is so goddamn big."

"Someone's been here. Look at that." Luke pointed to the graffiti sprayed on the walls. "We need to watch out for junkies and homeless people. They could be around here somewhere. Keep your guard up."

"I hear that. Legend has it the Pillsbury Doughboy haunts this place."

"Just pay attention. I'm serious, and watch out for rats. I'm sure this place is infested with them."

"Good point. Hold on a minute. We should probably have the Mace handy, just in case. It's not going to do us much good in the pack. Is it?"

They took off the packs, clipped the Mace on their belts, and kept walking.

"Hey look at that. What do you think?" Paul pointed to a black, fire escape stairway leading up to the roof.

"Let's check it out, see if it's safe. If it is, we'll get a good view of the layout from up there."

"You can go first," Paul said.

Luke started up. Paul followed behind, the red lamps shining off the wall in front of them.

"Seems pretty sturdy," Luke said. "I think we can make it."

"If you say so."

They made it to the top and looked across the one hundred yard span of the flat, black tar roof. The tops of the other buildings and towering smokestacks were spread out around them.

"Alright, if we go straight ahead that's the main entrance." Luke pointed to the left. "See way over there? That's where we came from. If we walk up further, we'll be able to see the guard shack and the access road that takes you in front of this building. You up for it?"

"Sure. How safe you think this roof is?"

"It's hard to tell, but our best bet is to stay toward the edge."

"I could use some more light," Paul said.

"We can use the low light lamp."

Luke powered on the small, rectangle lamp under the large, round one and adjusted it, until the beam shined on the roof, three feet ahead of him.

"This works. Turn yours on. We'll take it slow. Just watch for any holes or sagging spots. I'll lead."

They made their way across, stopped halfway and took a look around.

"It seems pretty sturdy," Luke said. "Let's go to the end and see what things look like out front."

Luke pulled back his jacket sleeve and looked at his watch.

"It's eight-thirty now. We'll look around some more and head out at nine."

"Okay, let's get some pictures before we go. I want a couple from up here with those big stacks in the background. No one will see the flash from over there. I want to post them to the website tonight."

"We can do that on the way back. Come on."

They continued toward the front of the building, until Paul stopped and raised his hand.

"Hey, hold up."

Luke froze and looked back at Paul.

"Check it out." Paul pointed at the headlight beams moving down the access road and heading toward the guard shack.

"They're probably lost," Luke said. "Better kill the lights anyway."

They shut off the lamps, crouched down, and watched the car pull up to the guard shack. Luke pulled the night vision binoculars out of his pack and looked though them.

"It's a fucking limo."

"No shit? How does a limo driver get lost? I thought all them things had GPS systems in them."

Luke, still looking through the night visions, gave Paul the play-by-play.

"One of the guards is talking to the driver. They should be leaving any minute now. Alright he's walking away. Shit, no he's not. He's opening the gate for them. Fuck, he's letting them through."

The limo went through the gates and the guard started moving them back into position.

"Come on," Luke said. "Stay low and follow me. Be careful."

They walked across the roof, headed toward the front of the building. When they got near the edge, they dropped onto their stomachs and looked over the side. The limo pulled to a stop in front of the loading dock platform below them.

"What the hell are they doing here? You said this place is abandoned," Paul whispered.

"It *is* abandoned. I mean someone must own the whole thing, but there's nothing in there."

The headlights of the limo stayed on, shining against the door of the dock entrance. The back door of the limo opened. Two men got out on the driver's side of the rear seating area, while another one exited from the opposite side. They met near the front of the car and started talking.

"Think it's a drug deal?" Paul asked.

"They look like business men, but who knows."

The passenger side door opened. A large, black man got out and walked over to the dock platform. He put both hands on the concrete ledge, jumped, and swung himself up onto the platform. He pulled something from his pocket, pointed it at the door, and it started raising.

"It has to be a drug deal," Paul said. "That guys looks like he's a bodyguard or something."

"This is like a movie man."

The noise coming from the door stopped after it rolled all the way up. The black guy went inside. A flashlight beam, coming from inside the building, flickered on and off against the windshield of the limo, then stopped. The black guy came out to the edge of the dock, lowered a wooden ladder to the ground, and rested it against the edge of the loading platform.

The three suits climbed up one at a time and went in. The black guy stood at the edge, looked around, and pulled the ladder back up. He waved toward the limo and went back inside with the ladder. The door started coming down and the outside lights of the limo went dark.

"The driver's still in there," Paul said.

"No shit." Luke took a second to think about it. "If this was a drug deal, you'd think another car would be coming here. What the hell are they doing in there?"

"Who knows? A limo, guys in suits, a body guard, all in an abandoned building. Must be something going down in there. We got more than we bargained for tonight. Now I'm curious. Aren't you?"

"Shit yeah." Luke rubbed his hands over his eyes. "What are we going to do?"

"We can't do much tonight but we can come back. We need more time to look around. Maybe we come back during the day, or at night, or both. We'll need to find a way inside somehow."

"That shouldn't be too hard in a place like this. There's got to be a lot of ways in. We definitely have to come back. This is too cool."

"Alright," Paul said. "Here's what we do. Let's go back to the truck. We can move it and park so we can see where the access road meets the main road and stake it out. When we see the limo leaving, we follow it, see where they came from."

"Who knows how long they're going to be in there. It could be hours. You going to wait *that* long?"

"You saw them. How long do you think guys like that are going to stay in a rat hole like this for?"

"You're right." Luke laughed. "It can't take too long to torture and kill someone."

"I already thought of that. If something like that was happening, we have to find out."

"We'd be famous."

"Or victims," Paul said. "Come on let's get out of here. If they don't leave by eleven we'll leave. Sound good?"

"Let's roll."

# WOODLAND HILLS

## September 2008

The ringing house phone woke me. I got up, went out to the kitchen to answer it. It was seven-thirty in the morning.

"Thomas, hope I didn't wake you?"

"Actually Joel, you did. What's up?"

"My conscience has been bothering me. I've been feeling bad about ruining your trip back East, and it just so happens that...is Bryce still sleeping?"

"I guess so, his doors closed. Hold on a minute." I went to the front room and looked out the bay window. "The car's still here, why?"

"Do me a favor. Go wake him up and put me on speaker phone. I've got some exciting news for the both of you."

"Hold on."

I banged on his door with my fist and foot at the same time.

"What do you want?" Bryce yelled.

I opened the door and walked in. Bryce was lying on his side under a sheet.

"Come on out here. Joel's on the phone. Say's he needs to talk to us about something big."

I walked back to the kitchen and put the phone on speaker.

"He'll be out in a minute."

"Tell him not to worry about his makeup."

"Don't worry about your rug either Joel," Bryce yelled from the hall.

"Somebody's having bitchy o's for breakfast this morning," Joel said.

Bryce came into the kitchen, dressed in boxers and a t-shirt. He went right for the coffee maker. I sat at the island as he filled the glass pot with water.

"Alright, we're both here. What's so important?" I asked.

"Like I was saying, I feel bad about ruining your trip, but I think you'll both agree that it had to be done. So, an opportunity has presented itself that will hopefully make up for it. I think the two of you will find it very intriguing. We will certainly meet to go over the specifics, but I can tell you, that you'll be in Boston for a few days, and then enjoy a weekend in New York City. Sound interesting?"

"What's the catch?" I said.

"Come now Thomas, what makes you think there's a catch? I prefer to look at it as an opportunity. A chance for both of you to satisfy the inner thespian desires that burn inside you. On the World's greatest stage no less."

"We're going there to *act*?" Bryce asked.

"Come on Joel get to the point. What's really going on?"

"Gentlemen, ye of little faith. Of *course* there are other objectives, and we will discuss them ad nauseam later today. I will tell you, that if your trip is successful, which I have absolutely no reason to believe that it wouldn't be, Kite Industries will prosper and we will all be the benefactors."

"So when is all this supposed to happen?" I asked.

"As I said, it starts today, and I would like the two of you to be at the house at six o'clock tonight. We will need a few days of preparation, and I expect you to leave after that. What do you say?"

I muted the phone and a few seconds later, Joel started whistling *"Girl From Ipenema"*.

"Please gentlemen, take your time. I don't mind being muted."

Bryce shot the phone with a finger gun and blew the imaginary smoke off it.

"You up for this?" I asked him.

"I'd like to know more, but going to New York would be pretty cool. Depends on what he's got up his sleeve."

"I hear you. Let's go over and at least see what the deal is. We can always say no."

"Yeah right."

"Time's up gentlemen. What's your answer? I'm about to start into some Manilow and believe me, you don't want that."

We both started laughing and I took the phone off mute.

"Yeah, we'll be over, six o'clock right?"

"Excellent. Make sure you lock up the house when you leave. You won't be back there for a while. Bring whatever ancillary items you'll need. Everything else will be taken care of. I have to go, my next patient is ready. A washed up B-list actress with lots of issues, should be interesting. Six o'clock, *sharp.* See you then."

"Later," I said and hung up the phone.

Bryce brought over two mugs of coffee and sat at the island.

"He must have some great stories," Bryce said.

"You know he does. With all the famous head cases he has for clients, he's got to have heard lots of good shit. Sometime we'll get him talking, especially after he has a few. Maybe tonight even. Who wouldn't be interested in a washed up actress's issues?"

"She'll probably leave his office with more problems than she went there with."

"What are you saying?" I started laughing. "The shrink should be seeing a shrink?"

"You know what I mean. He's really smart, but he's got a strange vibe about him. Maybe it's just the look. You know, the suits, the jewelery, the ponytail. Maybe it's the beard. If he shaved that, maybe took the ponytail out, and let his hair down, he'd look way different, not so stiff. It's like he has this cocky way about him. He looks just like that hair product guy. You know the guy. What the hell's his name?"

"The Paul Mitchell guy?"

"Yeah, that's him." Bryce said.

"Great call," I said. "That's perfect."


## THE MISSION


We drove the fifteen miles over to Joel's place. Because of an accident on the 101 in Tarzana, we didn't get there until after six-thirty. We pulled up to the gate and Joel's voice came over the intercom, before we could press the button.

"It's about time. Six o'clock means six o'clock. I'm out at the pool."

The gate opened and we pulled in front of the house. James met us at the door.

Bryce and I each gave him a hippy shake. As was his custom, James pulled you in close with his shaking hand and patted you on the back with his other hand.

"He's out at the pool."

"Yeah, he already told us. He sounded pissed," I said.

"Has a major hair across his ass too." He folded his arms across his chest and took a quick inventory of his arms. "The guy can be one moody son of a bitch sometimes."

"He should loosen up. Probably needs to get laid," Bryce said.

"I don't think it was you guys who got him going. He was already on a roll when he got back from the office. He's just looking for reasons to be a dick. You guys go back there and cheer him up."

"We'll have some fun with him," Bryce said, winking at me. "Won't we?"

"You know it. We can't have him messing with James' karma now can we?"

"Good fucking luck." James put an arm on each of our shoulders. "Go get'm boys."

We went out on the terrace deck and looked down at Joel sitting at the patio table, legs stretched out and a drink resting on his thigh. A folder was on the table along with an ice bucket, a couple glasses, and a bottle of Makers Mark.

Bryce put his finger to his lips, signaling me to be quiet, while trying to suppress a laugh.

"Check out the robe," he whispered.

Joel was wearing a thick, black, terri cloth bathrobe.

"Guarantee you he's got the Speedo on underneath that," I whispered back.

"Hey Hugh," Bryce yelled. "Where's all the bunnies at? They all quit on you?"

Joel was only semi-startled and glared up at us. Even from where we stood, his blue eyes looked like they were made of crystal marbles, like a Siamese cats.

"Get you're sorry asses down here...*now!*"

We made our way down and took seats on each side of him. The letters JWF were embroidered in white cursive on the breast pocket of his robe.

"What's the W stand for?" Bryce asked.

"Why, that's what it stands for. As in, *why* do I bother with you two, *that's* what it stands for right now."

"Come on," I said, "we hit traffic and couldn't help it."

"Let's see." Joel ran his hand over his beard and looked up at the sky. "Rush hour in LA and you hit *unexpected* traffic. You can do better than that. How about, Joel we didn't get our lazy asses out of the house on time. That works *much* better."

"Alright, we'll go with that," I said. "Now can we talk about the reason we're here?"

"We would have already been doing that if you two." He took a deep breath. "Never mind, let's not get into it. DreemWeever, as you know has made incredible progress so far, and it's almost at the point of reaching the vision I've had for it. There is however, one last stage before I can deliver the product that my investors were promised, and expect."

Joel pulled the white candle out of the top of the Makers bottle, taking time to admire the flame and the pattern of white wax that had dripped onto the fake red wax on the bottle. He passed the candle to Bryce and picked up the bottle.

"Rocks?" he asked us.

"No," Bryce said.

"Yeah," I said.

Joel poured the drinks, took the candle back from Bryce, and corked the bottle with it.

"As I was saying, DreemWeever has one last phase to go and that is the underlying purpose of your trip."

"*Do You Feel Like We Do*" started playing and interrupted his train of thought.

"An incredible song, by an incredible artist. I was at this show you know, when they made this album. One of the best I have ever been to. The voice box was ingenious."

I was temped to make a joke about the Frampton of today, but Joel seemed to be in a better mood and I didn't want to ruin his moment of glory. Bryce couldn't resist.

"Hey, this guy was good and all, but have you seen him lately? You'd never recognize him. I saw him on TV selling insurance, making fun of this song. It's a shame, I don't care who he is."

I braced myself for Joel's tirade, but surprisingly, he let it go.

"In this case." He looked at Bryce. "Let's remember what was, and not what is. Shall we?"

Joel opened the folder and placed two color pictures on the table. One showed an attractive lady with long blond hair. The lady in the other picture had shoulder length, light brown hair. She was good looking, but not as much as the one in the first picture.

"Take a good look at these photos because you will be getting to know these women very closely in the near future. The four of you, will determine the future success of DreemWeever. "

## BOSTON

Bryce and I left LAX on a United flight sitting in first class and arrived at Logan International in Boston at five-thirty in the afternoon east coast time. It was a smooth trip and we spent most of it sleeping, or listening to our MP3 players. It had been an intense four days at Joel's place, going over the plans, doing research, and rehearsing for the trip.

We got our luggage, went outside of C terminal, and made our way over to the taxi stand. The driver pulled up and lowered the passenger side window.

"Where are you going?"

"Back Bay, seventy-one Marlborough Street," I said.

He popped the trunk and motioned to the back of the car with his hand. We put our suitcases in and got in the back seat with our carry on bags. The driver entered our destination in the GPS, reset the meter, and headed for the exit.

"This definitely isn't LA man," Bryce said, looking out at the city in the distance.

"That's a good thing. This is where it all happened. Lot's of history here."

"This place better be nice," Bryce said.

"It's some friend of Joel's. He's a plastic surgeon, so I assume it's not a shit hole."

"Is he going to be there?"

"No, according to Joel, he's out of the country until next week."

I unzipped the side pocket on my bag, pulled out a set of keys, and dangled them in front of Bryce.

"That's why he gave me these."

Bryce snatched the keys from me, inspected both of them, then held one between his thumb and index finger.

"What kind of key is this?"

"It's a skeleton key. The kind they used in the old days."

"Wonderful, are we staying at a haunted house or what?"

"Yeah, it's possessed with Playboy Bunnies," I said. "They all left Joel's house to come here, and save his Speedo from eternal damnation."

Marlborough Street was lined with brick apartment buildings that looked like they were all attached to each other. Each building had three floors, a basement unit, and an attic loft. Elaborate, black, wrought iron fences extended from the front of the buildings out to the brick sidewalk. The individual buildings were divided in two by separate entrance doors at the top of the cement stairs.

"We're staying here?" Bryce said. "This looks like some kind of glorified projects."

"Joel called it a brownstone. This is an exclusive part of the city according to him."

"I'm not impressed."

The driver pulled up to number seventy-one. It had a flat front and the two buildings on each side of it had more elaborate facades and nicer windows.

The cab fair was thirty dollars. I gave him sixty dollars and he popped the trunk. We got our bags and walked up the wide, multi-colored, brick walkway to our building.

"They sure love their bricks here," Bryce said.

The stairs leading up to our double-door entrance had the same wrought iron railings on each side and another one in the middle to separate the entrances. The tall, light oak doors had individual panes of stained glass in the top halves of them.

Bryce looked up at the three stories of the building.

"This whole side is ours?"

"Bad news, we only get the bottom floor. This is the main entrance, to *this* side of the building."

"What are we staying in, the cheapest house on the block? What kind of plastic surgeon is this guy?"

"According to Joel, this isn't where he lives. He just uses it as an apartment. He's got a big house somewhere outside the city."

"That's more like it. So he basically just screws chicks here. Now it all makes sense."

The other key on the ring opened the door and we went into the shared entrance foyer. An oriental rug covered the hardwood floor and a large, master staircase lead to the units on the upper floors and attic. The lock on the door of our unit wasn't the right type for the skeleton key. The same key that let us in the building got us into our place.

"What the hell is this key for?" I asked Bryce as we walked inside.

"Must be for something in here. We'll have to check it out."

The hallway was made of polished hardwood and ran the entire length of the place. We dropped our bags in the front room, which also served as a parlor. The large bay window provided a perfect view of Marlborough Street.

I called Joel from my cell around seven.

"Hello Thomas. I was wondering when you were going to call. Where are you?"

"We're at the place, the brownstone or whatever you want to call it."

"I'm sensing sarcasm. What's the matter, not LA enough for you?"

"To say the least. I'm not a fan of minimalist chic."

"That's an eight hundred thousand dollar place, in one of the best sections of the city. Things are different out there. It's more of a conservative, pinstripe, old money mentality. Lot's of cash, but no flash."

"What's the skeleton key for?"

"I was going to get to that. There's a cabinet in the kitchen above the microwave. You'll find a strong box that you'll need the key for."

"What's in it?"

"Why don't you go find out? I have to go, my four o'clock is waiting. Call me tomorrow at three your time, bye."

"So what's the deal with the key?" Bryce asked.

"Come on."

We went out to the kitchen, which was small, but the marble counter tops and stainless steel appliances made it look somewhat modern, compared to the rest of the place.

"He said it's in there," I told Bryce, pointing to cabinet above the microwave.

"What's in there?"

"A strong box? I think it's like a safe."

Bryce opened the cabinet, pulled out a black steel box with an old padlock on it, and put it on the counter.

"Man this thing is old," he said.

I undid the lock and opened the box.

"Nice, I like that. Thought that was coming with the Fed Ex delivery," Bryce said.

"Me too."

Inside were: two bands of twenties, two of hundreds, an envelope with *Johnny* written on it, two boxes of Accuview 2 Colours Opaque contact lenses, two credit cards, and another envelope with nothing written on it.

Bryce took out the contact lens boxes and looked them over.

"Jade green…and chestnut brown? I'm taking the jade ones."

"Whatever, this guy must be pretty tight with Joel to leave this stuff. He has to know something about what's going on. He never told me his name though."

"That's a shock. Did you notice there are no pictures of anyone around here? There's no mail, no phone, not even a magazine."

"There's a TV and a DVD player, but no cable. Isn't that a coincidence? We just happen to have DVD's."

"He thinks of everything," Bryce said. "I bet if you dusted this place for prints, there wouldn't be any."

\*\*\*

I got up at nine the next morning and my first thought was to have some coffee. Fortunately, there was a full can in one of the cabinets and I started brewing some. I ate a couple of oranges while I waited for the coffee and reread the notes from the unlabeled envelope. At the top was *Always Use Accents*. On today's agenda was a twelve o'clock appointment at Azure Salon de Coiffure. My stylist was going to be Rhiannon and Bryce was with Renae. The only other thing for today was to again watch the *Wilde* and *The Adventures of Robin Hood* DVD's.

I poured two cups of coffee. There was no milk, so it would have to be black. I walked over to Bryce's room with the cups, banged on the door with my foot, and went in.

"Come on you better get up and hit the showers."

He sat up and I handed him a cup.

"My sincere apologies old boy as it appears that the butler has overlooked the need for milk this morning," I said.

He took a sip and put it on the table next to the bed.

"That's quite alright old sport," Bryce said. "It reminds me of my days in New Guinea."

"Indeed, would you care to join me in the parlor?"

"Splendid, I'll be right there."

"There's some fruit in the icebox, if you are so inclined. From now on, use the accents at all times. We still need the practice."

"Whatever," Bryce said. "Fix me some tea and crumpets then, Jeeves."

"More like a screwdriver in your case legend has it."

I went out to the front room and sat in one of the stiff, white leather chairs to drink my coffee and look out the large bay window at the people and cars passing by. The galley style kitchen didn't have a seating area, so the front room served as a dining area too. Bryce came out and joined me at the table.

"This is the most boring décor I have ever seen." He looked around the room. "Everything is square and white."

Bryce was right. With exception of the leather couch in the room we were in, and the ottoman in his room, everything was white. Even the bricks around the fireplaces were painted white.

"Where is this place?" Bryce said, looking over our itinerary.

"One thirty-two Newbury Street."

"How far is that?"

"We can walk there. It's less than half a mile. Let's go."

## NEWBURY STREET

"This is it," I said.

There was a large terrace on the second story that extended over the sidewalk. I could see a few people sitting at little tables.

"You sure it's on the second floor?" Bryce asked. "It looks like a restaurant up there."

"Positive. That must be part of the place, and a big reason we have to drop a grand here."

"Hey, it's not my money. We're worth it right?"

We walked up a staircase and through the entrance door. A receptionist sat behind a frosted glass desk, talking on the phone and typing on a computer keyboard. I could see part of the styling floor through the glass wall behind her.

She hung up the phone and gave us a 'Why are you here?' look.

"Can I help you?"

"Yes love, you certainly may. We have twelve o'clock appointments," I said.

"Ohhh kay...names?"

"Dorian Vane and Peter Blood."

She looked at the computer screen and moved the mouse around.

"Peter and Dorian, here you are. You're going to be with Renae and Rhiannon today." She turned around and scanned the stylist's area. "Unfortunately, they're still with clients. It shouldn't be too long though. If you want, you can wait out on the terrace and have a complimentary drink, or an espresso, or whatever. They'll come get you when their ready for you."

"That sounds like a splendid option. What do you say to that Peter?" I asked Bryce.

"An offer we mustn't refuse old sport. Please, after you."

"You've been so kind miss…my apologies, I don't believe you've told us your name."

"Oops." She turned around the name plate on her desk. Jessyka was inscribed on it. "Sorry about that. Everyone calls me Jesse."

"Well...*Jesse*," Bryce said. "Thank you for the assistance. We'll see you on the way out. That is, unless you would care to join us on the veranda?"

She started giggling.

"I don't think Gaston would be too happy about that."

"Gaston?" I asked.

"Yeah, he's the owner. He's not here yet, should be soon though."

"Ah, maybe we shall meet him later then. Let's go Peter."

We walked along the outside of the styling floor and went out to the terrace. Techno music was playing at low volume from speakers cleverly hidden within some fake plants that bordered the outside railings.

We sat at a small table on the edge of the terrace. The hustle and bustle of Newbury Street was two stories below on the other side of the railing. An oriental guy, sitting behind the small, Mahogany bar came over to our table. He was obviously a stylist in training and dressed in all black. The sleeves of his t-shirt were double cuffed to expose his skinny, but well defined arms. His black hair had red highlights in the front and was gel spiked upward in a purposely messy style.

"Hello, I'm Sasha. Welcome to Azure. What can I get you today? We have wine, cappuccino, espresso or maybe." He lowered his voice and cupped his hand over his mouth. "Something a little stronger perhaps?"

"I think I'll have a double espresso, black, Sasha," I said.

"Make that two, if you would be so kind," Bryce said.

"Two espressos it is. I'll be right back."

"You on the wagon mate?" Bryce asked me.

"Of course I'm not. I presume we'll be going out tonight to explore this fine city. There's plenty of time for spirit indulgence, like as soon as we get out of here. Plus, that coffee was nasty and I could go for some nice strong espresso."

"I can't argue with that. We shouldn't be here that long anyway."

"Indeed."

"Ah, here comes our good man Sashay now," Bryce said, trying to keep a straight face.

"A verbal faux pas I assume?" I asked, covering my wry smile.

"Here we go gentlemen."

Sasha put the tray on the table and placed the espressos in front of us. Each one had a Belgian chocolate biscuit on the side of the china saucer. He put a small, crystal dish of Altoids, a bottle of mineral water, and two glasses in the middle of the table.

"Let me know if you need *anything* else. Our wine selection is very good."

"I must resist your temptations for now," I said. "But you are a most gracious host, and I hope we will be inside enjoying the renowned services of Azure rather soon."

"It shouldn't be that long, but if you need anything just wave, tootles."

"We shall. Thank you Sasha," Bryce said.

I raised my cup to Bryce. "To Sashay and a splendid and adventurous trip."

He laughed. "Cheers mate."

Ten minutes later, a man came outside. He had a brief, private conversation with Sasha before he came over to our table. He was short, stocky with close-cropped, grey hair and dressed in all black. His silk, short sleeve shirt was unbuttoned to the mid-chest. He spoke with a French accent.

"Gentlemen, welcome to Azure. I am Gaston, the owner. Which one of you is Peter, and who is Dorian?"

I stood up and shook his hand.

"I am Dorian." I extended my left hand in Bryce's direction. "And this is Peter."

Bryce got up and shook his hand.

"Ah, the infamous Gaston. It is truly a pleasure to meet you."

"It is very nice to meet the both of you as well. I thank you so much for coming. I hope you will be happy with our services."

"I can assure you that we will," I said. "In fact, Azure has been quite intriguing so far and I think this will only continue."

"Yes Gaston, it is a *very* nice establishment you have here," Bryce added.

"You are very kind. Please, if there is anything I can do for you, do not hesitate to ask. They will be ready for you very soon and please, enjoy."

"You are too kind sir," I said.

Gaston headed toward the salon area, stopped, and whispered something to Sasha before going inside.

I poured some mineral water into my glass.

"You want some?"

"Sure, why not."

Five minutes later, two girls came over to the table. They looked like they were in their mid-twenties. Both around five-seven, and rail thin.

"Hey there," the one with straight, shoulder length, platinum hair said. "I'm Renae, welcome to Azure. Which one of you is Dorian?"

I stood up to greet her.

"Renae, what a beautiful name. I am Dorian."

"And I guess that makes you Peter," the one with the long, blond, flip-curl hairstyle said. "I'm Rhiannon, nice to meet you. You can call me Rio though."

Bryce stood up. "Rio, how exotic and totally charming, the pleasure is indeed all mine. It appears we are in very good hands Dorian."

"That is a vast understatement Peter."

"Alright, shall we?" Renae asked.

"We will follow your lead Renae," I told her.

"Please, you can call me Rena."

"Smashing," Bryce said. "Rena and Rio, how marvelous."

We followed them into the styling floor. I tapped Bryce on the shoulder and discretely handed him a few Altiods.

"Thanks," he whispered.

"No worries."

We were seated at stations next to each other in tan colored, leather, styling chairs. Marble counter tops in a light pink design topped the smaller cabinets in front of us. The smaller cabinets were book ended by larger cabinets on each side, forming a divider between the stations.

Various trade credentials were on display at the bottom of the huge mirrors lining the wall in front of us. The mirrors extended from the counter tops to the top of the sixteen foot high, stucco ceiling. It appeared that Rena had more qualifications, based on the *Assistant Creative Director* title under her name on the placard in her station.

"Looks like we have a lot of work to do on you guys today," Rena said.

"Please Rena, if you would be so kind, refresh our memory as to what we are having done today," I said, winking at Bryce in the mirror.

She put both hands on my forehead, pulled my hair back through her fingers, cascading the ends onto the top of my shoulders.

"You're getting this colored chestnut brown, ionically straightened, and a wash, cut and blow dry. Why would you want to do that to such awesome hair?"

"For no other reason than sheer boredom," I said.

"That's pretty drastic."

"Let's just say that it is in line with my personality. What about my cohort here Rio? What is in store for him?"

"Yes Rio, what *do* you have planned for me?" Bryce asked. "Although, I assume a straightening is not required."

Rio followed Rena's lead and stoked her hands through Bryce's dark blond, shoulder length hair.

"*You,* are getting an auburn brown coloring and a wash, cut and blow dry. What did you have in mind for the style?"

"I'm afraid it is rather drastic as well. I would like all of this removed, but still covering a bit of my ears. I envision using gel to comb it back. Kind of like a Pierce Brosnan look, if you will. Can you picture that?"

"Totally, I know *exactly* what you mean."

"Splendid, I put myself in your capable hands."

"What about the mustache?" she asked, referring to the razor mustache that Bryce had been growing since we went to Joel's.

"Ah, the mustache." He ran his thumb and index finger over it. "I prefer to keep that. Of course, I will reevaluate that decision after you are through, but for now it shall remain."

\*\*\*

Bryce signed for the FedEx delivery when it came at ten the next morning. It included two medium size boxes, one slightly larger than the other. He carried them into the front room. We opened them and took inventory. One box contained two DreemWeever headsets, and a portable Bose CD player. The other box had a black, leather, attaché style case inside it.

"Hey, you know what I don't see?" I asked Bryce.

"What?"

"The disc's for the headsets."

"Are you sure?"

"Positive," I said.

"Wait a minute."

Bryce pushed a small button on the side of one of the headsets. A red LED came on, but a disc didn't pop out.

"No luck," he said, "thought they might be in there already."

"I'll have to ask Joel," I said. "I can't imagine he'd forget it, if he packed the boxes."

"It's not like it's a minor detail you know."

## CRYSTAL

"How are you my dear?" Joel said over his cell phone.

"Actually, I'm getting ready to go to lunch. What's up?"

"I wanted to run something by you. It might prove to be a good opportunity."

"Oh, is that right. You know me, I'm all about opportunity. When it knocks, I'm right there standing naked at the door. No seriously, what's going on?"

"Through a client of mine, I've been made aware of a director and a screenwriter, who are going to be in New York this weekend on a working vacation. From what I'm told, they already have a deal, an extremely lucrative one I might add, to make the picture."

"And this is important to me...why?"

"It's important to you because they will be in New York to review locations and more importantly, because two large roles have not been cast yet. Roles I might add, that you could be a nice fit for."

"Now you have my attention baby. What's the catch though? As much as I'd like to believe that this is only about little 'ole me, I know there has to be something else."

"Can't this just be considered a simple act of kindness, done for no other reason than the worship of one of the most attractive members of the opposite sex?"

"Please, save it, come on."

"Well, if somehow these gentlemen, who I might add are relocating to LA, were to decide they needed to confide in a certain professional about their *issues* that might be considered a brilliant stroke of good fortune. Don't you think?"

"Now you're talking. So what's the plan? I'm presuming the plan doesn't include me investing any of my hard earned money. Does it?"

"Why of course not my dear, I think the two of you will be extremely happy with the arrangements."

"The *two* of us, who's the two of us?"

"Ah yes, like I said, there are two of them that are going to be out there and I can't very well send you out there alone now. Can I? I was thinking that your friend Leigh Anne might be persuaded to join you. Do you think that's a possibility? Of course, she wouldn't have to know anything other than it's a free trip to the greatest city in the world, outside of LA of course. What do you think?"

"I'll ask her, but no guarantees. I'll see if she's up for it. It's just a weekend right?"

"Yes, get there on Friday and back by Sunday afternoon. Get in touch with her and let me know, toot sweet. If she doesn't want to go, start thinking of a plan B person. Anyway, just let me know, I'll take care of all the arrangements. Five star all the way baby. Make sure you tell your friend that too, okay? Ciao."

"Later…Magic Man."

## VICTOR

Joel pulled the lever on the side of the sectional and the built in ottoman popped out. He stretched out his legs, reclined back, and reached over to the seat next to him to pick up the headset. He looked it over and used the sleeve of his robe to wipe off the smudge marks as he noticed them.

*Looks spectacular, has an evil Darth Vader look to it. Once the logo goes on, it will really look good. We have come a long way baby.*

He held it up in front of his face, admiring the light shining on the glossy, black paint as he moved it around.

"Showtime."

He put the strap over his head, pulled the DreemWeever down over his eyes, and adjusted the tension knob until it was tight to his forehead and cheekbones. With the headphone cups tight to his ears he started humming, to hear if it sounded like a bass in his head. It did. The design was right. The sound would be excellent.

*Comfortable, not tight on the nose or the temples. Fits like a glove.*

He reached into the side pocket of his robe, pulled out a mini CD disk, and slid it into the vertical slot on the right side of the DreemWeever.

"*Heartless*" started playing and DreemWeever VR, in blue letters scrolled by like a stock market ticker in front of Joel's eyes.

*Fantastic audio.*

The screen transitioned to a red, nineteen seventy-five Corvette convertible pulling up Joel's driveway. A woman with a mane of blond hair, wearing white framed, star shaped, sunglasses sat behind the wheel. She got out of the car, strutted up to the front stairs, and walked through the front doors of Shangri-La. Her body movements synchronized with the song, as she made her way through the house. She stopped in front of the closed door of the media room, pulled out a compact mirror and got the hair and lipstick in order.

The screen transitioned to the other side of the media room door. "*Straight On*" started, the door opened and she walked in, moving seductively toward the sectional. Her pink tank top was skin tight and the extra short, cutoff jeans had peace sign patches on the thighs. A yellow, banana comb stuck out of her back pocket and moved with her ass. She danced with her arms over her head, in perfect time with the music. A Strobe light came on and she looked right into Joel's eyes, lip synching the lyrics.

Joel pushed a tiny button on the left side of the headset. The music and video stopped. He took the DreemWeever off his head, rubbed his hands over his face, and smoothed his hair back to tighten the ponytail.

"Un-be-lievable."

He picked up his cell and called Ahriman.

"Hello Joel."

"Victor, how are you?"

"Doing okay, how about you?"

"I am absolutely fantastic, and you sir, are a genius. I can't talk now, but I had to let you know that things worked out very well, and I thank you for all your hard work. We are almost there.

"Thanks, I thought the same thing."

"How are you making out with the new project?"

"It's coming along, the video's almost done, and then I need to add the audio. I think you'll be very happy with it. It should be ready for you sometime tomorrow."

"Excellent, call me when it's done. I have to go, but I just wanted to tell you how impressed I am. I'll talk to you soon. Do you need anything down there?"

"No I'm good for now. I'll be coming up for air tonight, but I'll be back before morning."

"Excellent, thanks again Victor."

## SHATTERED

We were heading to New York to live deliberately. No contingency plans were made, nor were any reserve chutes packed. We harbored no desire to live with the "rats on the west side" or sleep with the "bedbugs uptown". During our journey we would have a five-star feast on the marrow we sucked from the cities bones.

"We'll be right down John." I snapped my cell shut and looked at Bryce. "This is it old boy, he's here. You ready?"

"But of course *Dorian*," Bryce said.

"Dorian, ha, I love the sound of that. Don't you...Peter?"

"Indeed I do old sport. Nice accent, almost as good as mine."

With that, we toasted the demise of our former selves with a shot of Absinthe. We would only be away for two nights, but the nature of our trip required us to take the four suitcases we carried out to the waiting limousine. Certainly, we could have flown, but considering the amount of luggage and the "sundry" items we were taking, this was the only feasible mode of transportation.

"John, long time, no see. How have you been my friend?" I placed a hand on Bryce's shoulder. "The dashing rogue is played by Bryce."

"I would say handsome rogue, not dashing," John said, shaking Bryce's hand.

"I'm afraid you are wrong John," I said. "The razor mustache makes him dashing. Without it, he would be merely handsome."

"Anyway," Bryce interrupted.

I winked at John and pointed to the luggage with my Faberge walking stick. "The bags aren't going to load themselves into the car."

"You're kiddin' me right?"

"Surely not sir. A dandy and a movie idol would *never* load their own bags. Maybe this will persuade you."

I pulled a large envelope from the breast pocket of my topcoat and handed it to him. It contained five thousand dollars in one hundred dollar bills. John pressed a button on his key chain and the trunk popped open.

Bryce started moving toward the door, but I held him back with my outstretched, gloved hand. I stared at the door, then toward John, and back at the door again.

John opened the rear door and looked at us. "As you wish my lords."

We climbed inside while John started loading the luggage. He finished and got behind the wheel, looking every bit the classic chauffeur.

"The Marriot Marquis, Times Square my good man," I said.

"By the way." John made eye contact with me in the rear view mirror. "I was talking with Joel and he-"

His words were cut off as the divider reached the roof. I shot Bryce a Cheshire grin and he started laughing.

"That was cold," Bryce said.

"He knows I'm joking."

"Here you go." He handed me a CD.

I put it in the CD player and *"Tumbling Dice"* started playing as we made our way down Marlborough Street.

We spent the four hour ride listening to music, discussing our plans, and when we reached Connecticut, started watching a DVD called *The Digital Man* starring Ray Liotta and Crystal Kelly. It was not good and Bryce ejected it by the time we crossed the border into New York.

We made our way through the superstructure gauntlet, down West Forty-Eighth Street, and turned on to Broadway. When we reached Times Square, Bryce was impressed.

"This is unbelievable, TV doesn't do it justice. It's the number one city in the world."

"Unless the category is verbal fellatio, then it takes second place to Los Angeles."

John pulled up to the entrance of the Marquis. The doors were opened for us and I immediately handed the doorman a fifty dollar bill. True to character, I purposely didn't acknowledge the fact that we had luggage, confident that it would be taken care of. As expected, we drew curious looks from others as we walked through the massive, forty-story atrium, headed toward the check in desk. A moderately attractive oriental girl directed us to her station with a beckoning hand gesture.

"Good Evening," I said, purposely tipping my Bowlers hat with my right hand so she would see the Jade scarab ring on my index finger.

"Checking in gentlemen?"

"Yes, Mr. Blood and Mr. Vane," I said.

"Welcome to the Marriot," she said, still typing on the computer. "I'll need a credit card on record during your stay. Shall I use the same one as the reservations were made with?"

"Yes, please do," I said, knowing that Joel had already taken care of this minor detail and there would be no trail, paper or electronic, that would lead back to him, or us.

"Okay, I have you on the forty-eighth floor, in an executive suite, with a Time Square view for two nights. And you'll be checking out on Sunday, the twenty-fifth."

"Splendid," I said.

She handed me a packet with the key cards tucked into the slot at the bottom.

"You're staying in suite four eighty-six and your key cards will provide access to the elevator as well as the concierge rooms on floor thirty-two. Enjoy your stay gentlemen."

"We shall, thank you my dear," I said.

We walked to the elevators, which looked like a high-tech amusement ride. The shaft was a massive circular tower that rose up through the middle of the atrium. The eight, glass encased elevator cars were spaced evenly around the outside of the shaft. From the lobby, they looked like a bunch of huge test tubes with humans inside of them, moving up and down at different speeds and intervals. We were the only ones in our elevator and made it to our floor without stopping.

We walked down the hallway to our suite and went inside.

"This is awesome," Bryce said.

I stopped and pointed the walking stick at him. "What the hell are you doing?"

"What?" He put his hands up.

"Your accent, what did we agree to?"

"I'm committed."

"No." I lowered the stick. "You're only participating. Don't be the hen mate, be the pig."

"*What?*"

"Breakfast."

"What the fuck are you talking about?"

"You know, breakfast. The hen participates, but the pig is committed. *You* need to commit."

"Where do you come up with this stuff old sport?"

"That's better," I said.

"You going to pay Joel royalties on that one?"

\*\*\*

The next morning we got off the elevator and strolled across the lobby toward the exit. A Lincoln Town Car was waiting to take us to Rockefeller Center.

"Hey, look at that." Bryce pointed at a stack of New York Post papers, visible through the window of the gift shop. We stopped to look at it.

*ARMANI BUTCHER CAUGHT* dominated the top half of the front page in bold, black letters. The bottom half had a color photo of a man with graying hair in handcuffs. He was smiling, wearing a dark cashmere overcoat, and flanked by numerous members of the NYPD.

"Poorly dressed amateur," I said. "That will keep them busy. Let's go, we need to be in the front row."

"Good day, sir," I told the gentleman who opened both the hotel and car doors for us.

Bryce rewarded him with a twenty dollar bill.

The driver turned to look at us as he pulled away from the hotel.

"How ya doin' this mornin' gents? I'm takin' you to Rockefeller Center correct?"

"We're quite well sir," I said. "Yes, that is our destination. Specifically, where the Today show is broadcast from."

"You guys here for business or pleasure?"

"You might say a little of both," Bryce said.

"Touche," I said, tipping my hat.

"Where you guys from?"

"I reside in London." I pointed to Bryce. "And he's from Los Angeles by way of Tasmania."

"You guys are lookin' sharp, must do well with the ladies. You guys actors or somethin'?"

"We're all actors in the game of life, are we not?" I asked him.

"Never thought of it that way, but I guess you're right."

"He's a writer and yes, I'm in the film business," Bryce said.

"Anything I might have read or seen?"

"Perhaps," I said, noticing we were approaching Rockefeller Center. "If you would be so kind to pull over there, that would be marvelous."

"My pleasure."

The car came to a stop and I pulled two, one hundred dollar bills from a sterling silver money clip and handed them to the driver.

"I trust that this will cover our fare," I said, knowing the total was seventy-five dollars. "Would you be so kind as to get the door for us?"

"Certainly, thank you very much. You guys have a nice day. I hope you enjoy your stay here."

"We shall if everyone is like you sir." I tipped my hat to him. "You are truly a noble ambassador of this great metropolis."

"Oh, before I forget." He opened the glove compartment, pulled out an envelope, and handed it to me. "Mister Fischer sends his regards."

I folded it in half and put it in my overcoat pocket.

"Please," I said, "if you happen to speak with him, let him know we are well, and do pass along *our* regards."

"I certainly will, and say hi to Johnny for me the next time you guys see him."

"We surely will. From whom shall we pass along the regards?"

"Names Nicky Z. Me and Johnny go way back. Used to work together you might say. You guys enjoy yourselves."

He opened the door for us, got back in the car, and pulled away.

"Laying it on a bit thick old sport, don't you think?" Bryce asked.

"I was just getting started."

"What's in the envelope?"

"Let's just say that the case of the missing mini disks has been solved, and leave it at that."


## LEE-LEE


Lester Holt mulled around inside the aluminum crowd control perimeter where the Today show broadcasts the outside portion of the show. The remote camera crew scanned the crowd of over one hundred fans on the other side of the barricade, as they waited for an outside performance by The Black Crowes.

"Look how crowded it is down there. I didn't know they had so many fans," Leigh Anne Ralston said, pointing to the television.

"Who?" Crystal Kelly looked up, while still bent over tying her cross trainers.

"The Black Crowes, I thought they broke up in the Nineties."

Leigh Anne looked at the flat screen as the Today show prepared to go to commercial break, the remote camera making the rounds of the waiting fans, and "*Hard to Handle*" playing in the background. Crystal watched and waited, knowing Joel's movie connections would be in the audience. She would bring them to Lee's attention, get the plan started. Leigh Anne pointed at the screen, saving Crystal the trouble.

"Did you see those two guys?"

"Hell yeah," Crystal said. "It was kind of hard not too, especially the guy with the top hat. There are all sorts of characters around here. Probably works at Jekyll and Hyde, or in a play. Are you almost ready? I want to get this over with."

"I have to brush my teeth. They said The Black Crowes are coming on next, I want to see that. I used to like them when I was in high school."

"Alright, what…ever. I used to like that song they were just playing, and the one about the girl talking to angels. If we wait much longer, I'm going back to bed."

Leigh Anne came back into the room, toothbrush still in her hand and fastening her dirty blond, shoulder length hair into a ponytail.

The Today show came back on, still broadcasting outside. An overhead camera view showed the expanse of the crowd, the band in the middle, standing on a makeshift stage, and then switched to a handheld camera scanning the front row of the audience.

"There's those two guys again. Pretty good looking, don't you think?" Leigh Anne asked.

"Yeah, but they don't look like they belong there. Who would dress up like that this early...*on a weekend*? Look at the rest of the crowd, they're all hippies. Obviously, they *want* to get noticed."

"You know all about that," Leigh Anne said. "Maybe they're still up from last night."

"Doubt it. Do they *look* like partiers?"

Lester Holt started talking, introduced the band, and they started into "*Goodbye Daughters of the Revolution*". Crystal and Leigh Anne sat at the end of one of the beds and watched.

"Sounds kind of country," Crystal said.

"Yeah, it does. Some of them are pretty good looking, especially that guitar player. I don't know his name but his brother is the singer, Chris Robinson. He got divorced from Kate Hudson."

"What did she see in *him*?" Crystal rolled her eyeballs. "He looks like Jesus."

"Hey, he's a rock star. Don't you actors love the rock stars?"

"Hush up. Don't all you doctors like other doctors, or lawyers for that matter? For your information, as you know, I met a really handsome lawyer last year."

"Too bad he was married."

"Aren't all the good ones?"

"It definitely seems that way."

Crystal zipped up her running jacket, pulled her blond hair back with her hand, and put on a pink, New York Yankees baseball hat.

"Okay, let's go, it looks nice out there. They said it was in the fifties."

***

Just as planned and by coincidence for all Leigh Anne Ralston knew, we passed by the ladies in Central Park after we left the Today show. Crystal Kelly had been briefed by Joel that we would be embarking on our daily constitutional. Bryce and I were playing Crystal and she thought, mistakenly, that she was playing us.

"Excuse me," Crystal said, "I swear we just saw you two on the Today show this morning."

"You are correct my dear," I told her.

## THE PRE-GAME

As we agreed to during our "serendipitous" meeting in the park, the night started out with drinks at the St. Regis Hotel. This was Joel's idea and he had also made arrangements that let us bypass the line of people waiting for a seat in the bar. We were seated at a great table, with a perfect view of Max Parrish's Old King Cole mural. Bryce and I had dressed for the occasion in our character costumes and Crystal and Leigh Anne didn't disappoint, wearing short skirts, tight tops, and high heels.

Together, we looked deserving of our VIP seats. Based on the discreet and the more obvious looks directed at us, the other patrons felt the same way.

We finished a round of Bloody Marys and while we waited for our shots of tequila to arrive, Crystal got down to business. Leigh Anne, who had told us to call her Lee Lee, took it all in.

"So, tell us more about your project," Crystal said, with an overdone southern accent. "What's it all about?"

I looked over at Bryce. "May I?"

"Certainly." He looked at both of them. "If you feel the need to bore them with the details, please do."

"Don't be silly." Crystal put her hand on mine. "We would love to hear it. Wouldn't we Lee?"

"Nothing I like better than trade talk." Lee Lee gave Bryce a flirty stare. "But I do find the movie business fascinating. I'd like to hear about it."

"Hell yeah," Crystal said. "Come on guys, let's hear it."

"Very well then," I said. "It's about a very successful stock trader in this fair city, who has many idiosyncrasies, the main one being, an insatiable desire to take other peoples lives."

"Please, it is about so much more than that." Bryce looked at Lee Lee. "It's an introspection on society as a whole."

"Stop." I put my hand up and gently lowered it on to Crystal's shoulder. "Let's not get too philosophical. Besides, I've just had an epiphany of sorts."

"Do tell old sport," Bryce said. "Surely, you cannot leave us in suspense any longer."

"Cynthia!" I lifted Crystal's hand off the table and looked her into her eyes. "I have found our Cynthia."

"Brilliant," Bryce said, following my lead.

"What the hell are you talking about guys?" Crystal asked.

"You my love." I kissed her hand. "Would be a perfect fit for the role of our stock trader's secretary, Cynthia."

"*A secretary?*" Crystal looked over at Lee Lee.

"She's much more than a secretary," Bryce said. "In fact, the role is a fairly large, and important one."

"Here you go." The waitress interrupted and put our tequila shots on the table. "Can I get you anything else?"

"Please, another round of Bloody Marys if you would be so kind," I said, handing her a twenty dollar bill for the excellent service.

Lee Lee raised her shot glass and we did the same as she started to speak.

"To new friends and bright futures. Cheers."

We drank our shots and I started to clap softly.

"Bravo, well done Lee Lee," I said, winking at Bryce. "We are surrounded by talent it seems. Tell us Lee Lee. Have you ever done any acting?"

"She's a natural." Crystal rested her head against my shoulder. "Just like me."

"A splendid stroke of luck," Bryce said. "Don't you agree old boy?"

"Indeed it is."

As the waitress brought over the Bloody Mary's, Crystal and Lee Lee excused themselves and headed to the ladies room.

\*\*\*

Crystal and Lee Lee stood in the same stall in the ladies room of the St. Regis Hotel.

"So, what do you think Lee?" Crystal took two power sniffs off the coke bullet, handed it to Lee Lee. "Is this a trip or what?"

"They are *so* good looking." Lee Lee hit each nostil twice. "A little eccentric, but my God, are they handsome."

"They're hot, that's for sure. It's really freaky, you know, how this all worked out. Don't you think?"

"Kind of, but we're in New York. What do you expect? I'm not going to complain."

"Me neither. Besides, you might just get your chance to be in the movies. Just let little 'ole Crystal work her magic on them."

Crystal took a couple more hits off the bullet and offered it to Lee Lee.

"I'm good, for now at least. Let's go."

"Okay." Crystal opened the stall door. "Our princes are waiting."

\*\*\*

We finished the round of drinks and after some discussion as to where the night would continue, we decided that our suite at the Marquis would be our next stop. Crystal and Lee Lee were more than interested in finding out more about our project and Bryce and I were eager to educate them. I called our new-found friend Nicky Z and told him we were ready to leave. I settled our tab, rewarded the waitress with a fifty, and the four of us got in the Town Car headed to the hotel.

# FOUR PLAY

The elevator door at the Marriott closed and we started rising above the rapidly shrinking people.

"Wow, this is really cool. I never stayed here before," Crystal said.

"I did, about eight years ago," Lee Lee chimed in. "But it wasn't this nice. The elevators are way different now."

We made our way into the suite and Bryce immediately grabbed the remote to the Bose. *"Double Vision"* started playing, while I took the ladies coats and hung them in the closet.

The curtains on the large windows were open, providing a spectacular view of the night skyline. Crystal joined Lee Lee at the window and they looked down at the spectacle of Times Square in all of its grandiose, illuminated glory.

"I am definitely going to stay here the next time I come," Crystal said.

"So am I."

"Please." I motioned to one of the two couches. "Do have a seat."

They sat down and I did the same on the couch across from them. A mahogany coffee table separated us.

"Do you mind if we smoke a little pot?" Crystal asked.

"Not at all my dear," I said. "Let your inhibitions run wild."

Bryce smirked at the Rod Stewart reference. "I'll rejoin you in a minute," he said, walking toward his room.

They passed a glass bowl between themselves about five times. When they finished, the good doctor pulled a tin of Altoids from her purse, put a couple in her mouth, then passed it to Crystal.

Bryce came out of his room with an oversized, leather attaché case and sat next to me. He placed it on the coffee table as the ladies, who were obviously stoned, stared at it. I'm sure they hoped it was filled with a kilo of cocaine. He pressed the latches on each side of the case and lifted the top, until it locked at a ninety degree angle.

"What is *that*?" Crystal asked.

"This my love...is an Absinthe kit," Bryce told her.

"A *what* kit?" She leaned forward, trying to look inside.

Bryce turned it, so they could see inside the blue velvet lined case. The items inside were secured to the bottom with black fabric bands that held each piece in its custom fitted compartment.

"Absinthe," he said, "to put it simply, is an alcoholic drink that was a favorite of Parisian writers and artists during the late Nineteenth century. There was, and still is, a certain fascination associated with it, which can partly be attributed to the method of preparation."

"Well done," I said. "Poe himself could not have provided a more eloquent explanation." I looked at Crystal and Lee Lee. "Would either of you care to join us in the ritual?"

"Sure, sounds intriguing," Lee Lee said.

"I'm in," Crystal said.

"Excellent. I think you shall enjoy it."

"We'll need some ice," Bryce said, pointing to the bucket on the credenza. "Would one of you be so kind and go fill that up? The ice machine is at the end of the hall if you take a left out of the door."

The music segued into *"Come Sail Away"* and Lee Lee looked at Crystal.

"Can you do it? I love this song."

"Sure, be right back."

Bryce started removing the contents of the case and placing them on the table: four oddly shaped crystal glasses, a dark green bottle of Absinthe, a small glass canister of sugar cubes, a slotted silver spoon, and a thing made of silver that resembled a flattened teapot sitting on top of a silver candlestick.

"Pretty elaborate set up," Lee Lee said.

She grabbed the bottle, pulled the cork out, and lowered her nose to the opening.

"Smells like Sambuka."

"Licorice may be more accurate," Bryce said.

"You're right," she said, putting the bottle back on the table.

Crystal came back into the room with the ice. She placed the bucket on the table and sat down.

"Alright then," I said, "shall we indulge?"

"By all means," Bryce said.

He went over to the credenza, grabbed the liter bottle of Evian water and sat down.

After pulling the top off the teapot, he filled it halfway with ice. Then he poured the water in slowly, until it was almost full. He put the cover back on. The lower portion of the glasses had a round chamber at the bottom that held an ounce of Absinthe. Bryce filled each one with the jade colored liquid and the strong licorice scent permeated the air around the table.

"That's a really cool color," Crystal said, looking at me. "It matches your ring."

"It does indeed," I said.

Bryce placed the slotted spoon across the top of one of the glasses, then took a sugar cube from the canister and put it on top of the spoon. He moved the glass under the thin spigot of the teapot and slightly turned a small valve. As he did this, the ice water started slowly dripping over the sugar cube and into the glass. The droplets turned an opaque color as they sank to the bottom and separated from the absinthe, which remained on the top layer. The sugar cube deteriorated with each drop. This continued until the sugar cube disappeared as well as the last traces of the jade color.

"That was totally fascinating, like watching a magic trick. How does it do that?" Crystal asked.

Bryce took a sip, handed the glass to me, and I had a taste.

"Very good sir, you are truly a man of many talents." I handed the glass to Lee Lee. "Please, indulge yourself in one of life's true pleasures."

Lee Lee sampled it, passed it on to Crystal, and she took a sip.

"Mmm." Crystal looked at me as her tongue circled her lips. "I *really* like this Absinthe stuff."

Bryce continued to repeat the process with the other three glasses, while I leaned back into the couch and enjoyed the rest of the drink.

The ladies enjoyed the drinks and the entertaining stories with which Bryce and I regaled them. The tales and quotes we used were of course based on our character's lives and not ours. They didn't seem to know this, so we pushed it as far as we could and it was extremely enjoyable.

"Does anyone care for another?" Bryce asked.

"I will," Crystal said. "What about you Lee?"

"Sure, only if I can make this round."

"What do you think?" I said, looking at Bryce.

"I think it's a marvelous idea, *if* she promises to carry on this great tradition when she gets back home."

Lee Lee raised her hand in the air, like she was taking an oath.

"I promise."

When the last of Lee Lee's round was finished, they were obviously feeling very good. Bryce asked if another round was in order and they both agreed to "one last one", and to meet up with us for brunch at the hotel in the morning.

Bryce prepared the final round as I told them about the thieves who tried to rob the Millennium Dome in London.

We were all about half finished with the drinks when "*Boogie Nights*" got Crystal off the couch and dancing by herself. She grabbed Lee Lee by the arms and pulled her up to join her. They danced over to the window arm-in-arm and started to put on a show, like they were dancing for everyone in Times Square below them.

Their performance culminated with an especially loud, and over theatrical sing along to "*Dancing Queen*".

They took a break and Lee Lee walked toward us, pulling Crystal along by her hand. They were visibly unstable on their feet and Lee Lee spoke with a noticable slur.

"You guys have the greatest collection of music. Is there any way I could get a copy of all these songs you've been playing?"

"Sure," Bryce said. "I have a laptop here. I can burn you a couple copies."

Crystal flopped down on the couch and Lee Lee joined her. Their heads were unsteady and turning sideways, as they tried to focus through the blurred vision they were experiencing. This was expected and caused by the tainted sugar cubes Bryce had used in their last round of drinks.

Bryce looked at his watch, nodded at me, and grabbed the remote for the CD player. He pressed it a few times and "*Sweet Emotion*" came on. By the time the song ended, Crystal and Lee Lee were slumped over, and unconscious.

"Finally," Bryce said.

"I hear that. Let's get this show on the road. Go get the suitcase out of my room will you?"

"Maybe we should think about staying a few more days."

"Stop it. You're painting lips on a duck."

"What do you mean?" Bryce asked.

"There was a contest, to see who could whittle the best duck out of a piece of wood. So this one guy looked at the ducks the other people were working on. He thought they all pretty much looked the same, and the judges would have a hard time choosing which one was the best."

"Yeah, and your point is?"

"So he decides that to give himself an edge, he'd paint lips on the duck's bill, to make his stand out from the others."

"Did he win?"

"Of course not, the judges humiliated him in front of everyone because a duck doesn't have lips."

"And this is relevant because?"

"If he had just done what he was told, stuck to the plan and followed instructions, he might have won the contest."

"Okay Joel junior, whatever."


## PROOF OF CONCEPT


Crystal and Lee Lee were next to each other on the couch, unconscious, their heads hanging down, like they were staring at the floor. To keep them upright and restrained, we secured their upper bodies to the couch with some custom-made Velco straps.

Bryce unrolled the AV cables and plugged the ends into the side of the DreemWeever headset that was strapped around Crystal's head. Lee Lee had her own headset on, but we only needed to connect Crystals to the television to enjoy the show. He plugged the other end of the cables into the AV connections on the side of the television.

"Okay." He pressed the remote, the television screen turned blue. "The headset is connected. We can put the disks in now."

"This will only take a minute, so get ready." I pulled a syringe from the inside pocket of my coat and took the plastic cover off the needle.

I injected Crystal with her dose of what Joel called 'dream juice' first. Next, I took care of Lee Lee. In less than two minutes they were awake, but their bodies were paralyzed from one of the drugs in the shot. Joel had told us there were three ingredients to the shot. Besides the paralysis drug, another one countered the effects of the drug we used in the Absinthe. The last one was the most important because, even though they were awake, they were completely disconnected from their existing environment. Joel called it a 'real trance' and the DreemWeever would cause them to have intense visual and auditory hallucinations that they would believe were real.

Their skin looked flushed. Joel had told us their heart rates would shoot up really high and that as long as I gave them the exact dose, we should have no problems.

"Their sweating and it hasn't even started yet," Bryce said.

"It's one of the side effects. As long as they don't have a heart attack or a seizure, we should be okay. James better have mixed it right."

"James? What do you mean James?" Bryce opened the envelope that Nicky Z gave us and then handed it to me."

"James is a chemist. You didn't know that?"

"No, I didn't. What the fuck are you talking about?

I opened the clear, plastic disk case and took both of the mini disks out. "Same thing is on each one. At least it's supposed to be."

"Better be." Bryce took one of the disks from me and looked at it. "What about James?"

"Long story short, he was a normal guy with a chemistry degree from Caltech. One thing lead to another and him and some college buddies got involved in the whole crystal meth gold rush thing early on. They made huge money, but ended up getting busted, and lost it all. He did eight years in jail, and now he works for Joel, putting his degree to good use."

"That is insane. I bet he was a nerd, until he came out of jail"

"That's *exactly* what Derrik told me." I pointed toward Lee Lee. "You take hers and I'll take the other one."

"On my count put it in," I said, moving behind Crystal.

Bryce lined up the disk with the slot on the side of Lee Lee's headset.

"One, two, three, now." I pushed the disk into the slot and it disappeared into the side of the DreemWeever.

"It loads itself, pretty cool." Bryce pointed to the television. "Nice, check it out."

I looked up as "*Sister Christian*" started playing from the television speakers. White letters populated the black screen, like a typewriter.

*Kite Studios Presents*

*A Haskins Brothers Film*

*Starring*

*Chrystal Kelly*

*Scott Haskins*

*Introducing*

*Leigh Anne Ralston*

A message came across the screen. Both Bryce and I started laughing when we saw it.

*This story is based on true events. Only the soundtrack has been modified to protect the ears of the innocent.*

# THE GOOD DOCTORS

The black screen dissolved into a view of the New York City skyline at dusk. The snow, falling hard, as the birds-eye-view on the screen moved rapidly above the tree line of Central Park and continued through the city, over Times square, Madison Square Garden, then slowly moved in on the outside of One Penn Station.

*December, 24 2007 4:00 PM* populated the screen as it zoomed in on a block of windows near the top floor of One Penn Station.

Scott Haskins sat behind a large desk, releasing the tension from his necktie and talking on the phone, while *"2000 Light Years From Home"* played softly in the background.

"Hey, it's me. I've been trying to call you on your cell for the last couple hours. It's ringing and going to voicemail. Hope everything's okay. Listen, the weather has turned really nasty here. It's a goddamn blizzard. I was going to take the two o'clock shuttle. Everything was delayed, and now everything's cancelled. I was going to rent a car but there's no way I can drive in this. I got a cab back to the office. That's where I'm at now. Call me here, or on my cell when you get this. The storms supposed to let up later tonight, and I don't think it's going to be headed your way from what I've heard. I booked a flight, five-thirty tomorrow morning, just in case I can't get out of here tonight. I'm sorry about all this, it's beyond my control. I'll talk to you, don't worry I'll be home, kiss the kids for me. I love you."

Scott stood, walked over to the window, and looked down at the snow-covered streets below. Then he walked over to the cabinets behind his desk, pulled out a bottle of Chivas Regal and poured some into a coffee mug.

The ringtone on his cell went off.

"Hello."

"Scott, how the hell are you? How did it go?"

"What's up Joel? Not so good, I'm stuck here overnight. There's a blizzard out here. I knew it was a bad idea. Merri's going to have my fucking balls."

"Sorry to hear that. Unfortunately, the weather is one of the few things I can't control. Other than that, how did it go with Crystal? Did she sign up with you?"

"Nothing official but-"

"Yeah, I know I just talked to her. She told me about the weather too. She's going to sign, just making you sweat it out. Told me to tell you she's staying at the New Yorker, *and* that she is going to be at Mustang Harry's later on. It appears you made quite an impression on her."

"Come on, it's Christmas Eve. If I could have one present, it would be to get the hell out of here."

"Alright, I'll let you go. Hopefully, you get out of there tomorrow."

"That's the plan at least."

"Okay, good luck. Talk to you soon."

"Bye."

Scott finished the drink in one gulp, moved the mouse around on the desk and typed some letters on the keyboard. He picked up the office phone.

"Hi, I need a room for tonight...That's all you have...I guess I don't have much choice then do I? I'll take it...Haskins, Scott Haskins. You have all my information on file...alright, thanks."

He hung up the phone, leaned back in the chair and poured some more Chivas into the coffee cup.

The screen went black and repopulated, showing the inside of a crowded Mustang Harry's.

Scott stood at the end of the bar section and emptied a shot glass, while he scanned the crowd and "*Shattered*" played loudly in the background.

The entrance door opened and Crystal Kelly stood in the threshold, dressed in a full length, faux-fur coat. Her blond hair, styled in a long, flip-curl. "*Hot Legs*" kicked off as she sauntered toward the back of the bar, slipping out of the coat. Her tight, faded jeans and black t-shirt with PINK written on the front in pink letters caused others in the bar to stare as she strutted.

Crystal noticed Scott and moved in next to him. The music stopped as she put her hand on his arm.

"Hey there handsome, buy a girl a drink?"

"Sure, what do you want?"

She looked at him with a mischievous smile.

"Oh, I don't know. How about…a slow, comfortable, screw?"

"You said it, I didn't."

The screen changed and showed the rowdy scene at the now overcrowded bar. People were dancing, singing out loud, bouncing to the House of Pain's "*Jump*". Crystal stood behind Scott with her arms wrapped around his stomach. She moved to the music and kissed his neck as he downed another shot.

The music changed to Guns N' Roses doing "*Don't Cry*" as Crystal reached for her drink on the bar and emptied it in one sip. She wrapped her arms around Scott's neck, pulled him in close and started kissing him as they slow-danced in the middle of the crowd. The screen went black and refreshed, the same tune still playing. Scott and Crystal walked in the snow, his arm around her and Crystal's head buried in his chest. As they disappeared into the driving snow, the screen changed to a street view of the New Yorker hotel, then went black.

Scott sat on the edge of a bed putting on his pants. He finished dressing, looked across the room at Crystal sleeping, then walked out the door.

"*Straight On*" started playing and the screen showed Crystal stretched out on the bed, talking on a cell phone. The music played very low in the background. Both voices could be heard.

"It went pretty good. It wasn't like I didn't enjoy myself. It's too bad he's married, because he's really hot, and *a lot* of fun."

"Great job baby. You still planning on being back here tomorrow?"

"You bet your ass. I have to read for that part, remember? Joel, *please* tell me it's still on."

"You know it is, just making sure. And don't forget to call the cell later today. You still have the number, correct?"

"Yeah, that and his house phone, have both of them. I know what to do. I *get paid* to remember stuff."

"Okay my dear, ciao and Merry Christmas."

"Later lover, Merry Christmas to you too."

"Don't go there. I don't play that."

The screen transitioned to a moving car view, rolling down Hollywood Boulevard and "*Dreamboat Annie*" started playing. The screen changed again, showing Lee Lee sitting at an outdoor table sipping a glass of wine, and slowly moved out until Crystal was on the screen at the same table.

"That sucks. How could you be *so* stupid?" Lee Lee said.

"Don't ask me. I was really hammered, it just kind of happened. I don't know, I guess I was just into it way more than I should have been. It was kind of romantic in a way. You know, the snow, the vibe, the whole thing. Whatever."

"Well, you know the drill. When can you come in?"

"How about Friday? That gives me the weekend."

"Yeah, that works. Can you do two o'clock?"

"Definitely, thanks. I don't need to tell you how much a appreciate it."

"Did you tell him yet?"

"Yeah, I have to call him tonight, to let him know about Friday. He's all worked up about it, especially since his wife found out about us, and threw him out. He might be moving out here, or at least leasing something. I know someone who's got a lot of business for him out here. We'll see. I just have to take care of this first."

"That's what I'm here for. It'll all work out. You want another glass?"

The screen changed to Crystal lying on a table in a medical procedure room, inspecting the pink polish on her fingernail. Her legs rested in the stirrups, a hospital gown covering her upper body and hips. The door eased open and Lee Lee walked in wearing scrubs, gloves, surgical mask, and cap.

"Sorry to keep you waiting. My other appointment took longer than I thought. You okay?"

"As good as I can be I guess, considering."

"I'll make it quick, I promise. Oh shit, give me a minute, I'll be right back."

Crystal ran her hands over her face, stretched her arms out behind her, and the screen faded to black.

The screen changed to an overhead view of Lee Lee, lying on a table next to Crystal, both in the same spread-eagle position. Their arms were restrained to the table, legs secured to the stirrups. White surgical tape sealed their mouths shut and they frantically looked at each other, struggling to get free. Tears and beads of perspiration ran down the sides of their faces, mucous dripped from their noses with each muffled scream.

The door opened, but no one entered.

Seconds later, two tall people entered the room, dressed in green scrubs, unbuttoned white lab coats, surgical gloves, foot covers, caps and masks. They wore sunglasses and held scalpels. One started playing air guitar to Blind Melon's "*Skinned*", while the other sang into his scalpel.

When the song ended, they moved up close to the end of each table and looked down at the ladies as Cat Stevens sang "*Wild World*" softy in the background.

The one in front of Lee Lee started to talk in my voice.

"Well, it looks like the silicon sisters have got themselves in a real mess, doesn't it?"

The one standing in front of Crystal answered in Bryce's voice.

"To say the least. What do you think, *Mom*?"

"Hey, don't take that tone with *my* stepmother. Where *are* your manners?

"My apologies, but getting your limbs sucked off can make you irrational at times."

"Let's not forget Dr. Love," my voice said. "It's very bad manners to leave someone out of the conversation you know, especially such a distinguished master of her craft."

"Ah, you're right, and I'm truly honored. The last time the good doctor and I met, it wasn't exactly a pleasant experience."

"But we digress," my voice said. "And I think we have other more important matters to tend to."

The one with Bryce's voice looked down at his shirt, then over at his partner.

"Sorry to interrupt, but we appear to have a slight problem."

Small, dark red stains started to appear on the armpits of their lab coats and thighs of their scrub pants. The stains grew as the blood saturated the fabric.

"Oops," my voice said. "I hate when that happens. Don't you?"

"Yeah, and there's never a doctor around when you need one."

"Well, that certainly adds a sense of urgency now. Doesn't it?"

"Yes it does," Bryce's voice said. "Five minutes by my estimate."

"Shall we?"

They took off their surgical caps at the same time. They had no hair, just blotchy, discolored skin and protruding veins. The sunglass arms rested on protruding pieces of flesh, not ears.

"Don't be frightened Mom," Bryce's voice said, looking at Crystal. "I love you. It's all good."

They removed their masks, exposing facial skin covered in raw, open sores. Blackened lips surrounded their toothless mouths. Dark holes were the only remnants of their missing noses.

"How about a big smile for the ladies," my voice said, "to show them how handsome you turned out."

"In time, I'm not at my best yet."

"How could I forget?"

They grabbed the arms of their sunglasses and together, tilted them down slightly and looked over the top of them, like perturbed librarians. They had no eyeballs, just jagged flesh hanging over the eye sockets. They took off the glasses and tossed them on the floor.

"I know, I know ma," Bryce's voice said to Crystal, "of all the times to forget the camera."

"I'm afraid the show is coming to the end ladies," my voice said, pointing the scalpel at them. "And unfortunately, we must get to the finale. The good doctor shall enjoy the pleasure of my company, while you two have a little family reunion, and spend some quality time together."

They raised their scalpels and bent down at the end of each table, while "*Love Hurts*" played and the screen went black

# VAMANOS

I turned off the television and then made sure that the small, green LED's on the top of Crystal and Lee Lee's headsets were still blinking. They were now seeing the "director's cut" of the DreemWeever feed. It was ten minutes of bonus footage that would determine their fate and terrify them beyond anything they had ever experienced. Bryce didn't know there was more and I didn't tell him.

"That was awesome," he said. "The music was great. I still can't believe how real that stuff looks. You would *never* know it was all done on a computer."

"It's come along way. The video quality is much better with these new headsets. Ahriman is good at what he does, that's for sure. He's a master with the music too."

"It's fucking incredible," Bryce said. "He duplicated our voices perfectly. Seriously man, think about it, why would you need actors anymore when you have something like this?"

"No shit. Well, you would still need them, but just to provide a voice sample and a picture. You can make up anything from there. Come on, we have much work to do Amigo. If you want to hit the showers, go ahead, while I clean up this mess. Time is of the essence."

"Is John ready?" Bryce asked.

"He's been on standby the whole time."

I pulled out my cell and hit the speed dial for John.

"What up Jeeves?"

"Cut the shit. You guys ready?"

"It's almost four now. We need forty-five minutes. I'll call you when we're coming down. Meet us out front. Be there."

I dropped the call and looked over at Bryce.

"What do you have for tunes?"

"How about the Kings of Leon?"

"That works, which CD?"

"The newest one, haven't even heard it yet myself."

"What are you waiting for man?"

Bryce put the CD in, track one started to play, and we listened to it unfold.

I liked the intro music and then the lyrics kicked in.

We looked at each other in disbelief.

I pointed my finger at Bryce. "You knew this was coming."

"I swear." He put his hands up and shrugged his shoulders. "I have *never* listened to this before."

"What's the name of this one?"

He grabbed the CD case and flipped it over to the back side.

"I can't believe this. *You're* not gonna believe it?

"Come on, what is it?"

He smiled and threw it at me. It was called "*Knocked Up*"

Unbelievable," I said.

"Alright, let's get moving," Bryce said.

Bryce headed for his room and I started the cleanup, which started with taking off the ridiculous clothes I had on. The only thing I wanted to keep was the walking stick. It had a sword inside it and fortunately, I never had to use it.

I noticed the LED's had stopped blinking on their headsets and that meant the show was officially over. I removed the DreemWeever's from both of them and packed them away in the cases. Their eyes were wide open and moving rapidly as they looked around the room, and at me. They knew exactly what was going on, but were still paralyzed. I pulled off the straps that held Lee Lee to the couch and she slumped over the arm. I did the same with Crystal and her body flopped against Lee Lee's.

I could hear the shower running and went into Bryce's room. Two suitcases were open on top of the bed. I walked over to the bathroom, kicked the door open, and Bryce screamed as he ripped open the shower curtain.

"What the *fuck* are you doing?" he yelled.

"Wanted to make sure you shaved the stache, but I see you already did."

"Get out of here, *asshole*."

"Lock the door next time."

Another track started playing. It was a good one called *"Charmer"*

*You got to be kidding,* I thought as I listened to the lyrics and looked at them staring back at me.

I took the phone off the desk and put it on the coffee table next to Lee Lee. I gathered up all the Absinthe accessories, packed them back in the case, and put the case and the headset bags in one of my suitcases.

I looked around the room, noticed the bottle of Evian water, and put it in with the other stuff. As much as I hated to, I shut down the music and packed it away. I had everything that needed to go.

I checked the clock. We had fifteen minutes left. I went to my room and changed clothes: a pair of Lucky Jeans, Thin Lizzy T-shirt with a picture of Phil Lynot's head, sneakers, and a black leather jacket.

"You almost ready?" I yelled to Bryce.

"Yeah, I'm just getting dressed," he answered from his room.

"Bring your stuff out here when you're done."

I double-checked to make sure we wouldn't leave anything behind. Luckily, I checked the closet and noticed Crystal and Lee Lee's coats hanging in there. I packed them and took all the bags out near the door.

Bryce came out, wearing tan carpenter pants, sneakers, and a Lucky Brand, track jacket with the Union Jack taking up the entire back of it.

"Looking good man," he said.

"You too."

"Here." I tossed him a Yankees baseball hat.

He put it on. "Nice."

I pulled up my hair and tucked it under a Red Sox hat.

Bryce pointed toward Crystal and Lee Lee. "What's going on with them?"

"Good question." I reached inside the pocket of my jacket. "And even better timing."

I showed him the two syringes and walked over to them.

"Ladies, it's been real. If we had met under different circumstances, I think we might have been seeing more of each other. But as Shakespeare said, 'all the worlds a fraud' and I think you understand that now."

I could see the terror in their eyes as I injected them, and watched as they nodded off into another round of unconsciousness.

"To answer your question, we have exactly fifteen minutes until they wake up. They'll be oblivious to anything that happened tonight. So, I suggest that we get a move on."

I called John.

"We'll be right down," I said and hung up.

"So what do you thinks going to happen to them? I mean, you know, in the future?" Bryce asked me

"I don't think about that. I don't look back."

"What do you mean?"

"Like when someone's driving and hits an animal. They know they hit something. They might have even seen it at the last minute and felt it go under the tires. If they keep driving, they don't know if they killed it. They know they tried to stop and *if* they saw it, the last image they have is of it being alive. If they choose to look in the rear-view mirror, all that would change. They could see it suffering or not moving. In either case, they now have a mental image of it, and they feel guilty. They may even be haunted by it. So the key is, to *never* look back and just continue on."

"Wow that's pretty good."

"And this time, it's my own, not Joel's. Come on, let's go."

We got in the elevator and I called John as we made our descent.

"We'll be there in one minute."

We got off and carried our bags across the lobby, making sure to keep our heads down, knowing that there had to be cameras somewhere around. There was only one attendant at the front desk and she was too preoccupied with the computer to pay any attention to us.

"It's about fuckin' time," John said when I got in the back of the limo.

"Hey," I told him, "we're going to try and get some sleep. You mind putting the divider up?"

"Nah." He looked back at us. "Go for it. I think we should stop for some breakfast later though. What do you say?"

"I'm up for it," I said.

"Yeah, me too," Bryce said. "But give us a couple hours."

"You got it," John said.

I pulled out my cell as the divider started going up. "Better get this over with."

"What?"

"Calling Joel, specific instructions to call him *the minute* we leave."

"Let me call him," Bryce said with a sly grin.

"That's alright, I got it."

I pushed a speed dial on my cell and held it to my ear for about a minute, then snapped it shut.

"I got his voicemail, that's strange. He must be indisposed."

"No comment."

I laughed. "That's even stranger."

"Man, I could really use some rest, so I'm gonna stretch out and relax."

"Me too. How about some lullabies?" I reached into my travel bag and pulled out a CD.

"What do you got?"

"The White Stripes first CD, I think you'll like it. It's really bluesy."

"Bring it on," Bryce said.

I slipped it into the CD player and selected a track to start us off with. "*Death Letter*" came on and Bryce smiled and we left New York headed for Logan Airport.

***

The phone went through three ring cycles before it roused Crystal and Lee Lee from their chemically induced sleep. Lee Lee reached for the phone on the table next to the couch.

"Hello?"

No reply, but she heard a clicking sound, like the caller had just hung up.

"Hello? Hello?"

Lee Lee hung up the phone, looked over at Crystal and put her arm around her shoulder.

"We need to go."

"I know." Crystal said.

Lee Lee helped her up off the couch and they walked toward the door, not realizing that the phone had triggered their pre-determined actions. Both of them heard "*Goodbye Yellow Brick Road*" playing in their subconscious.

They joined hands, left the room, and walked down the hallway toward the elevators. They stopped, turned towards the atrium, and dove over the half-wall.

## MISFIT TOY

**October 2008**

"What's up Joel?" Bryce asked.

"Where are you?"

"The 405, on my way to Huntington."

"What are you driving, the Bullitt or the Challenger?"

"The Challenger, Tom's got the Bullitt."

"Where is he?"

"Don't know. He was gone when I got up. He said something about an audition the other day. He might be doing that."

"Doesn't matter, I'll call him later. How far away from Huntington are you?"

"I'm in Santa Monica. Why?"

"I have this big deal I'm working on and I need to provide a demo for it. I was thinking I could use you, if, you're interested of course."

"Yeah, I'm up for it. When's it happening?"

"We can talk about that. There's a lot of computer work involved and Victor's working earnestly on that as we speak. What I need most, what I think is going to make or break the deal, is the score. That's where you come in. You have an ear, a sense for that kind of thing. Thomas agrees with me on this, although I know he thinks he could do it better. I figure I can run the script by you, and you can come up with the music that's going to put it over the edge."

"So what are you telling me?"

"I'm telling you to turn around and meet me at my place as soon as you can, *that's* what I'm telling you. Now what are you going to tell me?"

"I'll be there. Probably in around thirty minutes."

"Sounds good, we can go over everything when you get here. Take care of my car."

"Always, later."

***

Bryce reached out the window and pressed the intercom button at the gates. Joel's voice came over the speaker.

"It's about time. Did you drive, or take a rick shaw?"

The gates opened and Bryce pulled up to the house. Joel met him at the door dressed in khaki pants and a black, short sleeve, silk shirt. He had a Rolex Yacht-Master on his left wrist and a platinum link bracelet around the right one. He put an arm around Bryce.

"I was only joking with you, come on in. I like the new look. It's more your style. Although, I heard you were quite suave in New York. I wish I could have seen it. You and Thomas really got it done out there. He said you were excellent, and it only cost me an arm and not the leg too."

"Thanks."

"Are you hungry? I can call out for something."

"I'm good for now."

"You sure, I was just going to drink lunch. You want one?"

"Yeah, I'm up for one."

"Excellent. I'm glad you are here. We don't really get time to talk, do we? Come on, let's go relax and review the project."

Bryce followed Joel through the door and into the media room. The lights were dimmed, Van Halen played at a low volume, and CNN was on the plasma.

"Come on, get comfortable. What are you drinking? I'm having Crown rocks."

"That works. Heavy on the rocks, splash of water."

"Done."

Joel brought over the drinks, handed one to Bryce and sat next to him on the sectional.

"Cheers." Joel touched his glass against Bryce's. "Okay, before we get down to business, I want to see if I have the right guy for the job. A little test, if you will."

"What do you mean?"

Joel reached for the remote, turned off the music.

"David Lee Roth, or Sammy Hagar?"

"What are you kidding me, David Lee Roth. No David Lee, no Van Halen."

Joel nodded in approval, started smiling.

"Congratulations, you passed. Sorry, I wish it was that easy. Okay, here's the deal. I'm going to show you something. You haven't seen it before, and that was intentional. I instructed Thomas *not* to show it to you, to leave you out of it. It may be upsetting to you, but it is relevant to our goal today. If you can't handle it, that's okay. I can understand, and we'll have to work on it."

"Come on just get on with it."

"Okay."

Joel pointed the remote at the plasma and pressed a button. The screen showed Crystal and Lee Lee lying on the couch and the phone was ringing. Bryce watched the scene unfold and Joel monitored his reactions closely, trying to get a read on his thoughts. Joel stopped the video as soon as they dove over the half-wall of the Marriot. CNN came back on the screen.

Bryce sat there, not talking, fast tracking his thoughts back to New York.

*Tom made a call in the limo. Said he was calling Joel. What the fuck, why did he hide it from me.*

Joel knew he had misjudged Bryce's reaction. He figured sadness, not anger.

Bryce stared at the plasma, as it displayed the aftermath of an explosion in downtown Falluja. He started trembling and sweating, as he watched the chaos and devastation being shown. Joel knew it was a pre-recorded video, not a live CNN story, and realized that a "product defect" sat beside him.

"Bryce...Bryce, earth to Bryce, you with me?"

Bryce snapped out of it and looked over at Joel.

"Yeah, yeah what were you saying?"

"I want to know where you're at with all of this. Tell me what you're feeling."

"To be honest Joel, I'm pissed off. Why didn't Tom tell me about this? That's total bullshit."

"Hey, hey, come on, calm down. It has nothing to do with Thomas. I take all the blame. I didn't think you could handle it. If anything, Thomas felt like he was protecting you. The onus is on me. Now calm down will you. Have another drink."

Bryce downed what was left of his drink and held out his glass.

"Make it a double this time."

Joel took the glass, went over to the bar.

"Joel, do me a favor. *Never*, I mean never, do that to me again. You understand?"

"Wow, I really underestimated you. I promise, never again. You okay now? Can we get down to business?"

"Yeah."

Bryce grabbed the glass from Joel, took a big gulp and put it down on the table.

"The final scene, the Elton John song," Joel said. "I came up with that. I thought it worked well, some of the lyrics really fit. After seeing it again, I still think it works, but I'll ask you. What would you have gone with? Take your time."

Bryce thought about it for a minute and gave Joel his answer.

"The Black Crowes, *Descending*". I think that might have worked just as well. Give me a few more minutes and I'm sure I can come up with some more."

"No, you've proved your point."

"I think *Bohemian Rhapsody*" would have been the best choice," Bryce said.

Joel thought about it for a minute, putting the lyrics and music together, envisioning the scene.

"Brilliant, simply brilliant, Bryce. I knew you were right for this."

Joel bent over, pulled out a packet of papers from a draw under the coffee table, and spread them out on the table.

"Now, let's get to it. But first, we need to agree on something?"

"What's that?"

"As I told you, Thomas had absolutely nothing to do with not letting you in on what we just watched. Do you understand *and* believe that?"

"Yeah, I understand. I'm cool with it now. You just, you know, caught me off guard that's all. You can understand that...can't you"

"Yes, of course I can. I knew it was going to play out one of two ways, and I'm glad it went this way."

Joel looked directly into Bryce's eyes, took a sip of his drink.

"So, what's my point? My point is that you, under no circumstances, let Thomas know about this. It will not, and should not, change anything between you two. If anything, I hope it makes the both of you, the three of us for that matter, stronger in the future. Are we in agreement on this?"

"Yeah. What about the music thing, can I let him know about that?"

Joel laughed as he fell back into the sectional, stretched his legs out, and rested his shoes on the table.

"Sure, tell him whatever you want. He'll be glad for you. Maybe a little jealous, but hey, I know talent when I see it. Do you want to know about the project or what?"

"Isn't that why I'm here?"

\*\*\*

"Hey, where are you now?" Joel asked.

"The house," I said. "Why, what's up?"

"Bryce just left here. He's on his way there."

"Yeah, you called to tell me that?"

"No, I called to tell you we have a problem, a serious problem."

"What kind of problem? Derrick forget to wax the Mercedes?"

"Enough. Now is not the time. Bryce is the problem."

"What do mean he's the problem? What could he have done?"

"I don't want to get into it now, but he came by the house today. He was asking all sorts of questions about New York, sentimental kind of questions regarding our favorite actress, if you know what I mean."

"What the fuck. He hasn't said anything to me about any of that."

"That's because he doesn't want you to know. He made me promise not to mention it, but now I'm telling you. I don't want to get into it right now. We need to talk. Be over here in the morning around ten. *Do not* let on about this when you see him, business as usual. I could not be any more serious about this. Are we on the same page?"

"Sure."

"I'll see you in the morning."

"Okay."

## VEGAS, BABY

"Hey, what's up?" I asked Bryce over my cell.

"Same old, why?"

"I'm over at Joel's office downtown."

"Yeah, so."

"Feel like going to Vegas with us?"

"Fuck yeah, when?"

"He wants to leave later this afternoon."

"How are we getting there?"

"A private jet from LAX. We'll swing by and pick you up."

"Cool what time? How long we going for?"

"Just overnight, we'll be back sometime tomorrow. Unless we hit it big, then we're staying, right?"

"Alright man, I need to get my shit together. When are you going to be here?"

I looked over at Joel. "What time you want to pick him up?"

"Tell him we'll be there by three."

"We'll be there at th-"

"Three, I know I heard him, I'll be ready, just be on time."

"Don't worry we'll be there, later."

"Much."

***

"You need a refill?" Joel pushed himself up from the sectional and walked toward the bar area of the media room.

"No, I'm good." I said.

I reached over, grabbed the remote off the cushion next to me, and turned up the volume on the plasma. *The Midnight Special* DVD was on and Linda Ronstadt was singing "*You're No Good*".

"You know." Joel poured the Dewars slowly over the ice. "I used to watch this show when it was on. It's the best rock show that was ever made. I think KISS is coming up soon. Just got these DVD's, they are unbelievable. Anyone who was anyone was on *The Midnight Special*. What a spectacular show."

"If you say so."

"Check it out." He tossed the DVD booklet to me.

He started coming over with the drinks, but stopped and stood looking down at me.

"Where's your head at Thomas?"

"Where it needs to be, I'm cool."

"I hope so, just making sure. You want to shoot a game?"

"Sure, then we better get out of here."

"What do you want to play for? No, let me rephrase that. I know what you want to play for, and it's not possible. *How much* do you want to play for?

"The Mercedes?"

"Not an option, how about twenty."

"Thousand?"

"Dollars."

"Deal, you rack."

I beat Joel out of the twenty and two more times for double or nothing. He didn't pay and I hadn't expected him to. We left the house and went out to the driveway.

"Here, you're driving," he said, tossing me the keys to the Mercedes.

"I thought I was going to follow you? What about the Bullitt?"

"Leave it here. We'll be back later. Besides, you know how much I cherish your company."

We got in the car and Joel pulled a CD from the console between us.

"The *Very Best of Cream*, what do you think?"

"Not a huge fan of Clapton, but I like Cream."

"I have to agree with you there. Actually, I didn't really think much about them, until I saw their reunion show on PBS a couple months ago. It was very good. I bought the DVD if you're interested."

"Yeah, I'd watch it."

Joel pushed the CD into the player and *"Sunshine of Your Love"* came on. I watched in the rearview mirror as the gates closed behind us when we left.

\*\*\*

"We'll be there in five minutes," I told Bryce over the cell phone.

"Wow, you're early. That's a first.

"I have to pack some things too. You ready?"

"Yeah, see you guys in a few."

"Later."

We parked in the driveway. Joel reached into the back seat and grabbed a bottle of Crown Royal that was inside a blue, drawstring bag with the Crown brand logo on it. We walked toward the house.

"You guys taking good care of this place?"

"What do think?"

"Just asking."

We let ourselves in and walked toward the kitchen. We followed the sound of "*Mr. Brownstone*" until we were standing just outside of the entertainment room.

Joel held me back with his hand to stop me from going in and gave me the "quiet" signal with his index finger on his lips. He poked his head into the room and looked back at me with a grin on his face.

"Que Pasa!" he yelled, jumping into the room.

Bryce bounced up off the couch.

"Assholes, what the hell are you doing?"

"Just having some fun, calm down, will you." Joel said, trying to contain his amusement.

Joel scanned the room, like he was taking a mental inventory. One wall was lined with CD's and DVD's and another with all books. The third wall, with the large bay window, had two, framed, rock concert posters on each side of it. On the wall above the couch was a framed reproduction of *The Scream*.

Joel grabbed the remote off the coffee table and turned the music down.

"No offense Axl," he said. "I keep forgetting how much I like this place. I should come here more often. It's good to see you're taking care of it."

Joel held out the bag of Crown Royal by the drawstrings and started swinging it back and forth.

"You're getting thirsty...very...very...thirsty. Come on, we have time, I'm buying. I think I remember where the kitchen is. Be right back."

He winked and gave us the six gun symbol with his free hand as he left.

"That guys a trip," Bryce said.

"To say the least, wish I had his money though."

"Me too, what do you think he's worth?"

"I asked John, but he wouldn't give me specifics, he just said, 'More than ten, but less than a hundred'."

"Where do you think he gets it all? A shrink doesn't make *that* much, no matter how famous his patients are. I know he's into other shit too, but still."

"He's got connections everywhere, plus, John told me he was born into money and then his parents left him a fortune. The video stuff seems to be really taking off."

"Maybe we'll get some of it someday?"

"I'm hoping."

"Here he comes," Bryce whispered.

Joel walked in holding a tray with three drinks on it and gave one to me and Bryce. He took his and put the tray on the coffee table.

"Here's to Vegas." He raised his glass to us. "May lady luck have her way with us."

We bumped glasses and took a drink. Joel walked over to the wall of the CD's. They were all alphabetized by band name and he scanned them, like he knew what he was looking for. He pulled a couple out, looked them over, and finally decided on one. I couldn't see which one it was.

He put it in the CD player and grabbed the remote off the couch.

"Not sure where you guys stand on this band, but if you can overlook the pretentious lead singer, they are not that bad."

He pushed the remote and *"What's this Life For"* started playing.

"You got to be shitting me. Fucking, Creed." Bryce said.

"Yeah, come on Joel, you can do better that this." I said.

"Gentleman, you must look deeper than the band to the essence of the song. I'm afraid I'm revealing my sentimental side, as we enjoy our drinks and time together."

He was bullshitting us and I could tell Bryce was buying into it.

My gut told me that Joel had scripted this out long before today, right down to the music. He wasn't making this easier on me either as I listened, trying to contain my real emotions. In Joel's perverted mind, this was letting him experience some sort of sympathy.

Bryce and I were standing next to each other and Joel looked down at his drink, like he was in deep thought, then looked directly at both of us.

"My boys...*my boys, my* lost souls, what more could I ask for?"

I noticed Bryce's head was starting to droop and his eyelids looked heavy, like he was starting to fall asleep on his feet. Joel looked at him and started snapping his fingers.

"Bryce, what's matter? Are you with us?"

Bryce started swaying. Joel got right in his face, grabbed him under the chin, and lifted his head.

"Bryce, are you feeling okay?"

Bryce's glass crashed on the hardwood floor, his knees buckled, and he crumpled to the ground, landing on his side.

"Are you okay Thomas? I'm sure this is tough on you."

"You can't understand what I'm feeling right now. Let's just get this over with and get *the fuck* out of here."

"On the contrary, I know exactly what you're *feeling* right now. I make you feel, I decide what you feel."

"*Whatever*, I don't really care right now. Let's just finish this."

Joel put his hands on my shoulders.

"Control yourself and listen to me. Get him onto the couch and lay him down. Don't forget, this did not have to be done so respectfully. It could have played out much, much differently. In fact, you know if he was stronger, less susceptible to certain things, it wouldn't be happening at all. With every product there are exceptions, defects if you will. Unfortunately, he was one, and as such, was a risk. A risk we could not afford to take at this stage."

"Enough, I understand, I get it. Okay?"

I grabbed Bryce under the arms and pulled him onto the couch. He was out cold, but moving around a little and breathing heavily, like he was having a nightmare.

"*My own Prison*" started playing. It was a haunting song and I knew why it was on.

Joel came over and put his arm on my shoulder as we looked down at Bryce. As cold as he was, I knew Joel must be feeling something. He was trying to maintain his façade, but I could sense that this was at least uncomfortable for him. I was just glad Bryce's eyes weren't open. The song was eating me alive as I looked at him.

"Turn this goddamn shit off will you!"

"I can't do that. It's going to be therapeutic for you someday. You can't understand that now, but believe me, you will. It is needed at this time. You're thinking of the negative, you need to focus on the positive."

"You're crazy, what positive is there in this? He's going to die."

"Listen to me. Like you, he would have never had a life, and the life that he almost had, was ended with unimaginable pain and suffering. He has had the chance to live, enjoy, experience, and to feel things other than pain. Now that the time has come for him to leave, he is doing so free of pain. He has loved, and he has been shown love. You need to think about it that way Thomas. Does that make any sense to you?"

"Yeah, in some way it does. I just want to get it over with."

"You need a few minutes, alone? It's alright, I understand if you do. I think you should, it might help. I need to go out in the kitchen for a minute, then, we'll finish up and go get drunk."

I sat on the floor next to Bryce, holding his hand and looking at him. I started crying.

"I'm sorry man. Why did you have to look back? I told you never look back. Never, ever, look fucking back, ever. Look where it got you. Why didn't you listen to me? Think about me will you, we're the same. Someday we'll be together again. I don't know what else to say to you man. Just forgive me, that's all, Just know that I loved you man."

I saw Joel standing in the doorway, holding a syringe and adjusting the transparent gloves he had on.

"Are you okay? Do you need more time?"

I stood up, wiping my eyes and nose on the front of my shirt.

"No I'm alright. Go ahead."

"Okay."

He grabbed the remote and "*With Arms Wide Open*" started playing. I still wasn't sure if this was a game to Joel, or some kind of weird eulogy that he came up with. It was probably both.

"A fitting tribute, don't you think?" he asked.

I just stared at him as he walked over to Bryce, knelt down next to him, and stretched his arm out on the couch.

"No problem finding a vein. I thought I might need a belt."

He forced the needle tip into Bryce's vein, pushed the plunger down, and emptied it into his arm. He pulled the needle out, wiped the tip off with the glove, and put it in his blazer pocket.

"A moment of silence would be appropriate," he said.

Joel stood next to me and again put his arm around my shoulder as we looked down at Bryce and the song played in the background. I started crying again, as Bryce's breathing slowed and his lips started changing color. It didn't take long before he stopped breathing. He was gone.

Joel immediately grabbed the remote and ejected the CD. He took it out, wiped it off with a handkerchief he pulled from the breast pocket of his blazer, and slid the case back among the other CD's on the wall.

He pulled his cell from the case on his belt and made a call.

"We're ready, come on over. The doors unlocked, he's on the couch. How long you going to be? Alright, we're leaving now. We will see you back at the house later on tonight."

He put the cell back in the case.

"Let's go. Derrick and James are on their way. Grab the Crown will you? It's in the kitchen on the counter. I don't know about you, but I need a drink."

"More than you could know," I said.

We walked outside and headed toward the Mercedes.

"Oh, before I forget." Joel stopped at the front of the car. "I need you to do something for me tomorrow."

"What's that?"

He pushed the fob on his set of keys and the trunk of the Mercedes popped up. He reached inside and pulled out a large, black case.

"I need you to deliver this to someone tomorrow. By the way, you should use the garage. That's what it's there for. Open the trunk of the Challenger for me."

"I can't, the keys are in the house. I'll go get them, if I can find where Bryce left them."

"No need, I got it."

Joel opened the door to the Mercedes, reached inside, and flipped up the cover of the console between the seats. He stood up and pointed his hand toward the Challenger. The headlights flashed and he tossed a set of keys back into the Mercedes.

He walked over to the Challenger and put the case in the trunk.

"Let's go Thomas."

## EVAN

I woke up the next morning in my bed at the Woodland Hills house. Joel and I had way too much to drink at some new place on Beverly Boulevard called the Medusa Lounge. John ended up having to come get us in the limo. I didn't remember getting back to the house and as far as I knew, I didn't get sick.

I still found it hard to believe the Bryce was gone and less than twenty-four hours ago, he was in this same house. I got up and went through the kitchen toward his room. The door was open and the bed was made, but all of his stuff was gone. I opened his closet door and it was empty, like he never lived there.

I walked out to the front room, the last place I saw Bryce, and it looked the same as it always did. I went over to the window and noticed the Challenger was gone. I couldn't remember if it was there last night or not, but I figured James or Derrick must have borrowed it when they left yesterday.

I went out to the kitchen, took some Advil, and made coffee. I had a serious physical hangover and a mental one from what happened yesterday. I looked at the clock on the microwave. It was almost eleven-thirty. I opened the refrigerator to get some orange juice and noticed the bottle of Grey Goose on the side shelf. I filled a large glass with ice and poured the vodka slowly over it, until it was half full. I added the juice and drank it all in one fast chug. I wiped my mouth and twitched from the after-shiver.

I heard my cell phone going off in my room. I went to get it, feeling a little bit of relief from the drink. It was Joel.

"You're still alive?" he asked.

"I should ask you the same question."

"Alive yes, but it hasn't been a very pleasant morning. I trust I'm not alone on this?"

"I'm hurting, but what can you do."

"It was worth it. I had fun last night, going to have to get back there in the near future."

"I can't even think about that right now. Where's the Challenger?"

"What do you mean *where's the Challenger*? It's not *there*?"

"No, it's not out there Joel, I'm serious."

"Come on Thomas, I'm in no mood for this."

"You're not shitting me, are you?"

"No, absolutely not, and your telling me it's *gone*?"

"That's what I'm telling you."

"I'll call you later."

Someone stole the car. It didn't make sense. But right now, it was his problem, not mine.

I went back to the kitchen, made another drink, and went out to the front room. I sat in the black, leather La-Z-Boy and stared at the couch in silence, picturing Bryce laying there dying. It felt like his aura was still in the room. My eyes filled up and when I blinked, tears ran down my cheeks. I raised my glass towards the couch.

"Well man, you're still with me. How about some music? And none of that Creed bullshit either. I'll never listen to that again. If I ever do, I'll think of you, it's the best I can do. It's time for a fitting sendoff. What can I play for you?"

I took a big sip, almost half the glass, and got up to look at the wall of CD's. I picked one out and looked at the track list.

I put it in the CD player. "*We Die Young*" came on and I sat back down, sipped my drink and stared at the couch. I kept listening until "*Brother*" started playing. Halfway through the song, I broke down again and couldn't listen anymore. I had to turn it off. I went out to the kitchen, made another drink and poured a shot. I went back to the room and put the shot glass on the couch.

"Here's to you man."

I made another drink when the disc ended and put in the Kings of Leon CD that Bryce had brought to New York. I listened to the whole thing. When it ended, I was drunk and felt like I could deal with him being gone, at least until I sobered up.

***

Joel sat down on the edge of the sectional in the media room. He used the remote to turn on the plasma, pressed a sequence of buttons, and the screen populated with options for the surveillance system.

He selected an option named Woodland Hills and two separate picture-in-picture screens came on: a view of the driveway from the street entrance, and an opposite view from the front of the house. He selected the one that showed the driveway from the house and started rewinding it. He let it run and froze the image when he noticed a car pulling up the driveway. He let it play slowly until the car stopped thirty-feet from the garage. Joel froze the screen, zoomed in on the front license plate, then pressed play and watched as the person in the passenger seat got out of the car and jumped in the driver's seat of the Challenger.

Joel grabbed his cell off the table in front of him, scrolled through the contact list, and selected one.

"Hello," the voice on the other end said.

"Evan, its Joel Fischer. How are you?"

"Joel, how the hell are you? Life is all peaches and cream, I got no complaints. What's going on?"

"I need a favor, nothing big, won't compromise your standing on the force, just some information."

"Information can be dangerous you know."

"Just like knowledge. We both know a lot of things. Don't we Evan?"

"That we do. Anyway, what do you need?"

"Are you in the office, or on the road?"

"I'm in the office, was just about to head out though."

"Ah, good timing on my part then. I had a little incident the other day. No need to get into the details, not yet at least. I need you to run a license plate for me. I'm looking for a name and an address, if you would be so kind."

"That's it? No problem, what do you got?"

"It's a California plate, X, D, S, twenty, twenty-two."

"All right, that's xylophone, delta, station, two, zero, two, two. Is that it?"

"Yes, that's exactly it."

"Hold on a minute, let me type it in."

"Take your time."

"Bingo," Evan said. "You got a pen?"

"Of course, go ahead."

I show a two thousand one Chevy Malibu, registered to a Luke Wadely. Let's see, D.O.B of April sixth nineteen eighty-one."

*That's him,* Joel thought, looking at the still frame on the plasma.

"I'm not interested in how old he is. What's the address? "

"I was getting to that hold on. Let's see here, twenty-three S.C. Timbers on three oh one Vineyard Ave in Oxnard. Hold on a minute, let me look something up. Here we go. S.C. Timbers is an apartment complex. You got that?"

"Yes that's perfect, just what I was looking for. I told you it was a simple request."

"Anything I can help you out with on this?"

"No, as I said, it's just a small misunderstanding, nothing that can't be handled with a conversation. If it were more than that, I would certainly ask for your assistance, within reason of course."

"Of course you would. Okay, if that's all, I got to run."

"Get going, and keep protecting our fine city. Oh, before I forget, there is one more thing."

"Yeah, what's that Columbo?"

"I'm entertaining at Shangri-La tomorrow night. If you can fit it into your schedule, you should try and make it."

"I just might take you up on that. The wife and kids are out of town, so maybe I'll bring a friend."

"They'll be *friends* there too, if you can't find one."

"I hear that. I'll see you there then. Good luck with your investigation."

"Thanks again Evan. Oh, and by the way, things are shaping up for that new crime show I was telling you about. I'm doing all I can to get you some face time, if, you're still interested of course."

"No shit. Yeah I'm in, just let me know what you need. That's great news."

"Consider it done. I'll be in touch, soon."

Joel dropped the call, pressed another speed dial. Derrik answered.

"What up boss?"

"Where are you?"

"I'm at the gym. Why, what you need?"

"You need to take care of something and James is going to have to help you. Where is he?"

"How the hell am I supposed to know? He's probably at a skinhead anonymous meeting, or some shit like that."

"Please, I'm in no mood. Bottom line, I need the both of you over at my place yesterday. Get in touch with him now, and call me back. I'll be waiting."

"Come on, how you expect me-"

Joel snapped his cell shut, dropped it into his front shirt pocket and picked up the remote. He zoomed in on the still frame of the guy walking up to the Challenger, near the garage of the Woodland Hills house. He walked over to the bar, poured a glass of Crown Royal, and took a slow sip, while he glared at the screen.

*** 

"It's about time. Tell me you're here."

"Come on now. How my supposed to be there already, when I have to go pick up that lazy, bald freak? You know he was still sleeping, while I'm out taking care of shit, bustin' ass, and what not."

"That's admirable, but get to the point. *When* are you going to get here?"

"Well let's see now, presuming he's ready, that's twenty minutes, and then another twenty, so I guess, in about forty-five minutes or so. I haven't even had any damn lunch yet, so we might have to-"

"No, no stops, forty five minutes, no later than that. No screwing around, just get here. Time is *not* on our side."

He snapped the cell shut, tossed it onto the bar and downed the rest of the drink.

*** 

I had fallen asleep on the couch and when I woke up, the time on the cable box was five thirty in the afternoon. My head hurt and I was thirsty. I thought about the vivid dreams I had.

I was sitting under the Space Needle in Seattle high on heroin. A black SUV with smoked windows pulled up. I got inside it. I was in a dark room, strapped to a table with lights shining down on me. I couldn't see anything but the lights. Two guys in doctor's clothes with face masks were looking down on me. I could see their eyes. They looked familiar to me. They were talking in a foreign language. One stuck a needle in my arm. I fell asleep.

I got up and checked my cell. Two missed calls, both from Joel, and one new message that I knew had to be from him. I was in no mood to listen to it and didn't. I went to the bathroom, brushed my teeth and got in the shower. I leaned under the nozzle and the hot water massaged my neck and warmed my body. I closed my eyes and started to replay the dream in my head, trying to make sense of it.

I was in the middle of getting dressed when I heard my cell ringing in the kitchen. I grabbed it off the counter and looked at the display. It was Joel calling, again.

"Yeah."

"Were have you been? I called you a couple times already."

"Fell asleep. Why, what's up?"

"About the car, don't worry about it, it's under control. It must have been stolen some time after we left yesterday. I talked to John, and he says it wasn't there when he dropped you off last night, and that you were bitching about me letting James and Derrik take it. You had some choice things to say about me too, but we won't get into that now."

"To be honest, I don't even remember getting in last night. I couldn't tell you if the car was here or not. This morning, I figured James or Derrik took it yesterday."

"No need for explanations Thomas. It's unfortunate, that's all, and you do not need to worry about it. You will have it back soon enough, I assure you."

# MR.BOND

"I don't know man. I'm just telling you, something weird is going on, and I'm getting spooked," Luke told Paul over his cell as he pulled into the parking lot of his apartment complex.

Paul exhaled the smoke from the joint he was toking on, concentrating more on "*Whiskey in a Jar*" playing in the background than what Luke was saying.

"Calm down man, you're just paranoid. Why don't you come on over, and we'll mellow down easy."

"I can barely hear you. I'm serious, can you turn that down? It's drowning you out."

"Yeah, no problem, hold on."

Paul pushed the volume control on the remote, until the song was blasting from the speakers.

"Alright, how's that?" he asked, taking a big pull off the joint and muffling his laughter.

"Come on dickhead, turn it down, *now.*"

"Oh you said, turn it *down*. My bad bro. Sorry about that. Hold on a minute."

Paul lowered the volume.

"Now where were we? Oh yeah, we were at the part where you were whining about being scared right? Please, continue. Where are you anyway?"

"I'm sitting in my car. I just pulled into my place, and I'm telling you, twice today, someone called my cell and hung up as soon as I answered. I tried to call the number back and I get a message saying that the number can't accept incoming calls."

"That's what you're worried about? Come on, let it go. It's probably some prisoner running a scam. You can't return calls to jail man, happens all the time, relax."

"Yeah maybe, never thought of that, but it's still weird."

Luke got out of the car, walked across the lot, and into the main entrance of the apartment complex, still talking to Paul.

He stopped at the top of the second floor stairs and pulled out his keys. "Maybe I'll swing over after I take a shower."

"Now you're talking. Come on over to my teepee. We'll smoke a while and have a few cocktails."

"Okay mister Costner. Hold on a minute, I got to unlock the door."

"Dude, you have to learn to multi task."

"What the fu-"

The dark, plastic trash bag came down over Luke's head. His vision went black and his body jerked backward.

His feet came off the floor and he felt a huge hand covering his face as the bag tightened around his neck and he gasped for air. The sunglasses that had been on the top of his head were inside the bag, digging into the back of his neck.

Luke struggled, trying to pull the hand off his face and tear the bag off, but a massive blow hit his stomach and emptied his lungs. Paul's voice came from his cell on the floor.

"You there? Come on man, what's up? Hello."

Luke stopped moving. His limp body landed on the carpet.

Derrik stepped over him, picked up the phone and snapped it shut. He opened it and pressed the button to view the received calls, then smiled and looked over at James.

Luke started moving around on the floor. James put his boot on the side of Luke's head, pushed it into the carpet and held it there.

Derrik unzipped a nylon gym bag, pulled out a roll of silver duct tape and two pair of surgical gloves.

"Here." He tossed a pair to James. "Put these on."

Derrik duct taped Luke's wrists together behind his back.

"You can take your foot off him now."

Derrik stood over Luke, straddling his back. He grabbed a handful of hair through the bag and pulled Luke's head off the rug. He wrapped the tape around Luke's neck, securing the bag. The bag inflated and deflated as Luke gasped for oxygen. Derrik clamped one of his hands around Luke's mouth and with his other hand, pinched the nose area between his thumb and index finger. He pulled off a small piece of plastic.

He grabbed the tape roll and started wrapping it around the bag. When he finished, Luke's head was encased in silver, except for the nostril hole.

Rapid snorts of air mixed with nasal mucus came out of the hole. Derrik let go of Luke's head and let it drop onto the rug. Luke squirmed around on the rug, trying to roll on to his back. James dug his boot into Luke's spine and held it there.

"Easy Toro, calm down," James said. "You're not ready for the ring just yet. What the hell is that? Where's it coming from?"

The "*James Bond Theme*" ringtone played from the cell in Derrik's back pocket. He pulled the phone out and looked at the display window on the front.

"Pablo? Wonder if this is him? It's the same person he was just talking to, calling back. We'll find out soon enough. Too bad double oh seven can't come to the phone right now."

Derrik tossed the phone over to James. "Here you go Moneypenny."

"What do you want me to do with this?"

"Just hold on to it for now. We'll get back to it, as soon as we get Mister Bond here a little more comfortable. Listen up Mister Bond, I know you can hear me."

James bent over and flicked the tape on the side of Luke's head. "I'm not so sure. How's he supposed to hear you through that?"

"Good point. This might be a little tricky."

Derrik dropped to his knees and pushed his finger into the tape, probing for Luke's ear hole.

"This feels about right."

He eased the tip of the knife into the tape until it went through and then pulled it out.

"Direct hit, damn I'm good."

He made a small cross cut, folded the tape ends out to expose the ear hole, and leaned his head in close.

"As I was saying, if you want that boot out of your spine any time soon, you got to lay still. Cuz, if you start movin' around, you gonna get hurt. You hear what I'm tellin' you? Nod, if you understand."

Luke nodded.

"Good, long as we on the same page, things will work out just fine. Now, you gonna be still, right?"

Another nod.

James took his foot off Luke, but stayed close.

Derrik grabbed Luke's t-shirt at the neck and ran the knife down it, cutting it in half. He sliced each of the sleeves and pulled the shirt out from under him. He stared at the tattoo on his back. It was black, calligraphy style lettering with BLEED across his shoulders, THE centered in the middle of his back, and FREAK across the lower back, above the waistline.

"Whoa." Derrik took a step back. "Will you look at that. Our boys got some serious ink goin' on there. Look at them big ass letters. Bleed the Freak? What the hell's that supposed to mean?"

"Don't ask me." James shrugged his shoulders. "Probably some devil worshiping saying, or something like that."

"Nah, he don't look like no devil worshiper, not with that hairdo. All those blond streaks and the little soul patch thing going on. I bet he's a musician. What do you say Mister Bond, you a devil worshipper, or a musician?"

"How's he supposed to answer that? There's no signal for multiple-choice questions."

"Then let me rephrase." Derrik said, straightening an imaginary tie. "Are you a devil worshipper?"

Luke's head moved from side to side.

"Ha, I told you. Are you a musician?"

He nodded.

"I rest my case." He pointed a finger at James. "And put you, in your place."

Derrik used the knife to cut Luke's pants from the beltline, down to the ass crack.

"Damn, I was going to let him keep his drawers, but he don't have none on. Go to the bathroom and see if you can find a towel or somethin' like that. Mister Bond, if there was ever a time you needed to be still, this is it. Do you understand what I'm telling you?"

He nodded.

Derrik cut the pants down the inseam of each leg, stopping when the blade reached the tape at the ankles, then cut around the ankles above the tape. James came back with a white towel and threw it on the couch.

Derrik looked at James. "Pullin' a table cloth from under a table full of plates ain't shit for a trick. Watch this."

Derrik grabbed the waist of the pants with one hand and a piece near Luke's knee on the same side with the other hand. He gave a quick jerk and stood up with the pants in his hands, showing them around to an imaginary audience. Luke's body had barely moved and James laughed.

"Get the sneakers and socks will you. You need to see which toes you gonna smash, or cut off," Derikk said, winking at James as he walked toward the kitchen.

Derrik opened the refrigerator door, started inspecting the contents.

"Man you ain't got shit to eat in here. No wonder you so small and scrawny."

He opened the freezer door, moved some things around.

"Well now, what do we have here?"

He pulled out a sandwich bag half full of pot and waved it in front of his face.

"Our boy here's a chronic fiend. How'd you expect to be catchin' international spies and stopping world destruction, if you're all high on weed and all?"

He put the weed in the front pocket of his pants.

"I'm making a citizen's seizure. This is a matter of national security and shouldn't be takin' lightly."

He reached in the refrigerator, grabbed a can of cola.

"You want one."

"No, I don't drink that shit," James said from the couch he was sitting on. "Come on let's get moving."

Derrik emptied the can in one gulp, crushed it in his hand, and put it in the gym bag.

James got up and started looking over the CD collection on the shelves underneath the television. He pulled one out, pushed the power button on the CD player, and slid it in.

"*Sex Type Thing*" blasted through the room.

"Turn that shit down!" Derrik yelled.

James turned in circles, looking around the room. "Where the fuck's the remote?"

Derrik walked over to the CD player and pressed the volume decrease button a few times. The music stopped.

"Time we got down to business. Bring that chair out here from the kitchen will you? Need to make sure our boy here's comfortable."

James put the wooden, high back chair in the center of the room.

"Give me a hand here, will you? Take that side," Derrik said.

They grabbed Luke under his armpits, pulled him upright, and pushed him down on the chair.

"Hold him there for a minute," Derrik said, grabbing the duct tape.

He wrapped it around Luke's upper body a few times to hold him to the chair, and secured his shins to the front chair legs. James let go of him.

Luke moved around slightly, trying to ease the pain in his arms and shoulders. James sat down on the couch and looked through a stack of magazines, while Derrik stood directly in front of Luke.

"Alright, this is a simple game. You nod for a yes and shake for a no. You got that?"

Luke nodded.

"Good. Now there's a couple more things about the game I need to tell you about. First rule, there's no lyin'. Second rule, if you do good, you'll earn a reward. In this case, I'll cut a hole, so you can breathe out of your mouth. Third rule, well it's not really a rule, more like the grand prize. The grand prize, if you follow all the rules, and play the game, like I know you can play it, you'll live. Do you understand the rules?"

He nodded.

"Now, every game has a penalty. You know, like go back two spaces, lose a turn, or some shit like that. This one ain't no different. Now to be fair, you need to know this before we start, so listen up. Sitting on the rug, right in front of you, right at your feet, is a twenty-four ounce hammer and a big ass huntin' knife. They're just sittin' there right now, with nothing to do. You understand that?"

He nodded.

"That brings me back to rule number one, no lying. Now, I don't want to ruin your concentration, but if you break rule number one, well, that's where my friend over there on the couch joins the game, and trust me, you don't want that to happen. I won't tell you the details of the penalties, but if you break the first rule, the other two are null and void. Don't you get all nervous about all this, cuz really, I'm a nice guy, and I don't want to have to hurt you. Just think of me as Alex Trebek or Regis Philbin, or one of them other dudes, okay. You ready?"

He nodded.

"Alright then, let the games begin. Do you know why we're here?"

He nodded.

"Is it because of drugs?"

He shook his head

"Good, I had to ask that. I don't know what else you into."

"Do you know where, what we're lookin' for is?"

He nodded.

"Does the person you were talking to when you came in, know where it is?"

He nodded.

"Congratulations you won a reward. I knew you could do it. Now I'm going to cut that tape where your mouth is, and you're not going to do any yellin' or screamin' or nothin' like that. Are you?"

Luke shook his head.

"Cuz that would be a violation of the rules, right?"

He nodded.

"All right then."

Derrik felt around Luke's face, trying to find the exact place to cut, then pushed the blade up.

"Stop flinchin'. You don't want me to slip do you? Don't answer that, stay still."

He pushed the knife in and Luke's head jerked. The blade slipped across to the right an inch. Blood spewed out of the slit along with Luke's breath. Muffled screams came from beneath the tape and Luke snorted though the nose hole.

James grabbed his own mouth and winced like it had just happened to him.

"Shit, I told you to be still." Derrik pushed his finger into the slit trying to widen it. "Get your damn tongue off my finger."

Derrik held on to a piece of the tape, started slicing, and exposed Luke's blood stained teeth, lips, and tongue. As Luke gasped for air through the hole, blood dripped down his taped chin and onto his bare chest.

"Throw me that towel," Derrik told James.

Derrik wiped his hands, pushed the towel against Luke's mouth and held it there for a few seconds.

"It's not that bad. Gonna bleed a little, but it still feels good, don't it?"

"Yes," Luke mumbled.

"Go get him a glass of water."

James came back with a WGYN 107.3 plastic cup and handed it to Derrik. He rested the rim of the cup on Luke's bottom lip and tilted it up. Luke drank it all.

Derrik put the cup in the gym bag.

"Alright, we back from commercial break. In case you missed any of the previous action, Mister Bond here was just about to tell us who his buddy is, that took something that don't belong to him. Cause if he don't." He looked at James, extended his arm, queuing him to take over the recap.

James hunched over, got close to Luke's ear hole. "I'm going to start playing this little piggy with him. You know, like this little piggy got crushed, this little piggy got chopped off, and after they all go wee, wee, wee, all the way home. We're going to start playing this…little… pecker."

"Ohhhh." Derrik bent over, grabbing his crotch in mock pain.

Derrik regained his composure and got back in front of Luke.

"Okay now, enough fuckin' around. The name, give me the name I'm looking for."

"Paul," Luke said.

"*Paul*?" Paul what? Paul mall, Paul bearer, Paul the last fuckin' name, is who I'm lookin' for."

"Paul Roenik," Luke said.

"Paul ro-en-ick? Can't it be somethin' easy, like Jones or Smith?" He looked over at James. "See if you can find a pen and a piece of paper around here, will you? I ain't even gonna guess how you spell it."

James looked around the room and picked up the *Rolling Stone* magazines sitting on the floor near the couch. Kurt Cobain was on one cover, Layne Staley on the other.

He held them out, so Derrik could see. "It looks like our boy has a soft spot for dead rock stars."

James stretched his arms out to his side, still holding the magazines, and leaned one way, and then the other, like a human scale.

Derrik glared at him. "What the fuck are you doin'?"

"Hey, this is no easy decision."

"They both suck. There's your fuckin' decision."

James dropped the Cobain issue on the floor, tore the cover off the other one, and tossed it on the couch. "I don't see a pen around here. I can always jab him with the knife and finger paint it, if I have to.

"Where's a goddamn pen?" Derrik whispered into Luke's ear hole.

"Draw under the microwave," Luke said.

James walked over to the kitchen and came back with a pen.

"Alright then," Derrik said. "How do you spell mister ro-en-nick's name?"

"R...O...E...N...I...K."

He looked at James. "You got that?"

"Yeah."

"Now, the million dollar question, and then we'll be done here. Where can we find him? And it better not be no complicated shit, like his name."

"In Ventura, four eighty-six Troobain drive."

"Spell it."

"T...R...O...O...B...A...I...N."

"He live in an apartment, or he got his own place?"

"Own place."

"He live there by himself?"

"Yeah."

"What we're looking for? Is it there too?"

"Yeah, in the garage."

"Oh yeah, before I forget, on your cell phone, what's your voicemail password?"

"One, two, two, five."

"Congratulations, you win, game over. That wasn't so bad now was it? You don't need to answer that. Now when we leave here, I know, you're not going to be doin' anything stupid, like callin' him, or callin' anyone else, like the po-lice now. Are you?"

"No."

"I didn't think so, you bein' a car thief, and dope head and all. So we're gonna be leavin here Mister Bond, and you just gonna be forgettin' everything that happened here right?"

"Yeah."

"Good. Now I'm just gonna cut your hands loose, and leave it up to you to get yourself out of the rest. I think you can do that. Don't you?"

"Yeah."

"I thought so." Derrik looked over at James, pointed to the bag. "So you just need to stay still, while I try and cut your hands free. Okay?"

"Yeah."

"Alright then." He put his hand on Luke's shoulder and pulled him forward.

James stood right behind Luke, waiting with the tape roll. In one quick motion, he pulled an arms length off the roll. Luke's body stiffened. His back slammed against the chair. James slapped the tape over Luke's mouth hole, wound it around his head, and covered his nose with the next pass. He kept wrapping, trying to keep pace with Luke's flailing head. He stopped when Luke's head went limp and his body slumped forward.

Luke's bowels released.

"Oh man, *what the fuck* is that?" Derrik yelled.

James started laughing. "You shit yourself when you die. You didn't know that?"

"No, and I didn't need to know that. I would have let him keep his pants on, *if I knew that*. Let's get out of here."

James ripped the tape roll free, picked up the magazines and put them in the gym bag. Derrik grabbed the bag and they left the apartment.

# ROAD TRIP

Derrik drove the Tahoe out of the apartment parking lot, while James pulled out his cell and called Joel.

"Yeah, we're just leaving now," James said, looking at himself in the visor mirror.

"How did it go? It took you long enough, any trouble?"

"Nah, he told us where it is. It's in Ventura. We're on our way there now."

"Good, you think you'll be able to get it tonight?"

"Don't see why not. As long as it's where he said it is, should be a piece of cake, whether our friend is there or not."

"Okay, good work. It's seven-thirty now, so what time will you be back here?"

"Well, if all goes as planned, I'm thinking by ten, maybe ten-thirty."

"*That long*? Come on, you can do better than that."

"Man, we have to eat, we're starving here. We were thinking of getting a little something on the way back to tide us over."

"No stops. Just get back here as fast as possible. I'll order you whatever you want when you get here. Understood?"

"Yeah, yeah, okay." James put the phone on his crotch, pretending to hump it, while Derrik laughed. "Okay, we'll be seeing you soon, adios."

James closed the phone and Derrik looked over at him.

"You know where we goin'?"

"No, I was going to put it in the GPS. Give me the address," James said.

"Give *you* the address? You have it, you wrote it down."

"I know I did, but I gave you the paper. Didn't I?"

"You didn't give me shit. You wrote it down, and you have it. Check your damn pockets."

"You check yours."

"I told you. I don't...have...shit." Derrik jerked the wheel to the right and pulled over to the shoulder of the road.

They checked their pockets, nothing.

"You fuckin' idiot." Derrik slammed the dashboard with butt of his palm. "I ain't goin' back up there, you are. You lost it, and you're gonna go get it."

"I swear, I think I gave it to you. I'm not going back up there. We have his number in that phone. We'll just have to call him."

Derrik cringed and stared at James with purposely widened eyes.

"You even stupider than I thought. Number one, if that paper is lying around on the floor, or anywhere else up there, the cops are sure as shit gonna find it, and that's a bad thing. Number two, we just gonna call this guy up with his buddies phone, and say what? Hello Paul, how are you doing this evening? We just killed your friend, and while we're in the neighborhood, we were gonna come over and fuck you up worse. Would you be so kind and tell us how we get to your house?"

James cracked a half smile, trying to hold back a laugh.

"This ain't funny." Derrik pulled the Tahoe back on to the road. "Joel ain't gonna see the humor in it, I'll tell you that right *now*."

"Screw him, and we're getting something to eat, *before* we go back to his place too."

"There's a snack waiting for you all over the seat of that chair up there. All you can eat, *after* you get the paper."

Derrik turned the Tahoe around, headed back toward Luke's apartment.

"The bag!" James reached into the back seat and grabbed the gym bag. "Hold on, it might be in here."

He rummaged through it, pulled out the paper and waved it in front of Derrik's face.

"Yeah baby, I got it. Don't remember putting it in there, but we got it."

"Lucky for you." Derrik pointed at the GPS. "Put it in there."

James entered the destination, while Derrik turned the Tahoe around, headed toward Ventura. The female voice started giving the instructions.

Derrick opened the console between them and pulled out a stack of CD cases, inspecting them as he drove. He made his choice and tossed the rest into the back seat.

"Time for some real music, inspirational kinda shit."

*Insane in the Brain*" came on and Derrik leaned back into his seat. His upper body moved and grooved to the song as he performed a duet with the singer.

## PAUL'S PLACE

Paul cracked open a can of beer and walked from the kitchen toward the TV room. He flopped down on the couch, took a long sip off the beer. He pointed the remote at the entertainment center, lowered the volume of the Molly Hatchet song, and grabbed his cell phone off the floor.

"Wader."

The cell autodialed Luke's cell phone, while he listened on speaker.

*Voicemail again? Where the hell is he?*

"Hey it's me. What's the good word bro? I called you a couple times already. You not taking my calls or what?

Everything cool with you? Sounded like you fell down the stairs or something last time I talked to you. Are you still coming over? Let me know. I'm going out to sit in the ride for a while. Call me, later."

He closed the phone and thought about the last time he talked to Luke, while he finished the rest of the beer.

*He was nervous about someone calling his cell. That was nothing though. The car? No one knows we have it. Wouldn't have told anyone. In a couple days, it would be gone anyway. We'd be up twenty-five hundred bucks each. Just getting too paranoid, must be the weed. The car, the car, the car, could someone know we took it? No way, how could they? No one was at the house. They were some badass dudes that were there before us, but no one there when we took it, we saw them leave. It's just a car, quit worrying, he's fine.*

Paul got up, made his way over to the bedroom, and grabbed a set of keys off the dresser. On his way out to the kitchen, he went into the bathroom to take a leak. He looked at his reflection in the mirror above the sink as the piss stream hit the toilet water, without the guidance of his hand. He took the Dallas Cowboys hat off his head with one hand and rubbed the five o'clock shadow covering his head with the other.

*Need a shave in the morning, starting to be a pain in the ass. Should let it grow long again, less hassle.*

He zipped his fly, moved closer to the mirror, and stroked his chin beard and the soul patch above it.

*Should grow a stache, a nice porn star one. Let my hair grow out again.*

Paul pulled another beer out of the refrigerator and took a sip, while *"Get Ready"* played from the TV room. The groove broke his thought pattern. He started singing into the beer can as he walked toward the garage. He flipped the light switch on and admired the Challenger from the threshold.

*What a ride. This car is the shit. Too bad we have to get rid of it. Maybe Dad would buy me one? Never, he already threatened to stop paying for the house. I deserve a car like this, not that piece of shit truck.*

The thought of his truck, compared to Challenger, brought him down, reminded him of his shitty job at the body shop. The "discretionary" income he got from the owner for the occasional car theft was the only reason he stayed.

*Thing looks even more evil in the garage. Like a black demon, waiting to unleash its wrath on anyone who dares to enter the cockpit. Samuel Jackson in Pulp fiction, that's what this car is. One powerful, fearless, and badass motherfucker.*

Paul pressed a button on the remote key fob. The lights flashed and the door locks released. He climbed inside, put his beer in the holder between the bucket seats, and started the engine. He pushed down hard on the gas pedal. The engine roared and the windows on the rollup garage door trembled. He pulled his foot off the pedal and the engine gurgled as it settled down. He punched the gas one more time, just to hear the gurgle, and shut down the engine.

"God...damn," he said out loud.

He pushed the power button on the media center display panel. The color screen came to life and refreshed with Sirius Satellite radio showing on it. He scrolled through the music types, selected Seventies Rock, scanned through the channel options, and made his choice.

He turned it up and drank some more beer, while checking out the labels and buttons on the media panel.

*MP3, WMA, JPEG, Serial port, Navigation, Voice Recognition. A fucking hard drive? A car with a hard drive? Better than Night Rider. Got to take it for a ride, just a little cruise. It's dark, it's safe.*

He felt an aura, like the car was begging him to take it for a ride, but he fought it.

*Get pinched for OUI. Better not, too risky.*

After "*Christine Sixteen*" finished playing, Paul drank the last swig and shut off the electronics. He got out and looked at the key fob, ready to press the lock button, but noticed a trunk icon and pressed it. He heard the trunk lock disengage and watched it pop open.

He grabbed on to the spoiler, pulled the trunk door up, and let go when the hydraulics took over and raised it all the way open.

*What the hell's that?*

He stared at the large, black, rectangular case in the middle of the trunk space. It looked like a cooler encased in protective, nylon fabric. He ran his palms over the top and sides of it and then put his hands under the bottom to see how much it weighed. For its size, it was light, no more than ten pounds. He noticed the carrying strap attached to the sides, but the strap was behind the case. He pulled the strap over the top, lifted the case out, and rested it on the garage floor.

He moved his hand around the perimeter of the top, following the zipper line, until he found the clasp and pulled it all the way around outline of the case. He flipped open the top and looked at the contents.

*Looks like some kind of console or something. A video game?*

Paul reached in and unfastened the Velcro straps that secured the black, plastic device to the padded bottom of the case. He pulled the device out, held it up to the overhead light, and looked it over.

*DreemWeever VR? This is cool. Some kind of mask. Looks like high tech ski goggles with a smoked glass visor. Built in headphones, this is the shit.*

He pushed it onto his face. It covered the bridge of his nose and most of his forehead. The flexible sides covered his ears, like earmuffs.

*Can't see anything, has to be a video game. How's it work?*

He took it off and examined it for more details.

An LED was on the top, above the right eye side. A thin, vertical, three inch slot was on the left side of the front and the three small, input plugs on the right side were labeled RA, LA, and V.

Paul pulled the elastic strap back, slipped it over his head, and pulled the mask over his face. It fit snuggly to his head. The strap held the sides tight to his ears. He felt the pads of the built-in headphones pushing against them.

*Can't see, can't hear anything. This is wild.*

He took it off and looked it over again, examining every detail.

*How does this goddamn thing work? No power button, no power input plug. The three inputs in the side look like the kind DVD players have, but not power plugs. The game must go in that slot. DreemWeever VR...VR, virtual reality? Must be a virtual reality game. Where's the games. How does it power up?*

He bent over, looked inside the case, and noticed two zippered seams along both the short sides. If the seams weren't there, he wouldn't have noticed them. The compartments were built into the sides of the case, between the hard plastic of the inside and outside walls. He unzipped one, reached down inside, and pulled out three individually coiled cables. The ends were the same as the three inputs on the headset.

He unzipped the other panel and pulled out a sealed, tan colored, shipping envelope, about eight inches square and padded inside for protection. He peeled open the seal, reached in and pulled out eleven mini CD's that were inside clear plastic cases. Paul flipped through the stack, reading the labels on each one.

*S.Haskins, Bryce Surgery, M.Haskins. Bryce Abort, Big Apple, Thomas Surgery, Demo, PTSS, Thomas Abort, Process/DWVR Corp, Abductions.*

*These are the games? Weird names for games. How do you turn this fucking thing on?*

Paul put everything in the case and carried it into the house. He sat on the edge of the couch, the open case in front of him and grabbed the remote to lower the Van Halen song.

The missed call audio alert beeped from his cell on the end table. He stretched out to the left, grabbed it and looked at the display.

*Wader, twenty minutes ago, about time. No voicemail?*

He pressed the speakerphone button and said, "Wader." After the fourth ring, Luke's cell picked up. Paul heard music playing.

"Hey what's up Luke, where the hell you been?"

No one answered. The music got louder.

"What's up with the rap shit? It's bad for your health. Are you on your way over or what?"

No answer, only the music. He recognized the song, "*How I Could Just Kill a Man*", Cypress Hill.

"Come on man, turn that shit off. You got me, I give, uncle, whatever. You better be on you way over. You're not going to believe what I found in the car man. You're going to shit when you see it."

The music stopped. A deep, low, slow talking voice came over the speaker phone.

"It's not nice to covet thy neighbor's goods...Pablo."

The call dropped. Paul stared at the phone and hit the SEND button twice to redial. It rang six times and Luke's voicemail greeting kicked in.

"This is Luke, you know the drill."

"What *the fuck* is going on? What was that all about? Call me back *now*."

Paul closed the phone and reached for the half joint in the ashtray. He lit it, took a power toke, and fell back into the couch, holding in the smoke. He thought about the phone call as he blew the smoke at the ceiling.

*It's not nice to covet thy neighbor's goods. It's not good to take someone else's stuff. Pablo. No one calls me Pablo, except Luke. The car, whoever that was, knows about the car. How could he? Luke wouldn't have told anyone about it. Something's wrong.*

He took a couple more tokes, snuffed out the head of the joint in the ashtray and looked down at the bag.

*What the hell is this thing? How does it to work?*

He went into his room, sat down at the computer and launched Google. He typed in DreemWeever VR and looked through the results. Nothing, only a tree hugger's blog and a few links to a writer's discussion forum, by a user named dreamweaver.

*Whatever this is it's not on the market yet. The Cypress Hill song. He was telling me something, sending me a message. The guy sounded black. Got to be the guy from the house, the big black guy. How does he know I have the car? Only one way, Luke told him. He made Luke tell him, how? Doesn't matter, he has Luke's phone. Where's Luke? Would have called, if he could. The big guy is on his way over here, has to be. Have to get out of here. Where to? Luke's apartment, see if he's there. If not, he's in trouble. Need to get out of here, now.*

Paul went out to the TV room and paced around, trying to make a plan.

*What do I need? What do I need?*

He grabbed the keys to the truck, the bag of weed, the bowl, and looked down at the case.

*Have to take it. What else? What else?*

He grabbed his cell off the couch and tried to put it in his pants pocket, but felt the keys to the Challenger in there. He pulled them out and put the cell in.

*What do I do with these?*

Paul double timed it into the garage, left the keys on the hood of the Challenger and went back inside. He put on a pair of sneakers and pulled a black Oakland Raiders hoodie over his head.

*Anything else? Forgetting something. Wallet.*

He went into his room, grabbed the wallet off the bureau and put it in his back pocket. He checked the front and rear doors, made sure they were locked. He knew the garage was already locked, but checked it again.

He kept the kitchen and TV room lights on, turned all the others off. He grabbed a Stone Temple Pilots CD and put it in the player, hoping that if anyone came, they might think he's inside and not try to break in. He grabbed the case, slung it over his shoulder and went out the front door, headed toward the truck.

He got in the truck, pushed the case into the extra cab section and put the key in the ignition.

*Shit, what's that?*

He looked out the driver's side window and focused on the headlights of a big, dark colored SUV as it rolled to a stop in front of his house. He looked down the slope of the front lawn, trying to see who was in it, but all the windows were tinted. The headlights went out.

Paul stretched out across the bench seat and moved down onto the floor. He reached his hand up and pushed the door lock button. His chest pounded and adrenaline pumped through his body, as he listened for any sounds outside the truck.

# D-RAYNGED

The bass riff of "*I'm That Type of Guy*" reverberated inside of the Tahoe.

"LL is the man. *Damn,* he know how to rhyme, none better." Derrik said. "Built like a brick shithouse too. That's why the ladies, love, cool James."

"I'm not into the rap shit," James said. "But he's pretty good. How's he think of this stuff?"

Derrik lowered the volume.

"He don't do shit, except work out, and think up rhymes all day. If that's all I had to do, damn, I'd be just as good as him. I got a lot of ideas. Just need the time to develop them. One of these days, gonna' book me some studio time, and lay it down. Next thing you know, I'll be rollin' in the green, like you ain't never seen. Yes sir, some day, *dee ranged* will be surrounded by all the money, and all the honeys."

"Dee ranged, what the hell's that?"

"That's my music name, have to have it. You know, like I'm crazy. Yes sir, thinking about putting a patent on it, so nobody steal it. Customized it too, capital D, dash, R A Y N G E D. How you like that?"

James put it together in his head and started laughing.

"Go ahead and laugh fool. If you lucky, and somehow, I feel bad enough for your sorry, bald, ass. I might let you be my bodyguard."

"Okay *deeee raaaanged.* Mickey dee's is more like it. The only thing I'll need to guard is the refrigerator. To keep *you,* from assaulting *it.*"

"You just wait, soon as I ge-" The GPS voice interrupted him. "We'll finish this conversation later."

"This is it. Troobain Road, take a left," James said.

"I know that." Derrik turned into the road. "Look out for number four eighty-six. It's gonna be on my side."

Derrik eased the Tahoe up the road, looking to his left, counting the numbers on the mailboxes.

"That's four twenty-two, it's down further," James said. "Not a bad neighborhood. This guy must have some money."

"The stolen car business must pay well these days. Too bad he ain't gonna be around to spend none of it."

"Four eighty-two, four eighty-four, okay, pull it over right there."

Derrick stopped the Tahoe at the bottom of the lawn that sloped up toward the front of the house and shut off the headlights.

"Looks like he's here," Derrik said, pointing toward the house. "The lights are on. There's his truck in the driveway. The cars in that garage there. Now, how we gonna do this?"

"Before we do anything, shouldn't we make sure the car is in there? So we know we're at the right house."

"Yeah, but the car is secondary. He said on the voicemail that he found somethin' in the car. That tells me, it's not in the car. It's in the house, with him. Tell you what. You look like you belong in this neighborhood more than I do. Why don't you get up to the garage and look in, make sure the cars in there. Then, you come back, and we just go right up to the door. Better yet, you go up, and I'll stand off to the side, so he don't see me. You tell him you need directions or some shit like that. Once he opens the door, you know what to do. I'll be right behind you. The rest is easy. Now get goin'."

"Alright, keep an eye out though. Be ready to get out of here fast if something happens."

"Just get up there, nothin's gonna happen. The guy don't even have the outside light on. You can't see shit out there."

James got out quickly. The inside lights of the Tahoe blinked on, then off, when he pushed the door closed. He walked along the edge of the lawn, until he reached the end of the driveway and looked up at the house. He walked up the driveway, trying to keep the noise of his cowboy boots quiet. The truck was parked in front of the garage door. James crept his way up, until he was standing behind the tailgate and the tinted glass of the bed cap hatch door. He looked over at the house, ready to sneak around the side of the truck and get to the garage.

The truck engine turned over.

"What the fuck!"

The motor raced, the reverse lights came on, and the truck launched backward. The bumper smashed into James' thighs. He tried to grab the top of the cap to hold himself up, but his hands slid off. The momentum of the truck drove his body backward, sucking his legs under the bumper. His back hit the driveway and his head slammed the pavement, flattening the back of his skull. The undercarriage of the truck scraped over his body and the front passenger side tire crushed his right arm as it rolled over it.

The truck skidded when it got onto the street and came to a quick stop. The engine raced, the tires squealed, and the truck accelerated as it went past Derrik.

Derrik jumped out, ran across the lawn toward the driveway and made it to James, who wasn't moving. A pool of blood grew around the back of James' head and little crimson tributaries inched down the slope of the driveway. Derrik bent over to see if James was breathing. He wasn't.

Derrik grabbed James under the armpits and backpedaled, dragging the body across the grass toward the Tahoe. He dropped James on the ground beside the car and opened the back seat door. He rolled James on to his stomach, bent over, and wrapped his arms around the upper body.

He hoisted James off the ground and shoved him onto the back seat. The legs hung out of the door and the cowboy boots were touching the ground. Derrik went to the other side, opened the back door, and pulled the body across the seat. He slammed the door, ran back to the other side and pushed the feet up so they bent at the knees and stuffed the legs inside. He slammed the door closed, jumped into the driver's seat and sped off down the road

Derrik got to the main road and turned on the inside light. He noticed the blood on his hands and more on the front of his sweat jacket and pants.

## BUZZKILL

Joel sat at the granite island in the kitchen and looked through the latest issue of *The Hollywood Reporter*, while he nursed a glass of Chivas Regal and listened to "*Mistral Wind*" playing on the Bose. He was on edge, doing whatever he could to occupy himself, and waiting for the cell phone in front of him to ring.

He looked at the time on the cell.

*Nine-ten, Give them another forty-five minutes, then call, if they haven't by then. They better not have screwed this up. What if there were problems? How could there be? It was simple. They would scare the shit out of him, get what they came for, and take care of the unfinished business. Problem solved.*

Joel swirled the Chivas and crushed ice around in the glass, took a sip. As he put the glass down, the ringtone sounded. He snatched the cell off the counter.

"That was quicker than I-"

"We got huge motherfuckin' problems. James is dead and the guy's gone. What the fuck am I going to do? I'm headin' your way, and you better have a fuckin' plan."

Joel downed the drink, spit the ice pieces back into the cup, and killed the music with the remote.

"Derrik, Derrik! Slow down, calm down, right now! Compose yourself."

"That's easy for you to say. You ain't the one drivin' around with a fuckin' dead guy in the back seat of your car."

"All right." Joel paced around the kitchen. "I understand that you are in a difficult situation, but you need to focus. Can you do that?"

"Don't give me any of your fuckin' shrink bullshit. Just have a goddamn plan when I get there."

"I will. I promise you that, but you need to calm down. Where are you?"

"I'm in Camarillo, I'll be there in forty-five minutes, and you better be ready."

"I will, I told you that. Just get here, and we'll take care of it. Okay?"

The call dropped. Joel snapped his cell closed.

*This can't be happening. Those goddamn incompetent idiots. How could they screw this up? Need to know what happened. Need to act fast. Need to catch that little fucker.*

\*\*\*

Derrik pulled the Tahoe through the gates and up to the front of Shangri-La. He killed the headlights and got out. Joel met him before he was past the front of the Tahoe.

Joel noticed the blood on the front of Derrik's sweatsuit and tried to ignore it, but Derrik got right to it.

"Look at this shit. I need to get out of these clothes." He waved his hands in Joel's face. "And clean the fuck up."

"I know, please, keep your voice down. You need to get it together. First, we need to deal with James. That's the number one priority right now, okay?"

"Yeah," Derrik said.

Joel followed him to the rear door on the driver's side of the Tahoe.

The interior light came on when Derrik opened the door and they looked down at James. His contorted body was stretched across the floor, between the front and back seats. The left side of his face rested on the blood stained, gray floor mat behind the passenger seat. The back of his bald head was bloody and looked flattened and indented. His right arm rested on the back seat and his forearm was bent at a forty-five degree angle.

Joel pushed the door closed.

"Shit, what the hell happened to him Derrik?"

"He got run over by the guy's truck. Never even seen it comin'. I saw the whole thing."

"Where were you?"

"What do you mean where the fuck was I? That's all you got to say?"

"Never mind." Joel raised his hands. "I apologize, I'm trying to sort this out and come up with some way to fix it. Believe me, James was a good man and this is a tragedy, but we have to do something very quickly."

"What are we gonna do? *That's* what I want to know."

"Okay, let's start from square one. Cleaning up the blood in there doesn't look like it should be that tough. Besides the floor, and some on the seat, I didn't see much more. Obviously, we need to get him out of there, and dispose of the body somewhere. We can talk about how that's going to be done, but first, we need to get you inside and cleaned up. Before we go inside, I need to know right now. Did anyone see you?"

"No."

"Are you sure?"

"Yeah, I don't think the guy even saw us."

"What do you mean?"

"I mean it was like he was waitin' for us, like he knew we were comin'. One minute, I'm sitting in the car watchin' James creep up to the house, and the next thing, the fuckin' guy is backing over him with his truck, and he was gone. Just like that."

"Alright, this is not the place to be talking about it. Come on, let's go inside. We need to sort this out tonight. The party is tomorrow, and people will be here to start setting up by noon."

## WHERE'S MY MOTIVATION?

Paul stopped his truck in front of the apartment building and stared up at Luke's second floor unit, trying to see if any lights were on inside.

*Nothing in his bedroom.*

He focused on the slider.

*Can't tell, the curtains are closed over it.*

He drove around the side, saw Luke's Malibu parked under the carport, and pulled into the empty spot beside it.

*Cars here, got to be inside.*

Paul walked along the sidewalk and cut across the grass to get a closer view of the terrace.

*Can't see any lights, curtains in the way. Has to be home, maybe asleep.*

He went up the stairs, rapped on the door a couple of times and waited. He banged it a few more times and put his ear against the door, listening for the TV or some music inside. Nothing. Silence.

*Mi Casa, Su Casa.* Paul thought about the time Luke had said that, when he locked his keys in the car. It was after the Godsmack show. They were drunk. When Luke tried to open the apartment door, he realized he didn't have the keys. Luke had thought he might have dropped them on the way up, but they couldn't find them when they retraced their steps back to the car. Paul had suggested they should smash a window to get the keys out of the Malibu and report it as a break in.

"No worries man," Luke had told him. "I have a spare hidden on the terrace, under the plant."

*Worth a try.*

Paul went down the stairs, looked up at the terrace and saw the plant pot in the same spot as it had been that night. He looked over the privacy wall of the apartment under Luke's.

*The blinds are closed across the slider. Good.*

He jumped up onto the wall, held on to the terrace floor with one hand, and moved the pot with the other. He ran his hand over the decking and felt the key under his fingers.

*Got it.*

Paul clenched the key in his palm, turned around and jumped back to the ground, hoping the key still worked.

He pushed the key into the lock and heard the tumblers disengage when he turned it. He eased the door open a few inches and looked through the opening. It was dark inside.

*Where the hell is he?*

He pushed the door open wider and stuck his left hand into the darkness, feeling along the wall for the light switch, until his entire arm was inside.

*Shit*, he thought, trying to picture the inside layout in his mind, knowing the switch was somewhere on the wall close by.

He heard voices coming up the stairs toward him and pulled his arm out. He pushed the door open, stepped inside, and gently closed the door.

Paul faced the wall, listening for noises in the hallway and trying to process the stench in the air. His hand flipped the wall switch up and the lights came on.

*What fucking stinks?*

He turned his head to the left and he sucked in so much air, a reverse scream came from his mouth. His chest muscles constricted and his shoulders squeezed his neck.

"What the fuck," he almost screamed, but covered his mouth to muffle it. He looked at what was in the chair.

"Holy shit, holy shit," he mumbled, pacing, his hands clenched to the sides of his head, like he was trying to stop his brain from exploding.

*Have to get out of here. Shit. Call the cops. Can't, probably already looking for me. Can't leave him like that. Have to get out of here, call from a payphone. Those fuckers, how could they? I'm fucked.*

Paul walked over to the door, sucking in deep breaths to calm down. He turned around and looked at Luke.

"Don't worry man." Tears rolled down his cheeks. "Someone's coming to get you. I'm going to get those fuckers for you."

He pulled the bottom of the hoodie over his face and held it there to sop up the tears, while he breathed into it.

*Calm down, get it together. Have to get out of here, calm down.*

He pulled his sleeve over his hand, wiped the switch as he shut the lights off, and did the same to the doorknob on each side as he left.

***

Paul merged onto 101 South, put the lighter to the bowl and inhaled all the smoke his lungs could hold, as he drove in the travel lane, trying to figure out his next move.

*Can't go back to my place. Did I kill that guy? Felt like he went right under the truck. It was them. Saw his bald head and the black guy in the Tahoe. Definitely them.*

He took a couple more hits off the bowl and put it in the ashtray.

*Maybe he was just hurt and they took off. If they did, they won't be calling the cops. If I killed him and the black guy left him in the driveway, I'm fucked. The cops are looking for me. Need to do something, make a move.*

Paul pulled the cell out of his pocket, held it in front of his mouth. "Wader." After the fourth ring, Derrik answered.

"Was wonderin' when you was gonna get the balls to call."

"Fuck you cocksucker. I know what you did, and you and your fucking buddy are going down for murder."

"Hold on my man, chill out. I think you got your facts all wrong. You the one who's going down for a hom-o-cide, not me. I ain't the one who drove over my friend, and left his skull all over your driveway. Am I?"

"Screw you. You were going to do to me what you did to Luke. I know it. It was an accident. That's all I have to say."

"Whoa, slow down now, there's a way this can all be worked out...for both of us. You hear what I'm sayin'?"

"I don't give a shit what you're saying. I'm telling you, that my friend is dead, and I know you did it."

"Oh you do huh? I think you got a better chance provin' that Osama Bin fuckin' Laden did it. Now, we are gonna work this thing out, and after we do that, we all gonna go on our merry way. How's that sound to you?"

Paul pressed the mute button on the cell.

*See what he has to say, give me time to make a plan. He's going down no matter what he says.*

"You still there my man?"

Paul took a deep breath, took the phone off mute.

"Yeah, I'm listening,"

"Hello Paul," Joel said.

"Who's this?"

"That is not important Paul, and I truly understand what you are up against. Believe me, this is an extremely unfortunate situation, for both of us. But there is a solution. Are you willing to hear me out?"

"Yeah."

"Good. First, you need to know that the police are not looking for you. I know that must be weighing heavily on your mind, and I assure you, that they are not. My friend here has similar concerns, and the question is whether he can be confident in knowing, that at this time, they are simply just concerns. Is that the way you see it?"

"Yeah, right now, at this moment, that's how I see it."

"Excellent. Now, I know that you took the Challenger, and to be quite honest with you, I am willing to overlook that. In fact, it means nothing to me, but what I am interested in, is what you found in the trunk. I take it you have it with you now, wherever you are. Am I right?"

"Yeah, I have the video game, if that's what you mean."

"Good. Now all I'm asking, is that it be returned. There will be no questions, no explanations. No harm, no foul. Is that something that you are willing to do, tonight?"

"Yeah, but not tonight. It's late, and I need some rest."

"Then when Paul?"

"Tomorrow. I'll call you at nine in the morning, and we can do it then."

"You are not going to let me down are you Paul?"

Paul snapped his cell closed.

*** 

Derrik sat at the island in Joel's kitchen and scooped the dregs out of the pork fried rice container. Joel closed his cell.

"So, what's he gonna do?" Derrik asked.

"He hung up on me, but he's willing to meet us tomorrow to return it."

"How we gonna do that?"

"Good question, and I think the best way, is to invite him to a party. What do you think?"

Derrik grinned. "I think that'll work out just fine."

"Me too, but we have more pressing matters at hand. You're clothes should be dry in about thirty minutes, although." Joel raised his eyebrows. "I'm sure you would love to stay in that robe."

"It *is* nice and all." Derrik ran his hands down his chest, smoothed out the black silk. "But it's a little too snug for my likin'."

***

Paul lowered the volume on "*Fly Like an Eagle*" as he got off 101 South at the Lost Hills Road exit in Calabasas, heading toward the Good Nite Inn.

*This is alright,* he thought, pulling into the parking lot. He shut off the truck, got out, and walked toward the main building to check in.

*What's it going to cost? Got to get some sleep.*

He looked at his watch.

*Eleven-thirty, nine and a half hours left. Have to be on top of my game.*

He came out and went back to the truck with the card key to a standard room with one queen bed and a parking lot view.

*Hundred bucks. Hope the room's decent. At least it's close to the truck.*

Paul grabbed his knapsack, the case with the headset in it, and took the stairs up to the room on the second floor.

*Have to give this thing another shot. Why do they want it back so badly? What's so important about a video game? Wish Luke was here.*

The room was clean and he could see the truck from the window as he pulled off his sneakers. He flopped down on the bed, reached for the remote on the desk next to him and put the television on.

*Need something to drink and eat. Must be vending machines. Could use a beer. Cold soda, a couple snacks will have to do.*

He took out his wallet and removed the singles.

*Four bucks. Should be enough.*

Paul went out to the hall, noticed the vending sign pointing to the left, and found the vending machines in an alcove at the end of the hallway.

He sat at the end of the bed and unzipped the cover of the case, while he finished the Doritos and most of the Coke.

"Time to see what all the fuss is about."

He put the headset on the bed, took out the package of mini disks, and pushed himself back, so he could lean against the headboard.

He dumped out the disks, spread them out on the bed and put the headset on his lap. He looked at the labels on the disks.

*Bryce Abort?*

He took the disk out of the case and lined it up with the slot on the side of the headset. He started to push the disc in, but it loaded itself and the green LED on the front of the headset started to flash.

"Yes, it lives."

Paul held it out in front of his face, so he could see the inside of the headset screen that had turned blue when the disc loaded. Music started coming from the headphones. He held the straps to the back of his head, pulled the headset over his face, and pushed the headphone cups tight to his ears.

Alice in Chains blasted in his ears and *Bryce Session #3*, in white text, displayed on the black screen. The lyrics started and a fetus, suspended in a cocoon of amniotic fluid, populated the screen. Paul grabbed the sides of the headset and almost pulled it off his face, but kept watching when the strobe light effect kicked in. A man's face kept appearing on the body and changing back to the fetus' head.

Paul took the AV cables out of the case, plugged the connectors into the matching colors on the front of the television and connected the other ends to the headset.

He pushed the menu button on the television and selected the AV option. The screen turned blue and he pushed the disk labeled *Process/DWVR Corp* into the headset.


## THE PARTY


I pulled the Bullitt up to the open gates at Joel's house. Derrik stood there, dressed in a black tux and looked intimidating with his arms folded across his huge chest. He motioned with his head for me to go through and nodded hello as I drove past him. About twenty cars and SUV's were parked on the lawn, but I was able to pull up the driveway and park behind a red Hummer H3 with a California plate that had HEDGAME on it. Obviously, the driveway was for VIP guests only.

I got out and looked back at Derrik as he directed a teal, Porsche 911 toward the lawn parking. I walked up to the front door. It was unlocked and I went inside. As I went through the great room, I looked down the hall and noticed the media room door was shut.

In the kitchen, a guy and a lady dressed in chef's whites and hats were cooking, and preparing food trays. A waiter wearing a black tuxedo came into the kitchen, grabbed two trays of hors d'oeuvres, and I followed him out the slider doors and onto the terrace. He went down the stairs, but I stood against the railing and looked down at the scene around the pool. About forty people mingled in various groups. Some sat at tables, but most of them gathered around the three large plasma screens that were mounted on top of thin, black pedestals. One was next to the bar and the other two were on each side of the pool. The main attraction on all three was vintage Aerosmith performing "*Train Kept a Rollin*".

The pool water, which was chemically colored light purple, and the flames coming from the strategically placed tiki lamps, created a surreal atmosphere. The bushes, trees, and exotic plants that were all around, added to the ambience and I understood why

Joel called this place Shangri-La. It really did look like you were at an exotic resort.

I could see Joel talking with a group of four guys and within seconds, he looked up and made eye contact with me. He raised his arm and pulled his fingers into his palm, summoning me to join him poolside.

I went down the zigzag of stairs and walked up over to join the group. They abruptly ended their conversation when I approached them and I got the feeling that I had been the topic of discussion.

"Thomas, looking sharp as usual," Joel said, shaking my hand and rapidly snapping his fingers at the passing waiter to get his attention.

"Yes sir, what may I get you?" the waiter asked.

"What's your pleasure Thomas?"

The waiter looked at me for the answer.

"Stoli, on the rocks, with a lime."

"Certainly sir, one moment," he said, and walked away.

"Gentlemen." Joel put his arm around my shoulder. "For those of you who don't know, this is Thomas, a dear friend."

Saboro, one of the guys I had met from Vegas, reached out and shook my hand.

"Ah, it's good to see you again, Thomas. I hope you're doing well."

"Doing just fine thanks."

The other guy from Vegas, Ghede, was there too. He extended his hand and I shook it.

"It's a pleasure to see you again as well Thomas."

"Thanks."

"This." Joel motioned to one of the two other guys standing in front of him. "Is Doctor Stephan Erlik."

"Hello Thomas."

"Hi. What's your specialty?"

"I'm a plastic surgeon."

I figured he was the guy who owned the house Bryce and I stayed at in Boston.

"Please, you are being to modest Stephan," Joel said. "Miracle worker is far more appropriate."

I shook his hand and Joel pointed to a guy that had been staring at the ground since I joined them. "And this is Victor Ahriman, computer wizard extraordinaire."

"Nice to meet you." He barely looked at me and kept his hands in his pants pockets.

"Same here," I said, thinking he looked like the actor who played Mark Wahlberg's flunky buddy in *Boogie Nights*, only greasier.

"Here you go sir." The waiter handed me the drink.

I thanked him and drank half of it in one sip. Joel put his hand on my shoulder again and addressed the others.

"Gentlemen, I need five minutes with Thomas. Please, enjoy, and let's plan on meeting inside in about twenty minutes."

Joel raised his glass and the others and I did the same.

"Cheers." Joel patted me on the shoulder. "Come on, let's talk."

We walked toward the back, off to the right of the bar, away from the rest of the guests. He pointed over at the plasma where "*Cat Scratch Fever*" was on.

"What do you think of that?"

"Ted's cool," I said.

"Not Ted, the whole concept. I have all ten of the DVD's from *The Midnight Special* loaded to play randomly. I thought it was a novel idea. What's your take?"

"No complaints from me. It's classic stuff, good stuff. Not sure what some of the people here think, but it looks like most of them are into it. It's better than ninety-nine percent of the shit that's around today."

"Excellent. Now to get you up to speed on what's been going on. If you remember, I put something in the trunk of the Challenger, and as you know, the Challenger was stolen. I know who took it, and despite my best efforts, I have not been able to get it back." He looked at his watch. "I thought I would have it by now, but it appears that the gentleman who has it, has reneged on the agreement I had with him."

"Come on, I'm sure that-"

Joel put his hand up, cutting me off.

"Let me finish. You also need to know that during the process of trying to get it back, James had some extremely unfortunate luck, and as a result, is no longer with us."

"No longer with us, or no longer *with us*, like he's dead. "

"The latter, I'm afraid."

"What the hell's going on Joel? Don't beat around the bush. Just tell it to me straight, no bullshit. Okay?"

"This is not the time, nor the place, to discuss this in detail. There are things that need to be done, and there is very little time with which to do them. The Cliff Notes version is that some guy, who, despite our best efforts, we cannot seem to find, is in possession of certain things that will bring down the entire DreemWeever project, and *everyone* associated with it. We need to find this person, and get back what he has, or things will happen, that are beyond anything that you or I could possibly imagine. Is that the answer you were looking for?"

"Shit Joel, what's this guy have?"

"Everything Thomas."

He looked over toward the guys from Vegas.

"Those two gentlemen were expecting something to be delivered to them yesterday. You were supposed to bring it to them. They don't have it, and in ten minutes, I need to explain to them why they don't have it, and when they will get it."

"What are you going to tell them?"

"That's my problem, not yours. Your most important problem, is finding the guy who has what they need."

"How the hell am I going to do that?"

"You are going to work with Derrik, and do whatever it takes, that's how. We can discuss this more later. For the time being, enjoy yourself. You look tense, relax. Everything will work out, I assure you."

An attractive girl, tall with long, jet black hair, came up from behind Joel and wrapped her arms around his neck.

"Hey there Joel."

He turned around quickly, holding his drink in one hand, and wrapping his arm around her back with the other. I could tell that she was feeling no pain.

"Lilli, so glad you could make it. Are you enjoying yourself?"

"You know it. The place looks fabulous," she said, looking over at me. "Who's your friend?"

"Ah, how rude of me," Joel said. "Lillian Goodrich, please meet Thomas."

I extended my hand and she shook it with her fingers.

"Let me guess, an actor, or a client?" she asked.

"Neither," I said, "just a friend. And you?"

She glanced at Joel. "All of the above. Anyway, it's nice to meet you *Thomas.* I need another drink. I'll talk to you guys later."

She looked over at the plasma near the bar, where The Cars were doing "*Let's Go*".

"Whatever happened to The Cars? Is that guy still married to that supermodel? He must be so old now."

"Age is in the eye of the beholder my dear," Joel said.

"You should know." She fluttered her eyelashes, rubbed Joel's chest, and then walked away, headed toward the bar.

"What's the deal with her?" I asked Joel.

"She's a star rider with the head creeps, just like all the others my friend. Nothing more, nothing less." He raised his glass and smiled.

"Your livelihood, you mean," I said.

"Touche, at least for now it is. But I'm afraid I must go, and put on a performance worthy of the greatest actor. We'll talk later."

"Good Luck," I yelled to him as he walked away.

The same waiter came over toward me.

"May I get you anything sir? Another vodka?"

I noticed John coming down the stairs from the house.

"Please, same as before." I pointed to the area near the hot tub at the entrance to the pool area. "I'll be over there. And bring over a bourbon too, straight up, please."

"Right away sir."

# QUALITY CONTROL

"Gentlemen." Joel looked at Ahriman, Ghede, Erlik, and Saboro, who were seated around him on the sectional in the Media room. "I hope you are enjoying yourself this evening. It's been a long time, too long frankly, since we last got together as a group. I thank each of you for the effort and commitment you have shown me throughout this entire process."

Ghede stood up, glaring at Joel through the pink tint of his glasses. The pale skin on his face looked stretched across his skull and barely moved as he spoke.

"Enough talk Joel. You're always talking, but say nothing." He pointed to the plasma that showed a split-screen camera feed of the pool area, and the front gates of the house. "We should be out there celebrating. Instead, we are in here listening to you, waiting to hear more of your excuses."

"He's right Joel," Saboro said. "Please, just tell us what happened yesterday. That is what we all are interested in."

"Yeah Joel," Erlik said. "Do we have to be concerned? Is there something wrong?"

"I assure you all, that there is nothing to worry about. There was a slight problem, a small defect if you will, that was brought to my attention. And in the end, it will actually be an enhancement."

Joel looked at Ahriman. "You will need to make a modification that, given your expertise, will not take long. And when that is done, I will deliver the final product, a better product." He made quick eye contact with each of them. "And I'm sure, that is what we all want."

"When?" Ghede demanded, sitting back down.

"As I told you, Victor will need to make a modification and I need to discuss this with him." Joel pointed to Arhiman. "And he will let me know how long this will take."

Erlik pointed at the plasma, stood up, and walked toward it.

"What's going on out there Joel?"

The video feed of the driveway entrance showed the front of a white SUV stopped at the open gates. Derrik was stretched out on the ground in front of it. A man, on his knees, leaned over him. A dark haired woman in a black dress was waving her arms and pacing around in front of them.

Joel grabbed the remote off the table, pointed it at the plasma. The split screen disappeared and the driveway camera feed populated the entire screen. The other three men joined Erlik and watched as Joel maneuvered the camera with the remote and zoomed in on the scene. He abruptly turned off the plasma.

"Gentlemen, please," Joel told them, "if you would, go back out to the party, I will handle this. I will join you out there as soon as possible. Again, I assure you that everything is fine. Please, go now, and have some fun."

They left the room. Joel went right, toward the front of the house. The others headed for the kitchen, to get back outside.

"What do you think of this?" Ghede asked the others as they walked.

"I think he's not telling us the truth," Erlik said.

"There is nothing wrong with the DreemWeever," Ahriman said. "I should know, I built it and designed it. If there was a problem, I would have found it, not Joel."

Ghede stopped when they reached the terrace and motioned to the others to join him.

"Gentleman, you have all confirmed what I believe. I will find out what the truth is. I assure you of that. For now, let's try to enjoy ourselves."

# THE PAYBACK

I met John as he walked into the pool area. We shook hands and were happy to see each other. He was dressed for the occasion in a light blue leisure suit, matching silk shirt, and white leather shoes.

"Tommy, it's good to see you kid. Where's the king of *Shan-gri-la*?"

"He's inside with those two freaks from Vegas and two other guys."

"Oh, the come to Jesus meeting? Wonder how that's goin'? Did he tell you what happened?"

"Yeah, what do you think about it?"

"What do *I think*? Two words, *he's fucked. That's* what I think. But what do I know?"

"You know plenty. Get this, he thinks me and Derrik are going to somehow find this guy who stole the Challenger. How's he expect us to do that?"

"You're askin' me? From what I hear, the only things they got to go on, is his cell phone number, and what he looks like. Sherlock Holmes couldn't find him with that. It's gonna take more than that my friend. He's on the run. He ran over James, that's all he knows. Maybe he knows he killed him, maybe he don't, but he knows he's in deep shit. He don't know if the cops are lookin' for him. Their not, but he don't know that. If he finds out that James and Derrik killed his pal, you definitely ain't gonna see him around any time soon."

"What do you mean they killed his pal?"

"Did I say that? Oops, me and my big mouth. I thought you knew. Yeah, James and Derrik paid him a visit, made him rat out his friend, the guy you need to find. That's how they found out where the car was. Well, actually Joel doesn't give a shit about the car. He wants what was in it. So anyway, after this guy tells them what they need to know, they put him out of his misery, just like that."

The waiter interrupted, handed John and I our drinks.

"Thanks pal," John told the waiter. He raised his glass. "Always on top of things Tommy, salute."

He took a sip and I did the same.

John pointed to the plasma on the right side of the pool where Fleetwood Mac was doing "*Rhiannon*".

"She was one good looking piece of ass. What's her name?"

A wave of sadness overpowered me. I thought of Bryce, our time in Boston, and the hair salon. It hurt.

"Hey." John waved his hand in front of my face. "You listenin' to me?"

"Sorry about that. This song reminds me of Bryce. I miss him."

"You're not alone there. He was a good shit, like you. Damn shame, that's all I got to say about that." He raised his glass. "To Bryce, the next best thing to Errol Flynn there ever was."

"To Bryce," I said, half smiling and banged my glass with his.

"Speaking of the A Team." John pointed toward the stairs. "Here they come now, and they don't look too happy."

"The two guys from Vegas never look happy. That guy Ghede doesn't even look real, like his face is made of plastic. He's got that Mickey Rourke look, especially with those glasses. I barely recognized them in the getups they got on. Saboro kind of reminds me of Billy Bob Thornton.

"Good call," John said, smiling. "I can see that."

"Erlik told me he's a plastic surgeon, and Joel gave him some big compliment, like he's the best there is. In LA, that's saying something."

"He's not from here. He comes from back east, in Massachusetts."

"No shit. That explains a lot. How's Joel know him?"

"They go way back, met in New York when Joel-"

"John." Saboro joined us, flanked by the other three. "How are you this evening?"

John shook his hand. "I'm good. Tommy and I were just solving all the World's problems."

"Did you succeed?" Ghede asked. "If so we could use your services."

The other three found this amusing and laughed.

"Where's Mister Big?" John asked.

"It appears," Saboro said, "that there has been an accident out front."

"What kind of accident?" I asked.

"It looks like someone has been run over, near the gates in the driveway," Ghede said.

My cell rang. It was Joel.

"I need you out front at the gates."

"What's up? I just heard someone got run over out there."

"You heard wrong. Just get out here."

"I'm with John, what about him?"

"Bring him."

"Be right there."

I looked over at John. "Joel needs us out front, come on."

"Okay," John said, looking at the others. "Gents, duty calls. Hopefully, won't be long. See you in a bit. Tommy, shall we?"

\*\*\*

When john and I got out front I heard a siren, but it wasn't coming from the white Ford Expedition with the flashing blue lights in the grill. It was parked on the lawn, near the closed gates. The siren faded out and I realized it must have been an ambulance, leaving, not coming toward the house. Joel was standing in front of the Expedition talking with a guy. He noticed we were coming and waved us over to join him. The guy Joel was with turned toward the group of people hanging around in the driveway and put his hands up in the air.

"Everyone, please go back inside, there's nothing to see out here. It's under control. If you want to leave, it's going to be a while, so please, go back inside until then."

"Glad you're here guys," Joel said, looking at the guy that made the announcement. "This is Detective Evan Carleton, one of Los Angeles' finest. Unfortunately, he got more than he bargained for this evening by accepting my invitation."

"Evan," he said, pointing to me. "This is Thomas, and of course, you already know John."

"What happened? Who got run over?" I asked.

"No one was run over," Joel said.

"Wish it was that simple," Evan said. "It was a shooting."

"Holy shit," John said.

"It's Derrik," Joel said. "And I'm afraid, it doesn't look good."

Evan shook his head and looked at Joel.

"Come on Joel, you saw him. He's not going to make it, most likely already gone. It's going to be a homicide."

I noticed Evan had blood on his hands and that the dark marks on the sleeves and front of his navy blazer must have been blood stains.

"Do you know who did it?" I asked.

"Not yet." Evan pointed toward the gates. "Obviously, whoever did it was out here alone at the time it happened, because no one saw anything. In fact as luck, good or bad, would have it, I pulled in, and saw him lying there. I almost ran him over. Probably wouldn't have mattered at that point."

"Here, use this." Joel pulled the white pocket square out of his breast pocket and handed to him. "You can come inside and clean up, when you're ready of course. The security camera feeds might prove to be helpful as well."

"Thanks," Evan said. "It was at close range, I'd say no more than five or six feet, one to the face, and three more to the chest."


## KNOCK, KNOCK


On my way back to the Woodland Hills house, I listened to Aerosmith and tried to make sense of all the shit that had gone down the last couple of days. Bryce, James, and now Derrik were gone and Joel expected me to find the guy who had the DreemWeever. I decided that I wasn't going to do anything, until Joel came clean and let me know exactly what was going on. I knew there had to be more to it than what he was telling me.

I pulled the Bullitt into the garage, feeling a little better than I had earlier. I pressed the remote, the garage door started closing, and I thought about Bryce. It would have been a lot easier to deal with all this if he was still around. I wondered if Joel was thinking the same thing and having any regrets. It really didn't matter though, Bryce was gone and there was nothing that either Joel, or I could do about it now.

I pushed the door to the house open and flipped the light switch on.

"Don't move motherfucker! Stay right there or I'll blow your goddamn head off right now."

I put my hands up in front of me. "Take whatever you want. I don't give a shit, anything you want, just take it."

He moved in closer, still pointing the gun directly at my face. "Just shut up, and put your hands down. I'm not here to fucking rob you, so just be quiet and listen to me."

"Okay." I dropped my hands down, thinking that this guy looks like Fred Durst. "I'm listening. You don't need to have that pointed at my head."

"We'll see about that." He took a couple steps back. "You have a gun on you?"

"No, don't even own one."

"Alright, come on, over there." He motioned with the gun for me to move toward the entertainment room. "Believe me, I have absolutely nothing to lose at this point, so don't pull any shit, because I won't hesitate to put one in your skull."

For whatever reason, I believed him and I didn't think that he was here to kill me. He walked backward and I followed his lead into the room.

He held the gun on me with one hand and pointed at the couch with the other. "Have a seat right there."

As I sat down, I saw the case that Joel had put in the trunk of the Challenger sitting on the coffee table and I knew exactly who this guy was.

He looked down at the case. "You know what this is, don't you?"

"Yeah, I'm pretty sure, but to tell you the truth, I never had a look inside it. It's got you in a hell of a lot of trouble though." I stared directly into his eyes. "Hasn't it?"

"Listen, I didn't ask for this shit." He took a couple steps back, still pointing the gun at me, but at least it wasn't aimed at my head. "So, do you know exactly what's in there?"

"There's probably a headset in there, but other than that, I couldn't tell you what else. You took it before I ever got to see."

"Go ahead and open it."

I leaned forward, pulled the zipper around the perimeter of the top, and flipped the cover over.

He moved closer and looked down into it. "Take everything out, and put it on the table."

I pulled out the headset, noticed the DreemWeever VR logo on each side of it, and realized I was looking at the final version that I was supposed to deliver to the Vegas guys. I put it on the table.

"Get the rest of the stuff too," he said.

I took out the AV cables, put them on the table, and then pulled out a padded shipping package. He snatched it out of my hand and took a few steps back.

"You ever see this before?"

"Never," I said, leaning back into the couch.

He moved closer, turned the package upside down, and dumped out a bunch of mini-discs on the table. I could see labels on the ones that landed face up and noticed my name and Bryce's on a couple of them.

He looked down at me. "You know what these are?"

"They're disks for the headset, but I don't think I know what's on them. Do you?"

"Yeah I do... *Thomas.* It took me a while, but I figured out how to get them to play. You *are* Thomas, right?"

"Yeah." I leaned forward. "What's your name?"

He started grinning. "Paul, and I got some bad news for you Thomas. You ain't who you think you are."

"What are you-"

The ringtone on my cell went off inside my pants pocket and Paul stepped toward me with the gun pointed at my face, again.

"Can I see who it is?" I asked.

"Hurry up."

I pulled the cell out and noticed it was Joel. "I should answer this one. I'm not bullshitting you."

"Go ahead, make it quick."

I flipped open the cell.

"What's up Joel?"

"Where are you?"

"At the house, was just about to try and get some sleep."

"Listen, I know it was that bastard who shot Derrik. We need to find him."

"I'm not doing shit until you tell me exactly what the fuck is going on."

"I will do that, and maybe then, you will understand exactly what is at stake, not only for me, but you as well."

"I'm listening."

"Not now. I have other priorities that I need to take care of. Please, be over here at the house tomorrow morning at nine-thirty. I will fill you in on everything. I tried to keep you out of this, but I have no choice now. Be here, okay?"

"Yeah, I'll be there. Try and calm down, we'll set it straight."

"That is the only option Thomas. I have to go. I'll see you in the morning."

"Okay." I snapped the cell closed and put it on the couch.

My new friend Paul lowered the gun. "Let me guess, that was Mister Big, the guy with the ponytail, Joel, right?"

"You got it, and if you haven't figured it out yet, he wants your ass big time. If I were you, I would leave that case here, and fall off the face of the earth."

"You're probably right, that would be the smart thing to do, but if I was going to do that, I wouldn't be here, and I'd already be gone. You must be wondering why the hell I came here?"

"Yeah, and I thought it was to kill me, and maybe you do plan on doing that, but I don't think so. Why *are* you here?"

"Because, I figured maybe, if I tell you what I know, you just might decide to help me. If you don't, then I guess I'm going to have to find a way to disappear."

I heard a ringtone going off and recognized it was *"Secret Agent Man"*. Paul pulled a cell out of the side pocket of his sweatshirt and looked at the display.

"Well what do you know. It's the fucking Boss Man."

Paul answered the call on speaker.

"Hello Joel," Paul said, signaling me to be quiet with the barrel of the gun across his lips.

"Hello Paul, I guess you didn't want to join the party."

"Not my scene, didn't think I would fit in too well there."

"I hope you consider us even now. You have proved your point, and it's time that we settle this. Put an end to the game, call it quits. What do you say?"

"What do you suggest?"

"I'm thinking that we should make this as easy as possible, *and* make it worth your while to follow through on our arrangement this time."

"Details Joel, I need specifics. Get to the point."

"It's actually very simple. I would like you to meet a colleague of mine, and when you do, he gets what you have, and in return, you get ten-thousand dollars. It will be very quick and I assure you, very safe. Does that sound good to you?"

"On paper it does. Where and when?"

"I'm proposing tomorrow at twelve o'clock, and as far as the location is concerned, I think the parking lot of the Walmart in West Hills will be more than adequate. Does that work?"

"I can do that. How will I know who I'm supposed to meet?"

"You'll be looking for a green, Mustang Bullitt. And something tells me you know what one looks like."

Paul looked at me, rolled his eyeballs and smirked.

"Don't be a wise ass *Joel*. I'll be there."

He pressed the end call button and put the phone in his pocket.

"What a weasel that guy is." He lowered the gun and pointed it toward the floor. "So, it looks like I'm supposed to meet you tomorrow, but you know what? I don't see that happening, because dude, you're not going to want to do anything for him anymore. You've been screwed hard."

"How's that?"

"Okay, here it is. We can sit and watch every one of those discs, or you can take my word for what I'm about to tell you."

He walked over to the La-Z-Boy chair across from me, sat down, and put the gun on his lap.

"I'm getting kind of tired of holding this thing. You think I have a reason to need it?"

"No, I'm cool. Let's hear it."

"Good." He put the gun inside his sweatshirt pocket. "Stop me if you heard any of this before. Your name isn't Tom Haskins, it's Dan Barrett, and you didn't look much like you do now. You've had a lot of plastic surgery, and been brainwashed with that headset. You were a junky, and this sick fuck Joel kidnapped you in Seattle over a year ago."

"And you know this from those discs?"

"Like I told you, if you want to watch the discs, you can, it's all on there. There's another guy, or I should say, used to be another guy named Bryce right?"

"What's on there about him?"

"Almost the same story as you except they grabbed him from Portland, Oregon six months after you. His name was really Chris Reilly."

"You found out all this from watching the disks?"

"Not all of it, but, alright, I have to know right now, do you believe what I just told you?"

"Yeah, I'm thinking I do, but what the hell do you want from me?"

"I want you to help me take this guy Joel down. Right now, this very minute, my buddy Luke is rotting away in his apartment. Those two cocksuckers, the big black guy and the bald headed goon he was with, killed him. I know they were going to do the same to me, if I didn't get the hell out of my place in time."

"I guess you don't have to worry about them anymore though, do you?"

"Hey, the bald guy was an accident. He was just in the wrong place at the wrong time, but the other one got what was coming to him. It was a kill or be killed situation, at least that's how I saw it. I don't care how many people were at that party, something bad was going to happen to me. I was supposed to show up there and join all the other phony fucks that this clown Joel hangs with, but I'm not as stupid as he probably thought I was. I just waited for the right time, and now all that's left, is to take care of the Boss Man."

"Let me get this straight. I understand that you took the Challenger, and that's how all this shit got started, but how the hell did you even end up stealing it? It doesn't make sense to me?"

"Are you going to help me or what? Yes or no? Because if you are, we don't have a hell of a lot of time, and if you're not, I guess this is where it ends. You can have the case, and I need to vanish, *after* I call in an anonymous tip to the cops. I'll tell them about Luke, *and* everything else. Either way, I'm still calling in about Luke, but everything else I tell them, depends on which way you want to play it. What's it going to be?"

"I'm in. Let's take him down. What do you have in mind?"

"First, there's some things you might know, that I need to know more about. You're right about the Challenger. We didn't just all of a sudden pull in here by mistake and decide to steal the car. Me and Luke had just started getting into a new hobby. It's called urban exploration. It's kind of an underground thing that's getting pretty popular around the World. You heard of it?"

"No, what's it about?"

"It's pretty cool shit. You find abandoned buildings, or subways, or whatever, and you find a way in and explore them. Luke got me into it. Anyway, one night we're scoping out this huge abandoned complex in Ventura. We end up seeing what we think is a drug deal or something big going down while we're there. So we decide we're not going to let it go, and end up following the limo they came in when they left. That led us to a house in Sherman Oakes, which ended up being your boy Joel's place. Now, what I still don't know is, what the hell is going on at that warehouse?"

"Here's the deal. Joel owns it." I picked up the DreemWeever off the table. "And this headset is part of something much bigger than you know. He's building a whole corporation around this thing. In his big plan, the entire enterprise is going to be there. Almost like a combination of a movie studio, a manufacturing plant, and a bunch of other things. He calls it Kite Industries, and he sees himself as the head honcho of all of it. I've seen renderings of the whole thing and you wouldn't believe it. This headset is the final product, and he was supposed to hand it over to the people who invested a shitload of their money into it. They have their own plans for it."

"Wow, that explains why he's got such a hard on for it." He pointed to the discs on the table. "I think he's more concerned about what's on those discs. There's a lot of incriminating shit on them. I'll tell you what, that just raised the price to fifty grand. What do you think?"

"Sounds good to me. Back to the Challenger, how did it happen?"

"Oh yeah, so me and Luke are determined to find out what's going on, it's kind of like a game at this point, like we're undercover operatives trying to crack this drug ring. So the other day we're just fucking around, and decide we'll take a cruise by Joel's place, to get a lay of the land, kind of like a recon mission, so some night we can come back and sneak around the grounds, maybe start fucking with his head a little bit. As we're coming down his road, he goes by us in his Mercedes, but he's in the passenger seat and you're driving. We turned around and followed you guys all the way to this place. We parked Luke's car down the road, the same place my truck is now. We snuck on up, and start watching the house though our binocs."

I knew right then, that Paul and Luke got more than they bargained for that day. I needed to know exactly what they saw.

"So you guys must have been watching for a while?"

Paul smirked and nodded his head. "You bet your ass. We were about to split, and then we see you and Joel come out of the house and get in the Mercedes. We gave you guys a little bit of time and decided, fuck it, let's go up and get a closer look, see if we can find out more."

"How the hell did you get the Challenger? You even look at that car the wrong way and the alarms going to go off."

"Dude, I'm getting to that. You have to understand, I work at a body shop man, there's no car I can't steal, if I really want to. Anyway, we go around the back, and guess what? The sliders not locked, and we just walked right in."

It was worse than I thought and I knew they must have found Bryce, before Derrik and James got there.

"You found Bryce didn't you?"

"Yeah, didn't know who he was, but he was unconscious, looked like he was dead. As soon as we saw that, we got the hell out of there, but I grabbed a set of keys off the island in the kitchen. I figured they were for the Challanger, and I wanted to take it, but Luke wasn't up for it."

"You must have changed his mind."

"Not really. Just as we got back in Luke's car, a Tahoe drives by us and pulls into the driveway. Luke just wants to get the fuck out of there, but I tell him we can't leave now, we have to ride this out. So we just sat there and waited for about twenty minutes. Next thing you know, the Tahoe comes back out, and drives right by us again."

"You guys should have left then."

"No shit, but I tell Luke I'm taking the Challenger, and we can both make some cash, if I move it through my connections at the body shop. He tells me to go for it, but says he's done with all this bullshit, and I told him that's cool, because so am I."

"Didn't quite work out that way."

"I still can't believe it man. I should have just listened to Luke, and left when we had the chance, but I had him pull up the driveway, and I took the Challenger. Now I have to deal with it."

"No," I said, "*we* have to deal with it. I think I know someone I can trust, and he might help us. No guarantees, but it's worth a shot."

## THE PLAN

The gates to Joel's place opened before I had a chance to stop at the intercom. I watched them close in the rear-view as I pulled up the driveway. Joel stood in the doorway, waiting for me to come up.

"Good morning Thomas." He put his arm around my shoulder and held his watch out in front of me with his other hand. "You're uncharacteristically prompt, only a half hour late. Come on in. I think we are going to have a good day today."

We walked through the house and went into the media room. I could hear The Police playing and four split screens of color video feeds were on the plasma.

"I take it some things have changed since last night?" I asked him.

"Indeed they have." He motioned to the sectional. "Please let's sit down."

We sat across from each other and I immediately noticed two video feeds from the Woodland Hills house were on the plasma. One showed the driveway from the house and the other showed the house from the end of the driveway.

I realized how lucky I was that I had parked in the garage last night, because I was sure that Joel must have watched me leave this morning. I still had to do something, because Paul was in the house and I knew he would be leaving soon. If he walked out the front door, Joel might notice it. At the same time, I was pissed that I didn't know about the hidden cameras.

"I sensed your frustration on the phone last night Thomas, and I think that after today, things will be much better. Certainly, when compared to the present state of affairs. Now, what do you need to know?"

"First of all." I pointed to the plasma. "How long have you had the cameras at the house?"

"Ah, don't be concerned about that. I had them installed long before you moved in. It's nothing personal, just a simple matter of security. Although, they paid a handsome dividend recently." He took a sip of his drink and grinned. "How do you think I found out who took the Challenger? To be honest, I very rarely have an interest in what's happening over there. In fact, now that you're here." He pushed the remote and two of the screens disappeared and changed to a split screen showing the front of Shangi La and the driveway gates. "There's no need for them."

That was a relief, for now at least.

"You know Joel, at this point, what else is there I need to know? So let's get on with it. What is going on right now, and what do we have to do to make this right? What can we possibly do to get what you need back. What *exactly*, do we need to get back?"

"That's a fair question, and it deserves a frank answer. Quite simply, the case that was in the Challenger, that this person, this sneaky, little, goddamn prick took, had the final version of the DreemWeever in it."

"*That's it?* Can't you have another one made?"

"Of course I could, but there is more. Let me finish. There are other things, specific to the development and testing of the DreemWeever, which are highly confidential. If we do not get them back, the consequences will be grave. Without going into explicit detail, I can tell you that the testing in New York was well documented, and that is only one example, of the many such items that we need to get back. You should be very concerned about this."

"I get the picture. So, you said it might be a good day today. Does that mean you think you're getting it back?"

"Yes, and that's why you are here. I have arranged for you to meet this gentleman. His name is Paul, by the way. And at twelve o'clock today you are going to meet him, to exchange what he has, for what you are going to give him."

"What am I giving him?"

"Well, that's a good question. It was going to be ten thousand dollars, which I offered to him, but he has increased it to fifty-thousand."

"Wow, he's getting greedy. You're actually going to go through with this?"

"I'm afraid I have no other options. He has found out how to use the Dreeweever, and I know this because he was kind enough to provide some details, that he would have only known by using it. I made the mistake of underestimating him. In this case, desperation has proved to be his motivation."

"What's the plan?"

"He has agreed to meet you in West Hills, in the parking lot of the Walmart at twelve o'clock. I would like you to get there at eleven-thirty. He knows you will be in the Bullitt."

"How am I going to know who he is?"

"He will be driving a brown, Ford truck, with a cap on the back of it. You should have no problem identifying it."

"That's it? Just make the switch, and I'm out of there?"

"Essentially, yes, that's it. He has also agreed to tell you where the Challenger can be found."

I started to laugh. "Shit, you mean he's not driving it around. You know, one thing I can't understand is, why the hell he stole it in the first place? You must have thought about that."

"Of course I did. In fact, I posed the question to him."

"What did he say?"

"He told me that he saw the car one day, while he was driving down the 101, and followed it all the way to the Woodland Hills house. He made up his mind to eventually steal it, and then sell it to some people he knows, who specialize in such things."

"It didn't quite work out the way he planned it."

"No, it certainly did not. It's an unfortunate situation for everyone involved."

Joel's ringtone went off and he answered.

"Hello John." He pointed to the plasma. "Yes I know. I see you out there. Come on in, we're waiting for you."

As Joel put the phone down next to him on the couch, I watched as John pulled through the gates and up the driveway.

"What's he driving?" I asked.

"You like that? It's a rental." Joel picked up the remote and zoomed in on the car as John parked it. "And I believe that is an Impala."

"Why's he driving that, you downsizing the limo?"

Joel stood up, lowered the volume of the music and walked toward the door.

John came in a few seconds later.

"What happened? You couldn't get the Prius?" Joel asked with a deadpan look on his face.

"Listen to him." John looked over at me. "A fuckin' Prius. I should've got the Caddy CTS. *That's* what I should've have done. Instead I end up with that piece of shit."

"Calm down John. I told you non-descript, and that is a fine choice. We have some things to go over." Joel looked at his watch. "Let's get down to business. You guys need to leave soon."

"What do you mean *you* guys?" I looked at John. "You're coming with me?"

"Don't look so happy about it Tommy."

"Come on John. I didn't mean it that way. I don't give a shit."

"Not exactly." Joel put his hand on John's shoulder. "Come on, have a seat. John's not riding with you. He's going to be there in the rental, as a precautionary measure."

John took a seat across from me and Joel walked over to the bar. He came back with a black satchel bag, put it on the coffee table, and sat next to John.

"Here it is." He slapped his hand down on the bag. "Fifty big ones that I need to say au revoir to."

"My condolences." John motioned the Sign of the Cross. "May it rest in peace."

I laughed and Joel tried to keep a straight face, but broke down and smiled.

"Believe me, it pains me to give this to him, but at least he's not going to get the chance to enjoy it."

"I *knew* there had to be more to it," I said. "What's going to happen?"

Joel glanced at John and then back at me.

"There's nothing that *you* need to do. Once you have made the switch, you are done. You drive back here." He looked over at John. "You will follow our friend out of the parking lot, at a safe distance of course, to find out where he goes from there. My guess is that it won't be very far, because, as soon as you finish Thomas, you will call me, and at that time, an anonymous tip will be called into the authorities. Letting them know where they can find the person who shot Derrik. Depending on how fast they react, they might even get him while he's driving. And my instincts tell me that he won't go quietly."

"Hold on a minute," I said. "If you do that, don't you think the first thing that he's going to do is tell them about us?"

Joel raised his eyebrows, stroked his hand across his beard and glared at me.

"*Of course* I have thought about that, and there are a number of reasons why I think that this is the best course of action."

"The man with the plan," John said, trying to break the tension.

"I agree with you Thomas, and if given the opportunity, I fully expect him to try and implicate me. If this happens, I realize that questions will be asked, and I have thought about, and prepared for them. I also believe that the two of you have no reason to be concerned. Here is the way I see it. Please stop me, if you disagree with any of these points."

Joel stood up, walked toward the plasma, then turned and faced us, like a lawyer about to present his summation to a jury.

"Let's first look at what he is up against. My guess is that he has a gun with him, most likely the same one he used on Derrik. If he does, that's a bonus, if not, he's still got much larger problems. He could be charged with Grand Theft Auto on the Challenger, and a homicide for the cold-blooded execution of Derrik. As far as the James situation is concerned, and I say this with nothing but respect for James, but I look at that as a mulligan. Do you both agree?"

"Yeah, so far," I said.

"Me too," John said.

"Good. So what does that leave in his favor? He knows that his friend is dead, and he also knows, or at least he thinks he knows, that Derrik and James committed this crime. What does this buy him? Considering that both of them are no longer alive, absolutely nothing. He will certainly try to bring my name up as a conspirator, but again, there is nothing to support those claims.

As I see it, he is now in possession of the one thing, and by far, the most important thing to his advantage. And soon, that will be taken away. Do either of you have any concerns?"

"What about the money?" I asked.

"You read my mind," John said.

Joel smiled and locked his hands behind his head. "It really was a bad decision on my part to leave that much money in the trunk of the Challenger. I will certainly never make the same mistake again. In fact, upon its safe return, I think I might even donate a generous percentage of it to our outstanding law enforcement department." He winked at us. "What do you think?"

John pointed his finger at Joel and looked over at me.

"Walt fuckin' Disney couldn't have come up with anything better than that. If we ever get pinched Tommy, we know who to call."

"That's why he's the boss," I said.

"Please, flattery will get you everywhere." Joel looked at his watch. "It's time for you to get going. Hopefully, in a couple of hours, this will all be behind us."

I grabbed the money case off the coffee table and put the strap over my shoulder. Joel walked with us to the front of the house, shook our hands, and closed the door behind us as we left.

John and I walked toward the cars and stopped in front of the Bullitt.

"So," John said, "this is where it ends, huh kid? You sure there's nothing else I can do?"

"I think I'm good. I feel bad that you have to drive all the way down there for nothing. You sure you're going to be okay?"

"Don't worry about me. I can handle it. You know he's probably watchin' us right now, so we better get movin'."

As I followed the Impala out of the driveway, my cell rang. It was John.

"I need a pack of smokes. There's a Shell not far from here, you can follow me there."

"No problem, lead the way," I said.

## THE SQUEEZE

I followed John into the parking lot of the Shell station on Van Nuys Boulevard and pulled up beside him. We got out of our cars and John used the key to open the trunk of the Impala. He met me at the back of the Bullitt and I opened the trunk.

"Come to papa." John reached inside and pulled out the DreemWeever case. "The prodigal case returns. Who says you can never go home again?"

He put the case into the trunk and walked toward the driver's side of the Impala.

"Come on, get in for a minute," John said.

"One sec, I need to get something out of the Bullitt."

I opened the driver's side door of the Bullitt, leaned in and grabbed a grocery bag off the passenger seat. I had put twenty-thousand dollars in the bag during the drive from Joel's and now it was Johns. I had told him we could split the fifty-thousand, but he only wanted twenty, because, he said that, 'I needed it more than he did'.

I got in the Impala and dropped the bag on the floor.

"Pleasure doing business with you," he said. "By the way, great job back there. We should get Academy Award's for that performance."

I shook his hand. "Take care John, I'll be in touch soon. I promise."

"That reminds me. I'm not much into all this internet bullshit, but I do know about e-mail at least." He pulled a piece of paper out of his shirt pocket and handed it to me. "I somehow figured out how to set up a G-mail account for myself. The name of it's written on that. Why don't you do yourself a favor and do the same thing. And when you get around to it, send me somethin'. Just put salvation in the subject line, and I'll know who it's from."

"Sounds good. You sure you're going to be okay?"

"Like I said, I'll be fine. Oh yeah, one more thing." He reached into his pocket and handed me an envelope. "This should help you."

I opened it and pulled out a Washington State driver's license and a piece of paper with a social security number written on it. The name on the license was Daniel Barrett, with an address in Seattle.

"You recognize him?" John asked.

"No, but I know it's me, or it used to be me." I looked at the birth date. "What the fuck?"

"What's wrong?"

I'm *thirty-five*. Not twenty-six?"

John grabbed the license and held it out beside my head. "You don't look a day over twenty-seven now. Would you rather have that ugly mug? I figure you can get the picture redone. You might get some hassle, but what the fuck, you are who you are. You get your life back, that's the bottom line."

He handed me another envelope. It was sealed shut and nothing was written on it.

"That's Bryce's. His name was Chris Reilly. A fuckin' mick, just like you."

"Yeah I know. Paul told me last night."

"Anyway, if you can somehow, try and make things right with his family, *if* you can track them down. I don't know where they put him. I'd tell you if I did, but I don't."

"Thanks John, I really mean it."

He slapped me on the shoulder and winked. "Good luck Danny boy. I better get going."

"Good luck to you too."

I shook his hand and got out of the car.

After John drove off, I went inside the Shell and bought a fifty dollar pre-paid phone card and a bottle of spring water. As I left the store, I pulled the battery out of my phone, dropped it on the pavement, and crushed it under my sneaker. I walked around the side of the building and tossed it into the dumpster.

I called Paul's phone from a pay phone in the parking lot.

"Hey dude," Paul said. "How did it go man? You on your way?"

"I'm good, but we almost got screwed over. What time did you leave my place?"

"About a half hour ago. Why, what happened?"

I knew Joel had turned off the video feed right after ten o'clock. It was eleven fifteen now, so we were safe.

"The driveway and front of the house are wired with video cameras," I said. "When I got there, he was monitoring them, and I almost had a heart attack."

"He's a sneaky prick. Wouldn't have mattered anyway. I went out the back door, and through the side yard to get to the street."

"Listen, as you predicted, it was a set up. As soon as we made the switch, he was calling you into the cops. He had it all planned out, and believe me, the way he told it, you were fucked."

"Change of plans I take it."

"Yeah, but we can deal with it. Once he finds out he's been screwed, which will be in a little more than an hour from now, I think the first thing he does, is report the Bullitt stolen, to try and get me. He's not going to do that with you, at least not right away. We have to ditch this car as soon as we can. Where can we meet up? You at the Walmart?"

"Yeah, where are you at?"

"I'm at a pay phone in Sherman Oaks. Tell you what, meet me at Pierce College, it's only about five or so miles from you. Ask someone, they'll tell you how to get there, if you don't know. I should be there in about fifteen minutes. We can dump this car in one of the lots. Sound good?"

"Yeah, I know where it is. I'm on my away. Later."

***

Joel sat in a recliner out at the pool, waiting for the call that was due to come in less than a half-hour. For the first time in a few days, he felt semi-relaxed and sure of himself. The warmth of the sun, the Bloody Mary, and Crosby, Stills, Nash, & Young singing *"Almost Cut My Hair"*, helped to let him concentrate on "what's going to be", rather than, "what was".

He thought about Paul, the little prick who had tried to take him on. How Paul had no idea that the next hour would be the last time that he would be a free man. He tried to decide the best way to put Ghede, Saboro, and the others in their place, when they came over tonight to get the DreemWeever and see the presentation. They were going to be doing some Hollywood style ass kissing. Erlik, Ahriman, and even Mari were okay. They did their job and just wanted what they had coming to them, but those condescending bastards, Ghede and Saboro, he didn't owe them anything, other that what was agreed to. After tomorrow, it wouldn't be long until he sold his practice and was on permanent sabbatical.

Joel took a long drink and thought, *Kite Industries is a reality and the future starts now*.

***

We drove down the 101 in Paul's truck heading toward his house in Ventura to get the Challenger out of the garage. We had left the Bullitt in the student parking lot of Pierce College. If Joel called it in stolen, the cops would find it there, or it would end up impounded by the on-campus Sheriffs Department. Either way, it wasn't our problem anymore.

"Okay, ten more minutes until all hell breaks loose. What's our next move?" I asked.

"I figure we wait about a half hour or so, and let him savor the fact that he's been fucked. Man, I wish I could be a fly on the wall when he gets the news. Then, we really give him a kick in the nuts, by calling in the tip about Luke. Who knows, maybe they already found him, but I doubt it. Either way, it won't take long for the cops to start coming down hard on him."

"I think I know how we can make this work even better," I said.

"How's that?"

"I know he's tight with a detective who was at the party last night. His name is Evan Carleton. In fact, he almost ran over Derrik's body when he was pulling up to the gates. He ended up taking control of the scene, and I'm thinking he's involved with Joel somehow. Maybe not in this, but with other things."

"So what do we do?" Paul asked.

"You call up and ask for him. You say it's urgent. Hopefully, you get him real time, but if not, you leave him a message. You tell him where they can find Luke, and that you know the guy who did it is Derrik Jackson. He's going to know that name right a way, and make the association to Joel, without you having to tell him. What do you think?"

"I love it. If this cop's on the take, he's going to have some tough decisions to make, and it's going to get really uncomfortable for him, and Joel."

"Why don't we get off in Thousand Oaks, hit a Burger King or something, and we can make the call," I said.

"Sounds good, I'm starving." Paul reached back into the extra-cab, pulled out a knapsack and rested it on his lap. "By the way, I helped myself to some CD's at your place. I figured you wouldn't mind. That was some collection you had there."

He unzipped the knapsack, pulled out a handful of CD's and put them on the seat between us.

"You're choice," Paul said, tossing the knapsack behind him.

I looked them over, went with *Van Halen 1,* and pushed the disc into the CD slot. *"Runnin' With The Devil"* came on and Paul started to play the air bass as he drove.

"Excellent choice man," he said. "There's not a bad song on this."

"Your're right, song for song, it's one of the best rock CD's of all time."

As we drove and listened, I thought about Bryce and knew that if he was with us, he would have been having a good time. Paul was cool and I'm sure his buddy Luke must have been alright too. Paul and I had both lost our best friends and Joel was directly responsible for that. If we could take Joel down and somehow walk away from all this, it would be some sort of redemption for Bryce and Luke, as well as Paul and I.

***

Joel snatched his cell off the table next to the lounge chair as soon as he heard the first notes of the ringtone. He tried to process why the display showed it was John, instead of Thomas.

*John's being a good soldier, like always, keeping the general up to date.*

He flipped the cell open, answered it.

"Tell me something good."

"I wish I could. The rat bastard took off. Both of them did. They set us up."

Joel slapped the Bloody Mary glass off the table and it shattered on the patio. He pushed himself out of the chair and stood up.

"What the *fuck* are you talking about *John*? That's impossible. What do you mean they just *took off*?"

"Just what I said. It was goin' down just as planned. Tommy is sittin' there waitin', and the guy pulls up next to him. I'm a couple rows over watchin' the whole thing. Next thing, the both of them barrel ass out from where they're parked and are headin' separate ways. It happened so fast, by the time I pull out and try to follow the truck, I didn't have a chance. He blew through a red light and he was gone. Tommy's not answerin' his phone either."

"Please John, just be quiet. Keep your goddamn mouth shut, and get back here. Can you at least do that for me?"

"What the fuck are *you* talkin' about? I'll be back there. I'll tell you what though. I'm returning this piece of shit, before I do anything."

Joel hung up, stood with his face in his cupped hands. He sucked in deep breaths and slowly exhaled, trying to think his way out of the anxiety attack. He flipped his cell open, called Thomas, but it went right to voicemail.

*How could he do this? How long had he planned it? How could I not to see this coming?*

Joel mentally backtracked every conversation, call, and meeting he had with Thomas, looking for a clue, but came up empty. He made another call.

Evan Carleton's voicemail came on and Joel left a message.

"Evan, Joel Fischer. I have a rather urgent problem at the moment. I'm hoping you can expedite it for me. I will of course follow up by traditional procedures as soon as I hang up. My car has been stolen. It's a two thousand eight Mustang Bullitt. It's Green, and the plate number is four, winter, charlie, zebra, one, zero, five. Please call me back as soon as you get this."

He hung up and dialed another number.

"My vehicle has been stolen," Joel told the police dispatcher.

# THE MESSAGE

Instead of drive-thru fast food, Paul and I decided to take a short break and ended up getting Mexican at Rubio's in Thousand Oaks. Both of us passed on the fish tacos and went with burritos and iced tea. At one-fifteen we got back into the car, knowing that Joel had taken me off his Christmas card list.

We drove a little further up Moonpark Road and pulled into a 7-Eleven. I gave Paul the pre-paid card and he walked over to the payphone to call in the tip about Luke. He came back toward the car about three minutes later, smiling and giving me the double thumbs up signal. He got back in the truck.

"How'd it go?" I asked.

"It's our lucky day dude. I spoke directly to *the man*. We better move out, in case he has ways to trace the call. Who knows what kind of high tech shit they have now."

"Good idea."

Paul started the truck, put it in gear, and we headed back to the 101.

"No shit," I said. "You got through to him?"

"Oh yeah, short and sweet. I say I need to talk to detective Carleton about an urgent matter. The lady wants to know who it is who's calling, so I tell her it's Joel Fischer."

I started laughing. "Fucking beautiful."

"It just came to me, but it worked, because thirty seconds later he gets on the line."

"What'd you tell him?"

"As soon as he comes on." Paul used the pinky and thumb on his left hand to make a phone, while he drove with his right hand. "I tell him this is an anonymous tip, and not to bother asking any questions, and just listen carefully because I am hanging up in sixty seconds. He tells me to go ahead with what I have to say. So I lay it out for him, and then tell him that this is no joke, and everything that I'm telling him is absolutely true."

"Did he say anything?"

"He asked me why I'm telling him all this. At that point, I felt like I was on a roll, and it's coming naturally to me. So I tell him that he knows why, and not to bullshit me, because I'm going to follow up on all this in twenty-four hours, and if I find out nothing's been done, he's going down. Then I hung up on him."

The animated way that Paul told me this had me smiling, but when he got to the last part I was laughing like I never had before.

We got back on the 101 headed to Ventura to get the Challenger. When "*Little Dreamer*" came on, Paul cranked it up and started laughing.

"Dude, this is Joel's theme song. What do you think?"

"Good call." I put my fist out toward him and he bumped it with his. "I was thinking the exact same thing. Great minds think alike."

"Can't wait to hear some tunes in the Challenger. That sound system kicks some serious ass. I already nicknamed it Samuel Jackson after his character Jules in *Pulp Fiction*. You know, the part where he's in the restaurant and pulls out his wallet."

"That's perfect," I said.

***

John took out his cell as he pulled the Impala into the Hertz Car Rental in Reseda and called Diamond Limo to get a ride back to his place.

"Hey Len, its Johnny. I'm back at the Hertz. You wanna send someone back over here to take me home."

"Sure Johnny, about ten minutes. When are you going to come back here? You know I'll make it worth your while."

"Come on Lenny, you know I got a good gig where I'm at."

"Yeah, I know, and I still can't believe that you keep working for that pompous prick. He made my life miserable when he was a client. Well, I ain't going to stop asking you. We still miss you around here."

"Two years you been askin' and two years I been sayin' no. But, I'll tell you what. Lately I been thinking about a change, and you never know, one of these days, I just might make a move. Listen, I got to return this Flintstone mobile. I'll keep in touch. Have a good one."

"Okay Johnny, you know my number. Take care. The car will be there in a jiffy."

The Lincoln Town Car pulled over in front of John's house in Reseda. The driver noticed the black stretch Lincoln in the driveway.

"Nice ride, who you work for?"

"Private client," John said. "Used to work for Diamond a couple years ago though. How long you been with them."

"I just started a couple months ago."

"How you like it."

"Love it, helps with tuition. I could do a lot worse."

"What do I owe you kid?"

"Nothing. Strict orders that it's on the house."

John pulled out his wallet, handed the driver three twenties.

"Here you go, buy yourself something at the malt shop. And don't worry about the door, I got it."

"Thanks a lot. Have a good day."

"I'm trying."

John dropped the case on the floor when he got in the house, then went to the refrigerator and grabbed a Heineken. He checked the answering machine, listened to the new message.

"Hello John, your appointment is confirmed for four o'clock this afternoon. I'm sure I don't need to remind you to be prompt. Unfortunately, Jason and I won't be able to see you later on, but the others are expecting you at six o'clock. I hope all is well, and I'll speak with you soon. Take care."

He deleted the message, walked out to the parlor and reclined in the leather La-Z-Boy, noticing that the time on the cable box was two-fifteen. The twenty grand in the case was important, but small things in life, like the Marlboro he lit, the ice-cold beer, and the more than hour of down time in front of him, were what mattered, especially now.

He kicked off his shoes, put the TV on, and tried to enjoy what was left of Friday afternoon.

*\*\**

We made it to Paul's place by two-thirty. It was nicer than I expected, but he told me that his father owned it and more than a few times, had paid the mortgage for him. He also told me that his father, the girl he was seeing, and the owner of the auto body shop he worked at, thought he was still in Vegas. He had called them from a hotel in Calabasas the morning after he ran over James, and as far as they all knew, he was gone until tomorrow night.

We drove by the house to make sure everything was cool and it was, so we turned around and Paul pulled up the incline of the driveway. He stopped about twenty feet before the garage and pointed to some dark spots on the pavement.

"That's where it happened. I'm not sure how bad I went over him, but he was right behind me, so it must have been painful."

Paul pulled the truck up close to the garage, shut off the engine, and stomped down on the emergency brake.

"The garage is locked. I need to open it from the inside, come on."

As we went up the walkway toward the front door, I thought I could hear music coming from somewhere. A second later, Paul noticed it too.

"Shit, you hear that?"

"Yeah." I stopped a couple feet before the stairs. "Someone's inside."

Paul laughed. "No ones in there. I forgot all about that. The night I left, I put a CD on to make them think I was still home, and it's *still* playing."

The Stone Temple Pilots were on when we went inside and Paul shut off the CD player.

"Can you think of anything we need? I have to get some stuff from the truck, but anything else?"

"We have to buy some things for tonight anyway," I said. "So I guess if we need anything else we can buy it then. We should get going."

"It might be cold later. Let me grab a couple sweatshirts. I'm sure I got something that will fit you, come on."

We went into his room and Paul picked through a bunch of sweatshirts on the shelf inside the closet. He dropped one on the floor and threw a hooded, navy colored one to me.

"That should fit you. Sorry dude the USC one is mine."

I held it out in front of me. It had IRISH in big, gold letters across the front and I could see that it would fit me.

We went through the house and out to the garage. The Challenger looked intimidating and still had a nice shine on it. Paul started bowing, like the car was a sacred idol.

"I'm not worthy, I'm not worthy. Mr. Jackson is just like I left him. The keys are still on the hood. Pop the trunk, and I'll get the stuff out of the truck."

He pushed the remote button on the wall and the garage door started to roll up.

"No problem," I said. "This is the part where you take off with the money, and leave me high and dry right?"

Paul laughed.

"I was thinking the same thing when I was at the pay phone. Come on man, if I was going to do that, I would have found a way to grab the keys first." He pointed to the truck. "We'll leave the truck in here, after we get our shit out of it."

I took the keys off the hood, popped the trunk with the remote button, and went out to the truck to give Paul a hand.

"Here." He passed a knapsack out to me. "This was Luke's pack. It's got some stuff in it that we'll need tonight."

He passed me the money case, pulled out two more knapsacks and we put it all in the trunk of the Challenger.

"It's your baby," Paul said, "so you're driving. I'll back the truck out, and pull it in here after you get this out on the street."

I had to put the seat back before I could fit in the driver's seat. Paul's buddy Luke must have been about the same size as him, because which ever one of them drove it last, was a lot shorter than me. I started the engine and wanted to stab the gas pedal to hear the sweet sound of the engine, but knew this wasn't the place to do it. It was good to be sitting in Samuel Jackson again.

I pulled out to the road and followed Paul back up the driveway, until the truck was in the garage. He got out, gave me the one minute signal with his finger, and the garage door started coming down. Paul came out the front door wearing a blue bucket hat with the Superman logo on the front and got in the passenger side.

"Let's roll amigo," he said.

"Cool hat. You still look like Fred Durst though. Anyone ever tell you that?"

"All the time, it was like a joke with me and Luke, because he kind of looked like Sully Erna of Godsmack. He was small like him, and had the same look going on. We definitely got our share of wise cracks when we were together. Funny thing is, a year ago my hair was down to my shoulders."

I backed down the driveway, opened the console, and pulled out the Kings of Leon CD that Bryce had brought to New York.

"Where do you stand on the Kings?" I asked Paul.

"Them and the Black Crowes are the only good music being made nowadays. Velvet Revolver is no more, and unless STP, or Guns n Roses gets back together, the Kings and the Crowes are the only bands I'd pay to see."

"I couldn't agree with you more."

I put the CD in, started it at track twelve, and we left for the Ventura Beach Marriot listening to *"Camaro"*.


## FIRE IN THE HOLE


Joel closed his cell and obsessed about the arrogant sound of Saboro's voice and the indignant way that he had just spoken to him on the phone. It wasn't enough for Saboro that *he* was footing the bill for the five of them to stay at The Beverly Hills Hotel since Wednesday, now Saboro has the balls to tell *him* that he wanted John to pick them up tonight in *his* goddamn limo. He blamed himself for trying to impress them. Saboro, Ghedi, and Erlik, he could almost justify having to do it for them, but Arihman, and especially Mari, they lived in California and were just riding the Fischer gravy train for all it was worth. What could he say though? Saboro, and Ghede held all the cards now and *he* was going to be the one kissing major ass, when they arrived at six-thirty. This was bad, no doubt, but being taken to the cleaners by Thomas, was the real testicle crushing kick to the crotch.

Joel called John's cell.

"Hey, you're still talkin to me?" John asked.

"John, I apologize for being short tempered with you. I know it's not your fault. We were both blindsided by this."

"I still can't believe it myself. Tommy ended up bein' a real Benedict fuckin' Arnold. What are we gonna do?"

"I'm trying to figure that out. Where are you now?"

"Sittin' on my fat ass at my place."

"I hate to be the bearer of bad news, but you need to pick up our friends at the Beverly Hills Hotel at six o'clock."

"You've got to be shittin' me. Make them take a cab."

"I'm afraid not John. In fact, I just agreed to it before I called you. I appreciate it though, if that's any consolation."

"I know you do. Need me to do anything else?"

*Any chance you could murder five people for me?*

"No, just make sure you're there at six. If I do come up with something, I'll be sure to call you." Joel looked at his watch. "I'll see you in three and a half hours. Thank you John."

"My pleasure, it's what you pay me for. See you later."

***

We made a last minute change of plans and took the 101 to Oxnard, to see if detective Carleton had taken us seriously.

"Alright man, slow it down," Paul said. "It's right up there on the left. We can see his place from the road."

There was slow moving traffic in both directions as we came up on the main entrance and looked across the parking lot toward the rows of buildings.

"Holy shit, they found him," Paul yelled, pointing to the last building about fifty yards up ahead of us. "Check it out, that's why everyone's moving so slow."

I could see two police cruisers, a couple of unmarked cars, and an ambulance in front of the building. As we drove by, I saw a small crowd of people looking at what was going on.

"They must have just got here. They don't need the ambulance," Paul said.

"I'm really sorry about all this."

"It's not your fault. He was a cool dude. You would have liked him. This sucks big time. They really fucked him up bad. I don't regret for one minute that I shot that fucker, or ran the other guy over. Not one fucking bit. Come on let's head back."

"Alright, I'll pull it around up there. Hopefully, they'll be coming down hard on Joel soon, or maybe it's already started."

"I just wish I could be there to see it."

I turned the Challenger around and as we drove by the scene again, Paul stared straight ahead, like there was nothing to see. I ejected the CD after we made it past the apartment complex and we headed for the 101 to get to the Marriot.

***

Joel grabbed the bottle of Crown Royal off the coffee table, slumped back into the sectional and poured a second round for himself. He closed the bottle and put it on the cushion beside him. They would be there in two and a half hours and he still didn't have a plan. The booze and *The Midnight Special* playing on the plasma, calmed him down a little, but hadn't inspired him like he had hoped. As he looked at Rod Stewart doing *"You Wear it Well"*, it made him feel old and he thought about Crystal.

He had convinced himself that losing her was just the cost of doing business; his way of taking one for the team. Now there was no team, except for John. He thought back to the first time he met Crystal and her best friend Lillian. They had both moved to L.A. to make it in the movies, with nothing but their looks, and an obsession with Heart. To them, he was the "*Magic Man*" and that's what they called him.

Their story was exactly like so many of his clients before, and after them. They were inseparable at first, sometimes even in the bedroom; a fact Joel personally learned soon after meeting them. The coke, champagne, suites, his office, and Shangi-La flashed though his mind. In the end, Lillian found a producer and Crystal found the floor of the Marriott.

The ringtone on his cell snapped him out of the malaise. He snatched it off the cushion beside him and looked at the display, hoping it was good news.

"Evan, please tell me they found my car."

"Sorry, no news on that yet Joel, but I think that's going to be the least of your concerns right now."

Joel downed the rest of the drink, let out a long exhale.

"Why, what's going on?"

"That's what I need to ask you, because I'm trying really hard to understand it myself. Where are you now Joel?"

"I'm actually at the office, and about to see a patient. What's this about? I only have a couple of minutes."

"I'm down in Oxnard right now, and we just found some guy dead in his apartment. He's been rotting away in there for at least a couple of days. Looks like he was tortured too, and believe me it's not a pretty site up there."

"That's terrible, but-"

"Let me finish. The thing is, we found out about it from an anonymous caller, who told us exactly where to find him, and that a big, black guy named Derrik Jackson, is the one that did it to him. I think that name might ring a bell with you."

Joel tried to stay calm and focused, pacing around the media room.

"Well, that might explain what happened to Derrik. A case of retribution maybe? To tell you the truth, I really wasn't privy to what Derrik did in his personal life, and I'm not aware of any trouble that he might have been in."

"That's what I thought too, someone getting payback on him for what he did to the guy in the apartment, if, he's the one that did it. It's not that unusual, happens a lot around here, see it all the time. If you ask me, I think that's exactly what happened."

"Well that certainly seems logical to me. Evan, I really need to get back to work. Can we talk later?"

"The thing is, like I told you, I'm over here in Oxnard, specifically, at an apartment complex called S.C. Timbers off of Vineyard Ave. The victim's name is Luke Wadely, and I remember you called me, looking for some information about this same guy. Is there anything you want to tell me about this?"

"First, I need to ask, and I trust the answer is no. Have you shared this with anyone else?"

"No, I haven't done that, and I don't intend to. I would really like to get your side of the story though Joel. But, you're a busy man, and it doesn't seem like you have the time to talk it over."

"Hold on a minute."

Joel covered the microphone on his cell, just enough to make sure Evan could still hear him.

"Elaine...I need a few more minutes...I know that...it won't be long...thank you."

Joel took a belt off the bottle of Crown Royal, composed himself, and put the phone to his ear.

"Sorry about that. I just bought myself a little more time."

"Good. So, what the hell's going on here? I'm telling you right now, it's not going to be long, before one and one equal two, and you're the deuce Joel. There's nothing I can do about that, it's out of my control. They're going to be digging a lot deeper into the Derrik Jackson piece of this, now that they got a respectable white guy as incentive. And Derrik is going to lead them to you. So, what's the story? No bullshit, no games."

Joel hesitated, thinking, *I'm the deuce? Evan's practicing his acting shtick on me? Another goddamn pissant.*

"Evan, I think you're underestimating yourself. There is a story. In fact, there are many stories. There's the one about this detective I know. He's one hell of a cop, does whatever it takes to get the job done. I can certainly understand why he might occasionally need some female companionship, other than his wife, or maybe a little something to help get him through the tough times, and the good times for that matter. But I'm afraid, others might not be so understanding. What do you think Evan?"

"Fuck you, don't even go there. I didn't have to call you, but I did. So don't start playing games with me. I'm telling you right now that you better be prepared, because the heat is going to be on soon, and you better have your story straight. There is absolutely nothing that I can do to stop the way that this plays out."

"Please, calm down Evan. I have had a very stressful day, and I know you'll do all that *is* in your power to help out. I truly appreciate it, you know I do. Listen, I really have to get back to it. Are you free for lunch tomorrow?"

"I can be. Why?"

"Let's plan on meeting up around, say, one o'clock tomorrow. Does that work?"

"Yeah, I can do that."

"Marvelous, I'll call you in the morning, and we can decide where. I think we can easily come to a mutual understanding about all this. What do you say?"

"Let's get one thing straight. If there's *any* chance that I can help you out on this, you need to let me know *exactly* what's going on. If you don't, you can't expect anything. Do you understand that?"

"Certainly I do, and it will all be settled tomorrow. I can assure you of that. On a totally different note, I think I'll have some good news for you any day now, regarding your role in the show. It's going to be called the Viceroys. Pretty clever, don't you think?"

Evan laughed. "Yeah, just like you."

"Guilty as charged. I'll talk to you tomorrow, but please, don't hesitate to call me if anything urgent comes up in the interim."

"You can count on that."

# ABANDON SHIP

Joel took another drink from the bottle, thinking about his passport. Evan's call had made him forget about Saboro and Ghede, but now they were at the top of his "what the fuck am I going to do?" list.

He figured he could stall Saboro and Ghede for one more day at most, but the whole Derrik fiasco could get ugly, especially if Evan turned on him. Joel didn't think that he would, but Thomas proved that anything is possible. He decided that it could only play out two ways. He could stay, face it all head on, and hope that what got him this far in life pulled him through, or leave it all behind and go on a long international vacation. Joel knew he had to decide soon, because both options required a game plan, and he had two hours to make a move.

"*Midnight at the Oasis*" came on the plasma and Joel decided he needed a well-deserved vacation to Rio. He changed the plasma over to a split screen video feed of the front of the house and went to get his passport.

*** 

Joel sat behind the desk in his home office and searched the LAX website for a first class flight to Galeão International Airport. The check box to select a one way or return trip, made him realize that he had no intention of saying goodbye to LA forever. He needed distance, time, and a clear head to deal with it and sort things out. He entered a date that would get him home two weeks from tomorrow and clicked on the search icon. When the results came on the screen, he decided that for four grand and a connection in Miami, American Airlines would get his business.

He noticed the time on the computer was four-twenty and knew he had to make some quick decisions about money and his patients, after he fixed himself a drink. The ringtone on his cell went off as he walked through the kitchen. He answered.

"Good timing John. I was just about to call you. There has been a change of plans."

"I got what you're lookin' for. I'm on my way over now."

Joel tried to process John's words.

*What's he got? The DreemWeever, Thomas, Paul, the Bullitt, a combination of the four?*

"You there? Did you hear what I said?" John asked.

"Yes, I heard you. Specifics John, get to the point."

"I've got the case and everything in it. Tommy called me, told me to look out the window and check out the driveway. Sure as shit, I look outside, and there it is, just like he said. Do you fuckin' believe it?"

"Did he say anything else?"

Joel walked into the media room, uncapped the bottle of Crown Royal.

"Nope, he just hung up, and that was it."

Joel drank a mouthful and along with the booze, his confidence settled in his stomach. After another sip, he felt like he was back on top.

"You said you're on your way here. Where are you?"

"I'll be there in ten minutes. Don't worry. I got plenty of time before I have to pick them up."

"Never mind about that, just get here. John, I don't know what to say to you. I really am speechless. I will take care of you, I promise."

"You speechless, that's a fuckin' first. What did you want to talk to me about anyway?"

"It's not important now. Please, just get here. I'll be waiting."

"Will do."

\*\*\*

I pulled the Challenger into the parking lot of the Ventura Beach Marriott and shut the engine down in the middle of *"Gimme Three Steps"*.

"Sirius is pretty cool man," Paul said. "The night shit went down at my place, I gave the Seventies channel a try. It kicked ass."

"Yeah, I didn't listen to it much. I just plug my MP3 player into the auxiliary jack.

*"MP3 player*? Why not an iPod?" Paul asked.

"You saw the CD collection at the house. Almost anything I want to listen to is in there somewhere. Come on let's go."

"Cool. We can pay cash when we check out, but they're going to need a credit card. I got one we can use."

"Good call," I said. "I didn't even think about that. All I have is a driver's license and a Social Security number. The license might be a hassle, until I get the picture redone. I have so much shit I have to take care of."

"Don't worry about it now man. It's all going to work out, you just need some time."

"Fifteen grand and a driver's license, I guess I could be worse off," I said.

"The way I look at it, this is all a bonus. Both of us could have ended up like Luke and Bryce," Paul said.

"That's exactly how I see it too."

We checked in and got a room on the third floor with two double beds. The hotel was nice, but compared to the Marriott Bryce and I stayed at in Times Square, it seemed like we were in a Motel 6. Paul flopped down on one of the beds and I did the same on the other. It felt good to stretch out and relax and I'm sure Paul felt the same way.

"Okay," Paul said, "It's almost five now. We got some time to kill. I definitely need to take a shower."

"You and me both."

"After that, I figure we could go down to the bar, have a couple drinks, something to eat, and by that time, we should be ready to go."

"That works. You can use the shower first. I'll give you a few minutes." I grinned at him. "And then take off on you while you're in there."

Paul sat up, returned a smile, and pointed to the bag with the money it.

"That's why I'm taking that in the bathroom with me."

I started laughing and tried to trump him.

"Why would you take a bag of newspapers in there with you?"

"Man, you got me. I'll try and save some hot water for you."

I turned on the television, started surfing through the channels and decided to watch the KABC evening news. The anchor was saying something about a breaking news story in Oxnard and right after that, a field reporter came on live from the scene. Right away, I noticed he was standing in front of Luke's apartment building and describing it as a grisly murder. I turned up the volume, got off the bed and banged on the bathroom door.

"Hey, get out here now, you got to see this."

I didn't hear the shower running and Paul opened the door, wrapping a towel around his waist.

"What's up?"

"Luke's murder is on the news."

We stood in front of the television and watched as Detective Evan Carleton of the LAPD talked about it being treated as a homicide, not releasing the name of the victim until next of kin were notified, and how at this time, they didn't have any more details that they could share. The reporter regurgitated his sign off and the story was over.

"What a fucking weasel," Paul said. "We should call the tip line, and set them straight. He's nothing but a slick, LA cop, Josh Brolin wannabe. Fuck him."

"That's exactly what I thought when I met him at Joel's the other night. The hairdo, leather jacket, and the cocky attitude, everything about him reminded me of a movie cop. You're right, fuck him. He'll get a reality check soon enough."

"If there's any justice in the World he will."

Paul went back into the bathroom and I watched the news, while I waited for my turn in the shower.


## THE ROOSKIES


John pulled up to the gates at Joel's place and entered the code into the keypad. The gates didn't move. He tried again, nothing. Joel's voice came over the intercom.

"Don't bother, I disabled it."

The gates started to swing open and John eased the limo through. He grabbed the case off the passenger seat, got out of the limo and walked toward the house. Before he got to the door, Joel opened it and stood in the threshold. He looked out across the yard, then down at the limo. He stepped back into the house, opened the door wider and John went in. He closed and locked it as soon as John was inside.

"Sorry for the hassle, John. I'm a little uptight right now."

"No problemo, I understand. You got to be careful these days." He handed the case to Joel. "Hopefully, this will ease your worries."

Joel took the case, put his arm around John's shoulder, and they walked toward the media room.

"Come on, let's go talk. Are you up for a drink? You look like you could use one."

"You read my mind," John said, thinking Joel was already pie-eyed.

John followed Joel into the media room. He motioned to the sectional for John to take a seat, walked over to the bar and placed the case on top of it.

Joel looked at his watch. "It's a little after five, and as much as I hate to have you do it, you should leave here around six to pick up Jason, Robert, and the other three. They are expecting you at six-thirty."

"That's what I figured. Actually, it worked out pretty good. I was getting antsy hanging around my place. Rather kill the time over here anyway. I gotta' take a leak, if you don't mind. I'll have a Stoli on the rocks."

"Okay, make it quick though."

"Be back in a jiffy. I'll only give it two shakes. Anymore than that and you're playin' with yourself, or somethin' like that."

John left the room, walked down the hall toward the bathroom, and double-timed it into the kitchen. He opened a cabinet door under the granite island and knelt down. He reached inside, pushed a sequence of numbers on a keypad, closed the cabinet, and stood up. He went back down the hall, into the bathroom, and turned the faucet on. He pulled the cell from his blazer pocket and pushed a speed dial.

"Ready to go, give me five minutes."

John closed the phone, flushed the toilet and headed back to the media room. He pushed the door shut after he walked in. Joel was sitting on the sectional, a drink resting on his knee. John sat across from him, grabbed his glass off the table and took a sip.

"So, that's it?" Joel said. "He just drops off the case and that's that? Did he say anything else?"

John noticed the plasma was on and displaying a four way, split screen with views of the driveway and the back yard.

*Shit, gotta get that off,* he thought.

"You worried about the cops in New York?" John asked.

"What do you mean? What's New York got to do with this?"

"It's all over the news today. They got some leads on the two broads Bryce and Tommy visited. There's supposed to be a big press conference or somethin'. Maybe they already had it. Check out CNN or one of those channels. It's probably on there now, or at least scrollin' down the bottom of the screen."

Joel closed his eyes, put the drink against his forehead, and slowly rolled it from side to side. John reached across the table, grabbed the remote and pressed a couple buttons. The video feeds disappeared and cable TV replaced them. He started scanning the news channels and reading the scrolling banners.

***

Anton closed his cell phone and put it in the back pocket of his pants.

"Okay, it's time," he said to Sergey, in Russian.

"Too bad," Sergey said. "I could get used to being driven around in a car like this."

"Yes, me too, but it would be better to be sitting, instead of lying on the floor. Don't you think?"

"Maybe someday, we will have such luxuries. Besides, it could be worse." Sergey pointed toward the trunk. "We could be in there with the rats."

"That is true." Anton pulled a key out of his sock. "But now we must deal with the two-legged rat. Come on, let's go."

Sergey grabbed an oversized, brown, leather brief case off the floor of the limo and followed Anton out the side door. They walked up the steps and stood in front of the door. Anton put the key in the lock and turned it slowly.

"This is good. No alarm, just like John said."

# PARTS IS PARTS

Joel concentrated on CNN showing on the plasma, still waiting to hear or read something on the New York story.

"What are they saying? What did you hear John?"

"Not much. Just that, some hairdresser in Boston called the NYPD and told them she had some information about-"

The media room door burst open. John rolled onto the floor. Joel tried to stand. Sergey rushed through and pulled the trigger on a large pistol. The tranquilizer dart hit Joel in the chest. He staggered and flung himself over the back of the sectional, landing on the carpet. John stood up. Sergey slowly walked around one side of the sectional. Anton dropped the briefcase on the floor and walked around the other side.

They stopped halfway, looked at each other.

"Oh, where did he go?" Sergey laughed. "He wants to play games. Hide and seek maybe?"

"Yes," Anton said, "but what if he has hidden himself so good, that we cannot find him. What shall we do then?"

"We will take our chances. How do you play this? Ah yes, I remember, One, two, three, ready or not, here we come."

They went around to the back of the sectional. Joel was lying on his stomach, unconscious. Sergey jostled Joel's body with his foot and looked over at John.

"Would you please go out there, and bring us back a chair." He pointed to the plasma. "Turn that off please."

"Sure, any chair?" John asked.

"Not one of those fancy, cushioned chairs, just one with a high back, and arms on the side. Thank you."

"Be right back." John pressed the remote and the plasma screen turned black.

"Let us prepare, while he rests. Move that table out of the way. That is a good spot," Anton said.

Sergey walked to the middle of the sectional and dragged the coffee table toward the side of the room. He picked up the briefcase, placed it on a cushion of the sectional, and pushed the clasps on the front of it. The locks snapped open. He pulled out a large square of polyurethane and started to unfold it. He waved it up and down with both hands, until it was fully open.

He looked at Anton and motioned with his head toward the other end of the plastic laying on the floor. "Give me a hand."

Anton lifted his end off the carpet. They carried it to the middle of the sectional and waved it up and down, to get the creases out. They stretched it across the sectional, until it covered the carpet and all of the seating. Sergey walked around the middle of the plastic, flattening it tight to the rug, then made a final pass around the inside perimeter of the sectional.

John came in carrying a wooden, bar stool chair that had a wicker back rest.

"This is the best I could do." John pointed to the middle of the plastic sheet. "I take it you want it there?"

"Excellent choice," Anton said. "Yes, right there in the middle."

John walked on top of the plastic, put the chair down. Sergey grabbed the briefcase and placed it on top of the pool table, with the top open.

"Let's get him comfortable, he should be waking up soon," Anton said, looking at John. "You should look for what you need."

"Will do," John walked over to the wall of CD's.

Sergey and Anton looked down at Joel.

"You get his legs." Anton tapped Joel's shoulder with his foot. "I'll get this end."

Anton rolled Joel's body over on to its back. Sergey pulled the dart out of Joel's chest and tossed it on the rug. They carried Joel's limp body into the middle of the sectional and forced it down on the chair.

Anton held Joel's upper body tight to the back of the chair, while Sergey went over to the briefcase. Joel's head stayed slumped forward, his arms dangling at his side.

Sergey came back holding a handful of brown, leather straps and dropped them on the floor in front of the chair.

"Two should be good right here," Anton said, slapping Joel's chest. "Then I will help you with the rest."

Sergey wrapped a strap around the chair back and under Joel's arms. He pulled it tight and tied it off with three knots. Anton let go of Joel and moved to the front of him, while Sergey secured another strap around Joel's stomach.

"How much longer?" John walking over with a CD case in his hand.

"Five minutes," Anton said.

"You take that side." Sergey tossed two straps to Anton, who was kneeling at the right side of the chair.

They tied Joel's ankles and shins to the front legs of the chair. Anton held Joel's arms behind the back of the chair, while Sergey wrapped the straps around Joel's wrists.

"That is all," Anton said. "Now, how about a drink?" He looked over at John "Is there any vodka over there?"

"You bet. What kind you like? Stoli, Kettle One, Grey Goose?"

"Schmirnoff," Sergey said.

"Sorry boss, don't have that. What's your second choice?"

"Stoli will be fine," Anton said.

"Ice?" John asked.

"No," Sergey said, and Anton agreed.

"Comin' right up," John said.

They walked over to the bar. John put down three glasses, poured Stoli in two of them, Chivas Regal in the other.

"Here you go gents." John downed his drink in one gulp.

Sergey and Anton did the same.

"Another?" John asked.

"Not now," Anton said. "After."

"You guys need me to do anything else, besides the music?"

"No," Anton said, "we are good, just do your thing."

Anton looked at Sergey and pointed over at Joel. "Come on, he's starting to move."

Joel's head moved slightly. His chin started to lift off his chest, then hang back down as he started to come to. His eyes opened. The eyeballs rolled around in the sockets, like a blind man. Sergey grabbed Joel's ponytail and jerked his head to attention. He held the ponytail tight in his fist as Anton slapped Joel's cheeks back and forth with his palm and the back of his hand.

"Come on, time to wake up. Wakey, wakey," Anton said.

Joel's eyes stayed open as he fought against Sergey's grip on his hair, trying to avoid Anton's hand. Sergey let go of the ponytail and Joel's head moved from side to side with the flow of the slaps.

"You...dirty...rat," Anton said, sounding like a Russian James Cagney as he slapped Joel at a faster pace.

Sergey glanced at John across the room. They both turned their backs to laugh. Anton stopped. It took a few seconds for the cease fire to register with Joel and his head went through the motions, unprovoked. Joel's face was pink from the slaps, and stinging. Loose strands from the ponytail stuck out around his head.

"What do you want? You name it it's yours," Joel blurted out, forcing more saliva droplets to mix with the sweat that drizzled down the beard hairs on his chin.

"We already know that," Anton said. "If you had everything you were supposed to, we wouldn't be here. So we will take what we can, including you."

Joel stared at Anton and Sergey standing in front of him and then set his eyes on John.

"You fucking Judas! How could you set me up like this? You lousy, goddamn piece of shit."

John put his hands up and shrugged his shoulders.

Sergey walked over to the briefcase and came back with a cordless Makita Sawzall with a ten inch blade sticking out of the end, and a pair of clear safety goggles. He squeezed the trigger on and off a few times, like it was a machine gun.

He pointed the saw as Joel. "Let's just do this now, no need to wait."

Sergey squeezed the trigger again, held it down, and raised his voice over the noise. "Let me cut his tongue out, so we do not have to listen to him anymore."

He put the blade inches from Joel's face, still holding the trigger down.

"Where is the money Joel?" he yelled.

Joel squeezed his eyes shut and tilted his head to avoid the blade.

"Hold on, hold on, I'm sorry, hold on."

Sergey grabbed Joel's ponytail and sawed it off close to the back of Joel's head, then tossed the hair onto the plastic.

"Nobody where's a ponytail anymore, you stupid idiot," Sergey yelled into Joel's ear, then slapped him on the side of the head.

He walked back toward Anton and pulled his finger off the trigger.

"Come on now Joel," Anton said. "The money. Where is it? This is not the time for games."

"It's here, not all of it, but enough. There's more in the bank. I can get it for you. Just give me time."

"You have had too much time already. Your business partners do not have any more time. They have decided it is time to cut their losses. Unfortunately, you are a loss to them. A bad investment is what I was told you are. Now, where is it?"

Anton walked to the front of the plasma, stomped his feet around on the rug, and slid his foot across the carpet.

"Could it be in the safe? How do you get to it?"

"Fuck him." Sergey pressed the trigger on the saw and walked toward Joel.

"The remote, the remote, you need the remote," Joel screamed.

"Where is it?" Sergey yelled into Joel's ear, still holding the moving blade on top of Joel's wrist.

"Here you go." John tossed the remote to Anton and Sergey stopped the saw.

Anton glared at Joel. "What do I need this for?"

"Point it at the screen," Joel said. "Press two, two, six, seven, eight, four, six, six."

"Hold on, say it slower," Sergey yelled.

Anton entered the numbers as Joel repeated them. After the last digit, the safe started rising from the carpet in front of the plasma.

"Well I'll be damned," John said. "I guess you didn't trust me as much as I thought."

"I trusted you more than anyone. You piece of shit," Joel said.

"Shut your mouth," Sergey yelled. "How do you open it?"

Joel let out a long breath. "Five, four, five, five, seven."

The three of them stood in front of the safe. Anton bent down, pushed the numbers on the keypad, turned the handle, and opened it.

"Ah, the secret treasure," Anton said. "How much is in there?"

"About a million," Joel murmured.

"Get us a bag or something to put this in," Anton told John.

"Be right back."

Sergey started pulling the packs of hundreds out, letting them fall onto the carpet.

"What about these folders?" he asked Anton.

"We are to take everything. Those are more important than the money."

"Here you go," John said, handing a green trash bag to Sergey. "It's the best I could do."

Sergey filled the bag with the money and the folders, then picked it up off the rug, spun it around a few times and tossed it toward the door.

"Okay, it looks like we are done here," Anton said, looking over at Joel.

"What about our invention?" Sergey asked, picking up the safety goggles. "Surely, we cannot leave without showing him."

"You are right Sergey. We must not leave without showing him. He is a man with many important relationships. He might be able to make us millionaires. After all, it is an improvement on his design. He must see it."

Sergey walked toward Joel, stopped in front of him, and spun the goggles around his finger by the elastic strap.

"What was it you called your big invention, the dream catcher, the dream machine?"

"Dream...weaver," Joel mumbled.

"Ah yes," Anton said, "the dream weaver, the ten...million...dollar...dream weaver. From what I am told, it is magic. It can make ten million dollars disappear. Is that right?"

"I told you," Joel pleaded. "I have more. I can get them their money back, if that is what this is all about. I can get it tomorrow, all of it, even more than that."

"You are a fool," Anton said. "This is not about the money. It is about your stupidity, your arrogance, and your lies. *That* is what it is about."

"Enough talking from you Anton." Sergey pushed the goggles over Joel's eyes and snapped the strap on the back of his head. He bent over and put his lips next to Joel's ear. "And you will talk no more. I will do all the talking from now on."

Sergey reached down, picked up two leather straps, and twisted them together. He moved behind Joel, holding the straps outstretched between his hands. Joel twisted his neck, trying to see behind himself. Sergey extended his arms over Joel's head and pulled the straps tight around Joel's neck.

"No! *Please* don't do-" Joel gasped for air as his body shimmied in the chair.

Sergey pulled the straps tighter until Joel stopped resisting and almost lost consciousness.

Sergey released the tension on the straps, lined them up with Joe's mouth and jerked them, parting Joel's lips and teeth. He tied them off around the back of Joel's head. Joel gagged as he tried to talk, his words indecipherable. Vomit spewed onto his lap, dripped off his beard, and onto the front of his shirt.

"You filthy pig." Sergey punched Joel directly on his ear hole. "You *filthy, foul, pig*."

Anton put his hand on Sergey's shoulder. "Please we have kept him in suspense long enough. Let us demonstrate *our* dream weaver for him."

Anton looked at Joel. "You see, we have beat you at your own game. Your dream weaver promised to give an experience that was supposed to be so real, people would not know what is real, and what is not. Maybe it did this, maybe it didn't."

"He does not seem to be impressed," Sergey said.

"Then we shall have to make him a believer."

Anton stood in front of Joel and grabbed the sides of the goggles.

"Ten million dollars, this is too much money. You are now wearing the greatest reality vision technology, and we have invested only ten dollars. Let us demonstrate, and you may be the judge."

Sergey walked toward the plasma and picked up the Sawzall off the floor. He pointed the blade toward the ceiling and squeezed and released the trigger as he stared at Joel.

"Please John," Anton said, "we must have the music, just as Joel's did."

"I thought you'd never ask. Comin' right up."

John took a sip from his drink, put the glass down on the bar, and looked at the CD case in front of him. He walked over to the CD player, grabbing the remote on the way.

John put the CD in, sat back down behind the bar and pushed the skip track button, until number six showed on the LED display. He pressed play.

"*Let It Be*" started playing over the surround sound. Sergey and Anton nodded their heads in approval at his selection.

"Louder, please," Anton told John.

"You got it."

Anton moved his thumb in an upward motion, to instruct John, as he increased the volume. He gave him the "okay" hand signal and John put the remote down.

Anton put his arm around Sergey's shoulder and whispered into his ear, "If it is reality he wants, then it is reality he will get."

Anton walked over to the bar and sat next to John.

Sergey walked slowly toward Joel, the Sawzall blade pointed at the floor. Joel's body stiffened, his head flailed, and he screamed through the leather straps as Sergey closed in.

"You must take all of the camera videos when we leave," Anton told John.

"Not a problem." John pointed to the velvet curtains on the wall near the pool table. "The computer is over there, behind the wall. We'll take it with us. It's all on there."

"Excellent," Anton said. "You better get going. Our other guests won't like it if you are late picking them up."

"Fuck them." John lit a cigarette, took a drag. "They should be hoping I don't show up."

"On with the show," Anton yelled over to Sergey.

Sergey nodded, pressed the trigger on the Sawzall, and brought the blade down hard on the middle of Joel's left thigh.

## COME TO MAMA

### 10 Minutes Later

"I am so glad you are here with me Jacob."

"Please Mother, my name is Joel now."

"Your *name* is Jacob. I do not care what you call yourself, I am only happy that you are here."

The stifling heat fueled the constant perspiration that excreted from their naked bodies.

"Are you frightened Jacob?"

"Of course I am. Why can I hear you, but not see you?"

"Don't be scared. The light will come soon, it always does. Until then, you must keep still."

"Why?"

"I cannot, I mean, I am not able to tell you why. That is how it is, and you must listen to me."

"Where are we?"

"I cannot tell you that either. You will need to find that out for yourself."

"What *can* you tell me?"

"I can tell you, that I am sorry. It is because of me that you are here."

"What do you mean? What did you do?"

"I did what I had to do for us to stay alive, after your father and sister were taken from us. You were such a young boy, and I know you saw me do very terrible things to those women. But at that time, I was only thinking about our survival. I hoped that because you were so small, you would not remember, but you did. And that is why you are here now. Do you understand this?"

"Yes, I think so. After all, I *am* a psychologist, and it's all about suppressed memories, subliminal desires, and the mother is always to blame. I didn't do what you did though. So, *why* am I *here*?"

"Jacob, maybe you did not do it in the same way, but it is the same thing in the end."

"What are you saying? Please tell me what-"

A powerful, hot wind moved over their bodies and continued to grow stronger.

"We must be quiet for now Jacob."

"But, I need to know-"

"Shhh, we will speak later."

Loud squealing noises, sounding like hawks invaded the silence and rapidly intensified and multiplied, until they reached an ear piercing volume. Strong bursts of wind hit Joel's body with such force, he felt a sensation of vertigo, until a cold, slimy hand grabbed onto his and held it tight.

The winds began to die down. The squealing slowly faded away, until both completely stopped. The hand Joel held slipped from his grip and he felt vibrations under his feet that reminded him of the many earthquakes he experienced in California.

"What's going on? What's happening?"

He did not get a response.

"Mother, where are you?"

Silence.

A small hole in the ground appeared, traces of orange light emanated from it. Joel could see he was standing naked and alone on a small wooden platform, one hundred feet above the light.

As the hole expanded, the black earth plummeted into a chasm of boiling magma, forcing a fountain of orange fireballs to shoot up out of it, illuminating the darkness like a massive, fireworks display.

Joel felt his body quivering. He tried to lay down on the platform, but couldn't move. He screamed, but no sound came from his mouth.

The hole stopped growing. The boiling liquid inside it ignited, transforming it into a caldron of flames that rose fifty-feet into the air. The light from the inferno allowed Joel to see his surroundings clearly. Joel felt like every cell in his body had constricted when he realized that he was in the middle of a coliseum, like the ones of ancient Rome.

Thousands of cherubs filled every seat. They sat motionless and silent, staring at him through their iridescent eyes. They looked like perfect wax figures.

In unison, they turned their heads toward the opening at the end of the coliseum. Joel looked across the chasm to the opening and saw the shape of three figures entering in a single file line.

"Jacob." He heard his mother's voice, but could not see her.

"Mother, where are you?"

"I am here, but I cannot be with you."

"Why?"

"That is just the way it is."

The three figures, dressed in black, hooded robes, walked with bowed heads and continued toward the chasm. They stopped when they reached the edge and stood next to each other.

Joel looked down, horrified. They pulled back their hoods, exposing their hairless, oblong, white heads. Two black holes, where eyes should be, were the only interruption to the network of red veins that traversed the fluorescent glow of the semi-transparent skin covering their heads.

They turned toward the entrance. Large black wings came from out of their backs. Their wings began to move and propelled them off the ground. They rose together and stopped when they reached Joel's eye level. The cherubs fixed their eyes on Joel, as the three figures rapidly flapped their wings to maintain the same altitude.

The three moved forward, until they stopped in front of Joel. The scorching wind powered by their wings, burned his body as it blew over him.

Joel tried to look away from them, but his eyes didn't respond. His eyelids wouldn't close to block them out.

"Who are you?" Joel screamed, but no sound came from his mouth.

"They do not speak," his mother's voice said.

"Mother, help me. Please help me! Who are they?"

"Jacob, you must not ask questions. There are no answers."

"But it hurt's. I feel like I'm burning. Can't you make them stop?"

"I cannot. I can tell you who they are though, if you will listen."

"I just want them to stop hurting me, and *looking at me.*"

"On the left is Ghede. Next to him is Orobas. In between-"

The figure in the middle rose above the others and stopped twenty feet above them.

"He is the leader, Abbadon. I must go now Jacob. I will see you soon though. I promise you."

"Mother, don't go. Please stay with-"

Abbadon started to expand in size. His wings generated fierce, cold winds and rapidly chilled Joel's body. He stopped growing, raised his arms to the blackness above him, and looked upward.

"Corpus Edimus," Abbadon bellowed. His voice echoed through the coliseum. He lowered his arms and bowed his head. "Sanguis Bibimus."

Ghede and Orobas rose until they flanked Abbadon. In unison, they yelled, "Ave Satani!"

Their words reverberated through the coliseum. They turned their backs on Joel and started flying away from him, until they disappeared into the darkness.

The cherubs' wings began moving. They started rising off their seats and into the air, blanketing the darkness above Joel, like an ominous storm cloud.

They started squealing. The noise shattered Joel's eardrums. He screamed from the pain, but could not hear anything.

The cherubs descended and swarmed around Joel. He could see each face and iridescent set of eyes as they passed by him.

The force of the arrow that pierced Joel's back caused him to move toward the edge of the platform. He tried to keep his balance as he looked down on the inferno below.

Arrows started to rip through his flesh, muscle, and bone from every direction. Joel tried to keep his bloody body on the platform.

The arrows abruptly stopped. The cherubs started flying away from Joel, who stood hunched over and looked like a bloody, human porcupine as he cried from the pain. Joel looked up and saw a boy cherub with curly, blond hair hovering directly in front of him. He put an arrow in his bow, pulled back on the string, and pointed it at Joel.

The arrow pierced Joel's right eye, blinding him. He held the arrow with both hands and staggered around the platform. The cherub reloaded his bow, pulled back, and the vision in Joel's left eye went black. The cherub started to fly away.

Joel shuffled his feet around the platform, trying to judge the boundaries of the wood under his toes and keep his balance, until he felt nothing under his left foot. He felt himself falling, hearing in his head, MISTRAL, MISTRAL, MIS, MIS......TRAAAAAAAAALLLLLL.

## FIXING A HOLE

By the time Paul and I had showered up, it was after six o'clock. We went down to the bar to run through the plan for later that night. The bartender brought over our Heineken's and we both ordered a burger and fries from the bar menu. Under any other circumstances, we probably would have sat there and got shit-faced, but we set a three-beer limit on ourselves. We knew that by eleven o'clock, we would be drinking top shelf somewhere and watching the news showing the future site of Kite Industry headquarters, as it burned to the ground.

"So, after tonight, where do we go from here man?" Paul asked.

"I been thinking about that a lot, and I think I'm going to New Hampshire as soon as I can. What about you?"

"I have no fucking clue, but I know I have to leave LA. I mean, I want to leave LA. Why would you go to New Hampshire?"

"A fresh start I guess. In my case, it really is a new life. At least that's how I see it. There is a reason though, and I'm not sure you would understand."

"Dude, after what we've been through, I can pretty much understand any fucking thing. Come on, let's hear it. I just might decide to join you."

"How many discs did you actually watch?"

"Not all of them. I didn't have the time, or I would have watched all of them. I saw the ones that showed a bunch of stuff about you and Bryce. It showed a lot of shit about you guys, before and after stuff, they were like documentaries. In one of them, you were on an operating table and Guns N' Roses is playing "*Coma*", while a doctor was carving up your face. Then there was this really sick one that showed a fetus, and it kept changing into Bryce's head, then your head, and then it kept showing these two chicks really fast. It just got really disgusting, like I mean nasty. The fetus started boiling, and then its arms and legs were getting ripped off its body. The whole time, Alice in Chains' "*Grind*" is playing, and this crying baby noise is tracking over it. It was the sickest thing I ever seen in my life."

"Joel is one sick fuck. Is that the only one you saw?"

"No there was another one, it was like a movie. The disk was labeled New York, and I noticed the two chicks who kept flashing over in the baby one were in it. They were both pretty hot looking, especially the blond one. At the end they dive over a railing, while they are holding hands. What the fuck."

"That's all in the past." I raised my beer to Paul and he clanked his bottle against mine.

Paul drained the last of his beer. "So how does this relate to New Hampshire?"

"I was getting to that. Joel had this patient named Scott Haskins. He was an entertainment lawyer. He lived in New Hampshire, but worked on both coasts. He met Joel at a bar in LA. one night while he was out here on business. They start shooting the shit, one thing leads to another, and Joel ends up taking him on as a patient. This guy starts spilling his guts to Joel, and Joel decides that he's the perfect candidate for some tests he wants to start doing with the concept of the DreemWeever."

"No shit. What happened to him?

"He's in the psyche ward at Napa State hospital. He lost everything. Joel destroyed him, and his life. Now, here's where New Hampshire comes in. This guy Scott had a wife and a couple of young kids in New Hampshire. His wife, Merri was smoking hot, I mean like Cameron Diaz hot, but with curly blond hair. From the moment I saw the videos of her, I couldn't get her out of my head. I figure I got nothing to lose, so maybe I'll head back East and look her up. If nothing else, I'd just like to see her in person. I'm not talking about stalking her or nothing but, who knows. I figure it's worth a shot."

"You dirty dog. Now I'm definitely thinking about going with you."

"I'd love to have you go too. Anyway, that New York video pretty much explains how everything went down. Joel set this guy Scott up big time, and the next thing you know, He's divorced, and living out here in LA, and Joel has him right were he wants him to test a revised version of the DreemWeever. Joel used the DreemWeever to make this guy think he was insane. The next thing you know, he's living at Napa State. What you didn't see, is that while this guy Scott is stuck in New York City on Christmas Eve, Derrik is at the wife's house, testing out the DreemWeever on her. Joel found out that they'd been together since they were fifteen, but they aborted a baby when they were sixteen. Scott made the mistake of letting Joel know how much it still bothered him. Joel used this as a way to terrorize both of them. You saw the videos, it is more than realistic, but none of it's real. All he needs is a picture of someone, and the facts, and anything can be created after that."

"Come on, there's no way that what was on that New York disk wasn't real."

"Every last frame of that was created digitally. Joel has this computer wizard, a guy named Victor Ahriman, who does it all. I don't know much about him. Heard his name a lot, but I only met him one time, at Joel's party. John told me he was a big shot in the video production world, until he fucked up, did time, and now he's a level three sex offender."

"Sounds like a real nice guy."

"Like I said, I only met him the one time, but somehow, Joel ended up finding him, and spent a shit load of money to set him up with a lot of technology. Joel had him by the balls.

What's a pervert like that going to do? It's not like he had a lot of employment opportunities."

"No shit. Man, the more I learn about Joel, the more I wish we could take him out too."

"Leave it alone. We got one more thing to do, and it's over, we're done, end of story."

I met eyes with the bartender and signaled for another round. He refreshed our beers and a few minutes later, he brought over our food. While we ate, Paul decided that we should both head to New Hampshire tomorrow and I agreed. We ordered another round, paid the tab, and took the beers with us. We wanted to keep the bottles, because we would need them later that night.

*** 

We left the Marriot at eight o'clock and stopped at a Lowe's Home Improvement on South Mills Road to buy a five gallon gas tank. It was eight-thirty when we left Lowe's and nine by the time we had stopped to fill the gas tank and were headed to the warehouse. Paul had already been there with Luke, so he knew exactly how we could get into the complex from outside the security fences. As we drove, Paul checked out the CD's we had with us and handed me a Limp Bizkit disc.

"We need to get motivated dude. Put this in, track four should get us in the mood. What do you think?" Paul said.

"If it doesn't, nothing will."

I put the CD in and "*Break Stuff*" came on. Paul turned it up loud and we cruised down 101, while Paul did his best Fred Durst impression, like he was in the music video. The song pumped me up and I joined in. By the time we pulled in the parking lot of a company near the warehouse, we were both ready to finish what we had to do.

I shut down the Challenger and looked over at Paul.

"You ready?"

Paul bumped my fist with his. "Like cousin Freddy. Let's do it."

We put on the backpacks and grabbed the gas can out of the trunk. Just like he said, Paul knew his way and we were inside the security fence fifteen minutes later. We each had a headlamp on and I followed Paul up the fire escape stairs, until we were standing on the roof of the building. It was the same building that Paul and Luke had seen Joel, Derrik, Saboro, and Ghede go into the night they got themselves in the middle of all this shit. I put the gas can down and Paul pointed to the smokestack off to our left.

"The night me and Luke were here, I wanted to get my picture taken in front of that. Man, I still can't believe all the shit that's happened. If we had never come here in the first place, just think of how different things would be."

"You can't change anything, shit happens for a reason. I'm convinced of that. It's all beyond our control, so stop thinking about it."

"I hear you. Tomorrow we'll be out of here, and in a weird way, justice will have been served and we can leave it all behind."

"Amen. Let's get this over with, so we can go get properly drunk."

"Okay," Paul said, "there's got to be hole in the roof somewhere up here. We just need to find it, dump all the gas down it, and then light it up with a couple of Molotov's. Then get the fuck out of here."

I followed Paul's lead. There was a full moon and we could see where we were going without the headlamps. We were far enough away from the guard house that no one was going to see us walking around. Paul stopped when we were just about at the middle of the roof, pulled a flashlight out of the side pocket of his pack, and crouched down.

"Bingo." He shined the light across the roof and pointed to an area about twenty feet ahead of us. "There it is."

I crouched down next to him, followed the light beam with my eyes, and put the gas can down. The hole was about two feet round and looked like an exhaust pipe or something used to be there. It must have been removed sometime, probably by a salvage crew, or more than likely, thieves who stole metals for cash. We both got on our knees and Paul took the two empty beer bottles and a t-shirt out of his pack. He handed me the bottles.

"Fill those and I'll rip up a couple pieces of this to stuff down the necks."

I filled the bottles until they were more than half full and Paul stuffed each one with a piece of the shirt, leaving about six inches of cloth hanging out of the bottle necks.

"This is it man." Paul stood up and put his pack back on. "I'll take the bottles, you grab the gas."

We looked into the hole and Paul shined the light into it.

"Look at that," I said, "the floors made of wood. This is going to go up quick."

"Yes it is." He held out the bottles and tilted them a little, so the end of the shirt cloth hung down, away from the bottlenecks. "Pour a little bit on the end of these, then dump the rest down there."

I tipped the can on its side and poured all the gas down the hole. I heard the empty can hit the floor below us.

Paul handed me a bottle and pulled a lighter out of his pocket. "Alright, this is it dude." He held out his bottle so it was close to mine. "As soon as the cloth catches fire, we throw them down there and move out."

He pressed down on the lighter and touched the flame to the end of the gas soaked cloths. They caught fire instantly and we held them for a couple of seconds as the fire burned closer to the neck of the bottles.

"Now!" Paul yelled.

We dropped the bottles down the hole and ran toward the fire escape at the other end of the roof. I was in the lead and Paul was tailing me. About twenty yards from the end I heard Paul yell something from behind that I didn't understand. I looked behind me and he was gone. I stopped, saw a jagged hole in the roof, and ran toward it.

"Fuck!" I dropped to my knees, got down on all fours, and crawled toward the hole. "Paul, are you alright, what the fuck. Can you hear me?"

He didn't answer. I pulled off the headlamp, pushed the power button, and crawled on my stomach to the edge of the hole. I looked over the edge and shined the light down it. Paul was lying face down on the floor in a spread-eagle pose, not moving, twenty feet below. I could see blood had started to flow on the floor around his head. Paul was dead and there was nothing I could do about it. I couldn't look back any longer, or I would be dead too.

## THE HUMMER

### Two Weeks Later

I was lying on my bed at the Radisson in Nashua, New Hampshire listening to the Racontuers, contemplating how I was going to start a new life, and at the same time, put the pieces back together of my life before Joel. I had e-mailed John a few times since I got to New Hampshire last week, but had not got anything back from him.

The pre-paid cell I had with me started vibrating in my pants pocket and broke my concentration. I pulled it out and looked at the display.

Salvation? What the fuck.

My body tensed and my heart rate skyrocketed.

Who's got John's phone? Can't be him, someone found it, or took it from him. Who? It's got to be the police, or Joel...shit.

The phone kept vibrating and John's face dominated my mind.

What if it is him? Have to answer it.

"Hello."

"Hey, Danny me boy, how *the hell* are yah lad?"

Sounds like John. How can I be sure?

"Okay," I said.

How do I know it's really him?

"Okay? That's all you got to say?"

I know.

"Sorry, it's just that, you know, I was expecting an email. When I saw that it was your phone calling, I don't know why, but I was thinking about that time we went to John Wayne, and that song we heard on the way there. You know, the one about the father and the son."

"You mean "*Cats in the Cradle*", that one?"

It was him.

"Yeah, John that was it. Where are you man? I missed you. I thought I'd never see you again. You didn't reply to my emails. What the hell happened to you?"

"It's a long story and I don't have the time. It doesn't matter where I am. What matters, is that I know where you are. I do check my emails by the way. I thought you might need a lift. Do me a favor and come around the back of the hotel, will yah."

"What are you talking about, where are-"

He hung up on me. I tried to call him back, but it went straight to voicemail. I closed the cell, paced around the room and looked out the window.

Could still be a setup? Joel could be with him. Walk out there and get shot. No, John wouldn't do that, he wouldn't set me up. What does he want? Fuck it, have to find out.

I took the elevator down to the lobby, went out one of the side exits, and scanned the front parking lot.

He said around back.

I stayed close to the side of the building, on the grass, and walked toward the rear lot.

What's he driving? Never told me what kind of car he's in. Two-hundred cars out here, could be in any of them. Take it like a man, don't be afraid.

I took a deep breath and started walking through the lot, looking into every car as I passed it. No one was inside any of them. I was almost halfway across and I could hear the sound a car coming up fast from behind me. It was a black, Hummer H2 and I could see John behind the wheel, smiling.

Run or stay here? Can't see through the tint if anyone's in the back. Too late, he's right in front of me.

The driver's side window started going down.

"Danno, you look like shit."

"You alone?"

"What do you think? See for yourself."

The back window on his side started going down. No one was in there.

"Come on get in. Let's get out of here. We got a lot to talk about."

John stuck his hand out and we had a long shake. I looked into his eyes and could tell that everything was okay.

"You got shit up in the room?"

"Yeah."

"Go up and get it and check out. I'll meet you out front. I'm starving. You want to get somethin' to eat?"

"Big time."

"Hey, hop in, I'll drive you around."

I jogged around the front and got in the passenger side.

John put the Hummer in drive. "Just like old times huh?"

"Where's Joel?"

"Don't worry about him. Like I said, we got a lot to talk about."

John stopped the Hummer in front of the entrance.

"Give me five minutes," I said.

"No problem. I'm not going anywhere."

I went up to the room, grabbed my stuff and checked out.

I walked toward the Hummer and John stuck his arm out the window.

"Come on, let's go."

I opened the rear passenger side door and noticed there was a tinted divider, like in a limo, separating the third row seating and trunk space from the rest of the inside cabin. It wasn't there before and it made me nervous.

I knocked on it, trying to gage John's response. "Nice touch."

"What can I say, old habits die hard."

I laughed, tossed my suitcase and travel bag inside, and then jumped in the seat next to him.

"Were do you want to eat Danno? There's Outback, Olive Garden, Chili's. You name it. They got them all up here."

"I don't care. Outback I guess."

"Then Outback it is."

John pulled out and headed for the exit. We were halfway down the long, winding, access road and he pulled over to the side shoulder.

"Do me a favor, reach behind you, and get me that black bag, will you?"

"Now?"

"Come on just get it."

"Whatever."

I reached back, grabbed the leather gym bag, and handed it to him. He unzipped it and pulled it open so I could see inside.

"What do you think?"

It was stuffed with packets of hundred dollar bills.

"Where did get that? How much is in there?"

"Somewhere around a hundred G's, give or take. Now that I think of it, we better put this in the way back."

"Good idea."

"While we're at it, put your bags back there too. Chop chop."

John grabbed the gym bag and got out. I pulled my stuff out of the back seat and we walked to the back of the Hummer. He pulled open the rear door and there was a steel beer keg taking up most of the space.

"Planning a party? What the fuck is that for?"

He rapped it a couple times with the knuckles on his right hand.

"Like I said, you don't need to worry about Joel anymore. He's lost his head." He smirked and rapped the keg again. "And hands and feet too."

"No fucking way."

"Put the suitcase in, will you. Let's go."

John closed the door and winked at me. My head was spinning as we got back in the Hummer.

"What are we going to do?" I asked him.

"I heard South Beach is pretty nice. We'll stop somewhere on the way, and say goodbye to our friend."

John turned on the radio, raised his eyebrows, and looked over at me. "How app-ra-fuckin'-po."

He turned it up and we listened to Johnny Mathis singing "*99 Miles From L.A.*" as we merged onto Route 3, heading south.

# THE PACKAGE

## One Month Later

Merri Haskins sat at the kitchen table of the Nashua, New Hampshire apartment she and the two kids had been living in for the last six months. She pulled the CD from the 8x11 envelope that came in the mail, along with the collection notices and bills. The clear, plastic case didn't have a label, neither did the CD. She pulled out a piece of paper from the envelope and read it.

*Play Me? What the hell is this?*

Merri put the disc in the DVD drive of her laptop, clicked on the wave file. It loaded and *"Girl from A Pawnshop"* started playing. When the lyrics started, the volume decreased, a man's voice came over the laptop speakers.

*Merri, this is not a joke. I knew your husband Scott. I never met him, but I know enough about him, and what happened to him, that I can promise you that what I am about to tell you is absolutely true, and you have to believe me. I know what happened between you and Scott, and the most important thing you need to know, above anything else, is that it was not his fault. He was set up, and the person responsible for it was a Doctor Joel Fischer in Los Angeles. He's a psychologist and Scott was one of his patients, even before all the shit went down between the two of you. This Doctor Fischer was a cancer. I know this because me, and other people I knew, where also victims of his experiments, and unfortunately they're not around anymore. I was lucky enough to survive, and I hope that Scott can somehow salvage what's left of his life, with your help. Please do whatever you can to right the horrible wrongs that have been done to him and your family. I can tell you that Doctor Fischer is dead, and you'll never have to worry about him. It is up to you to take it from here. You'll receive another package tomorrow that will have certain things that you'll need to help you do this, including cash. That is all you need to know. Good Luck.*

The volume of the song increased when the voice stopped. Merri pushed the laptop across the table, dropped her head into her folded arms, and started crying, while the chorus played.

## DR WINTROP

### Five Days Later

Scott Haskins sat on the edge of his bed in the psychiatric ward of Napa State Hospital and looked over the liner notes of the White Stripes *De Stijl* CD that a staff member delivered to him earlier in the morning. It came in the mail for him the day before from an address in Florida.

He put the headphones of his compact disk player over his ears, pressed play, and "*You're Pretty Good Looking (For a Girl)*" came on. Scott smiled and turned it up. The music invigorated him and he tapped his feet on the floor to the beat.

*This is good.*

He stretched out on the bed and closed his eyes.

In the middle of track six, a hand lightly jostled his left foot. Scott's eye's snapped open and he pushed himself up with his elbows.

"What the fuck," he yelled, louder than normal because the music still blared in his ears. He pulled the headphones off. They landed beside him on the bed.

"Please, calm down, I'm sorry about that. I couldn't tell if you were sleeping, or just tuning out. I'm very sorry Scott. I didn't mean to startle you, believe me."

"What do you want?"

He pulled a chair over to the side of the bed, sat down, and faced Scott.

"It's nice to meet you too," he said, a friendly tone in his voice. "I'm Doctor Peter Winthrop." He extended his hand and Scott shook it.

"You caught me off guard. I didn't mean to yell at you. Sorry about that."

"No worries Scott. How are you doing today?"

"Same as everyday I guess. Not much changes, if you know what I mean."

*This doesn't even look like the guy in Fischer's file,* Peter thought, comparing the man in front of him, to the handsome guy with the styled, brown hair and chiseled features in the file photos that he reviewed during his debriefing yesterday.

*Poor bastard. If he cut the long, greasy, grey hair, lost the beard, and the unibrow, it might look like him, but the teeth would need a lot of bleaching to get them back to-*

"Where's Doctor Mari?" Scott asked.

*That's what a lot of people want to know.*

"He won't be coming today Scott. In fact, that's why I'm here. Why don't we go somewhere where we can talk, if that's alright with you?"

"Yeah, I guess, might have to wait a couple minutes. They're going to be coming with my meds soon."

"You're not going to be getting any medication today, at least not what you're used to. Please, let's go talk. I think the visitor's room works. Sound good?"

Scott grabbed the headphones off the bed, put them around his neck, and stood up. He slid his feet into a pair of sneakers, bent over, and fastened the Velcro straps across the top with one hand, while he held the CD player in the other.

"You need a couple minutes to buff up?"

"Nah, I do have to piss though."

Scott shuffled into the bathroom and closed the door

Peter obsessed over Scott's condition.

*Cheap khaki sweatpants. Matching sweatshirt. Beaten down and haggard. Can't imagine him in an expensive suit, all tanned up, smiling. Big time entertainment lawyer, made more in a month than I make in a year, reduced to a shuffling zombie. Fischer destroyed him. Asshole. How do I tell him he's not really insane?*

The bathroom door opened and Scott came out.

"I'm ready, we can go now."

A Muzak version of *"Raindrops Keep Fallin' on My Head"* played softly through the overhead speakers as they walked toward the back of the visitor's room.

"How's this?" Peter pointed at an empty table in the back corner of the room.

"It works." Scott took a seat across the table from Peter. "So, what's this all about?"

"Well." Peter let out a long exhale. "Scott, you've been the victim of a terrible, terrible crime that was committed by Doctor Fischer."

"*What?*" Scott's eyes widened and he leaned forward in his chair. "What are you talking about? What *kind* of crime?"

"Please, calm down, it's going to be okay. I promise you, but try to stay calm. Can you do that for me?"

Scott rested his arms on the table and held the CD player in his hands.

"Yeah, okay, I'm calm. Can't you tell? Now get to it. What *the fuck* is going on?"

Peter wanted to say, *that goddamn psycho maniac Fischer, used you as a human guinea pig, ruined your life, and you would have ended up dying in this shit-hole, if his house of cards didn't come crumbling down*, but he kept it professional.

"During your treatment with Doctor Fischer, and to some extent, Doctor Mari, they used some very unorthodox methods, that they never should have, and because of-"

The ringtone on Peter's cell phone started playing. He pulled it out of the case on his belt and looked at the display.

"I'm sorry Scott." He put the phone to his ear. "This will just be a minute."

Scott grinned at Peter. "Saved by the bell."

"This is Doctor Winthrop. Excellent...okay...I'll be right there."

Peter closed the phone and dropped it in the side pocket of his lab coat.

"I apologize. Listen, I need to leave for just a couple minutes, but I'll be right back. Just stay right here." He reached across the table, put his hands on Scott's arms, and looked directly into his eyes. "It is going to be okay Scott, it's over. Please wait right here."

Peter walked quickly toward the door and left the room.

Scott slumped back in his chair as the Muzak changed to a song about Pina Coladas. He leaned forward and grabbed the CD player off the table.

*Where did I leave off? Track six? Yeah, track six.*

He pulled the headphones off his neck, put them over his ears, and started track seven. "*Sister, Do You Know My Name?*" came on and he leaned back in the chair and waited for Peter to get back.

*Good song, like the others. The White Stripes. Need to find out-*

The door opened and Scott saw Peter, who stopped and held it open for someone behind him.

Scott watched, as the song played in his ears, and a woman came through the door following Peter.

"Oh my God."

Scott's sinuses burned and tears streamed down his cheeks as he looked at her.

"Merri?"

He pushed himself out of the chair, pulled the headphones off, and tried to wipe the tears off his face with the sleeve of his sweatshirt.

Merri ran by Peter and when she reached Scott, wrapped her arms around him and buried her face into his chest. Mascara tainted tears ran down her cheeks and stained his sweatshirt. Scott's tears dripped down into her curly, blond hair.

## THE LIFE OF REILLY

### December 2008

"Alright," Ricky Sherman told his two workers, "this is an easy one, just tear it all out. If it's carpet, it goes. It's all being done over with hardwood, and I need that to start tomorrow. You guys cool with that?"

"Yeah," Manny Herrera said, "piece of cake."

"No problem, probably four or five hours," Hector Reyes said, looking at Manny. "What do you think?"

Manny nodded his head. "Yeah, sounds about right. A couple hours to strip it, get it out of here and in the dumpster, and another couple hours to pull up the padding and tack stripping, and clean it all up."

"That's what I like to hear," Ricky said. "Call me when you're finished so I can let the floor guy know it's a go for tomorrow. Hopefully, we're going to be starting on the main house by next week. So do it right, this is a big one."

"No problem," Manny said.

"Good, talk to you guys later." Ricky walked over to the door and looked back at them. "Call me when you're done."

"Will do," Manny told him.

Hector and Manny walked over to the corner of the main room where the tools were and put on their kneepads.

"This place is the shit," Manny said.

"Man, what kind of sick money do you need to make to live like this?"

"Big time money my friend. More than we'll ever know."

Hector reached in his pocket, pulled out a plastic bag, and showed it to Manny.

"You want to get high first? We can go outside, no one's around."

"Sure, come on," Manny said. "We can check out the pool."

\*\*\*

Manny took a sip of Gatorade. "Let's get this over with. It's not going to get any cooler in here. It sucks there's no power, would have been good to have some tunes. I figure we can start in the bedroom, work our way back through the hall, finish in here."

"That's cool," Hector said, picking up his toolbox.

They went into the empty bedroom and looked around.

"I'll start in the closet," Hector said.

"Alright, let's do it man."

Hector put on his work gloves, grabbed a utility knife and a hammer, and walked into the closet. He got down on his knees and pushed the blade out of the knife.

"Damn, this is bigger than my bedroom," he yelled out to Manny.

"I hear that," Manny pushed the blade out of his knife, bent over, and started slicing the rug, working his way across the middle of the bedroom.

"Hey," Hector yelled, "come see this, get in here."

Manny walked over to the closet door. "What's up?"

Hector sat in the back corner of the closet, under the double row of mahogany shelving that ran along the sixteen feet of the back wall.

"This place is on a slab, right?" Hector asked.

"Yeah."

"That's what I thought, but look at this." Hector pointed to the indents on the rug. "Must have been a bureau or something like that on top of this before they took everything out of here."

Hector hooked the hammer claw under the corner of the rug, pulled it back, and a three-foot square of padding, still attached to the underside of the carpet, came up with it. The rest of the padding stayed secured to the floor and surrounded the plywood square.

"Check it out." Hector banged the wood with his hammer. "It looks like some kind of trap door or something. If I put the rug back down, you can't tell it's there. It fit's perfectly. See how it's just a little lower than the cement. You can walk on it, and not feel any difference when the rug's back over it. Think we should open it?"

"Maybe," Manny said, "but look at all those screws. It would be a pain in the ass to undo them all. How many are there?"

Hector counted them. "Six on each side, so twenty-four."

Manny bent over, rapped his knuckles on the wood. "Sounds hollow, must be something under there."

"Yeah, maybe it's a stash for something valuable."

Manny raised his eyebrows up and down a couple of times. "Or illegal."

"We should find out. Go get a couple of screwdrivers, Phillips heads."

Manny came back with the screwdrivers and Hector pulled the carpet back far enough to give them room to work. They got down on their knees.

"You take these two sides," Manny said. "I'll do the others."

Manny got the first screw out and looked at it. "Two inch screws. These will be a pain in *the ass* to get out. Wish we had a cordless."

***

"Don't take that last one all the way out," Hector told Manny. "We'll need that to pull it up. It's too tight to fit the claw between the spaces."

"Good idea," Manny said, finishing the last couple of turns.

Hector picked up his hammer. "The moment of truth."

He hooked the claw on the top of the screw head, pulled back, and the wood came up.

Manny's face soured and a second later, Hector's did the same.

"What the fuck is that smell?" Hector pulled his shirt over his nose, pushing himself back from the hole.

Manny cupped his hands over his face and used his foot to push the plywood over the opening. "Holy shit, that's fucking nasty."

"Let's get the fuck out of here," Hector said, through the shirt."

They scrambled to their feet and left the room.

***

"On a scale of one to ten, this is an eleven. Should never have gone down," Evan Carleton told Detective Lydon, as they stood on the patio that surrounded the pool. "I feel bad for the fucking patrolman who answered the nine-one-one call. He's a new guy, Trinadad. He thought it was just some dead animal or something down there. So he jumps down, and he's so fucking horrified when he sees what's down there, he tries to get back out, but he can't pull himself back up. Lucky for him, the two workers who called it in were there and pulled him back out. They had to take him out of here. He was puking and all fucked up. I can't blame him for that. I still can't get the fucking smell out of my nose. Add the visuals to the smell, and it's going to be a day to remember for him."

"What do we know so far?" Lydon asked.

"There's a bunker under there, like a bomb shelter. The walls and ceiling are all concrete, but it looks more like an apartment than a bomb shelter.

"No shit."

"Swear to God, and there's no record of it ever being built. No permits pulled or nothing. It looked like you could have lived down there, if you wanted to. There's power, air conditioning, heat, stove, the whole nine yards. At least there was, must have all been shut down for some time now. The main room was set up with a bunch of computers, but they were all smashed up. One of the rooms looked like an operating room in a hospital, and the other must have been used to mix chemicals or something. A Hazmat team is on the way here."

"How many are down there?" Lydon asked.

"Depends what you're talking about." Carleton cracked a half smile. "There's three badly decomposed humans, without heads or hands, and about twenty dead rats, that probably ate themselves to death, if they didn't suffocate first, or die from eating from the trays of D-Con that are down there. It looks like a slaughterhouse. My guess is they were tied up and still alive when their heads and hands were taken off."

Lydon grimaced, ran his hands down his face. "So, obviously there's no identity on any of them yet. You know they still haven't found the owner of this place. Think one of them is him?"

"Yeah I know. I thought the same thing, but the strange thing is, they all had wallets on them. Money, credit cards, driver's licenses, all still there, and none of them says Joel Fischer."

"Who are they then?"

Carleton pulled a small notebook out of his back pocket and flipped back a couple of pages.

"Let's see. There's a Victor Ahriman, a Doctor Vincent Mari, and a Doctor Stephan Erlik."

Lydon's ringtone went off, he answered.

"What's up Sully? No fucking shit. When? How the fuck did they pull that off? Just what Bush needs huh? Should be interesting. I'll call you later."

"What's up?" Carelton asked.

"Someone just whacked Vladimir Putin. Shot him, then killed himself."

"No way. What the fuck."

"They're saying it's an American that did it too. Someone named Christopher Reilly from Oregon."


### Author's Note:

Thank you for reading MINDJACKER. I sincerely appreciate it. I can be reached at spreardon81@gmail.com and would love to hear from you.

My blog is: http://seanpatrickreardon.blogspot.com

**Special thanks go out to**: my lovely wife Vikki, my two beautiful children, Nana and Pa and the rest of my family and friends, Tom Sherman, who listened to all my crazy ramblings, Adrian McKinty and Declan Burke, who inspired me with their terrific novels and blogs, and finally, I would like to thank Mark Coker, the founder of Smashwords, for all the hard work, encouragement, and opportunity that he has provided authors.

I am currently working on my second crime novel.

Peace,

Sean

1/25

Made in the USA
Middletown, DE
12 August 2018